ARIEL TACHNA

CHERISH
THE LAND

DREAMSPINNER
PRESS

Published by
DREAMSPINNER PRESS

5032 Capital Circle SW, Suite 2, PMB# 279, Tallahassee, FL 32305-7886 USA
http://www.dreamspinnerpress.com/

Cherish the Land
© 2015 Ariel Tachna.

Cover Art
© 2015 Anne Cain.
annecain.art@gmail.com
Cover content is for illustrative purposes only and any person depicted on the cover is a model.

ISBN: 978-1-63476-087-4
Digital ISBN: 978-1-63476-088-1
Library of Congress Control Number: 2015904661
First Edition June 2015

Printed in the United States of America
∞
This paper meets the requirements of
ANSI/NISO Z39.48-1992 (Permanence of Paper).

Readers love the Lang Downs series by ARIEL TACHNA

Inherit the Sky

"…a well-crafted, beautiful book that I would recommend to anyone looking for a love story that takes courage."
—Guilty Indulgence

"This story is beautifully, realistically handled."
—Joyfully Jay

Chase the Stars

"I loved the opportunity to revisit Lang Downs… I enjoy the world and the characters enough to be eager to spend more time there."
—Reviews by Jessewave

"Ms. Tachna has the talent to take everyday life and weave it into something special that leaves the reader sitting back just feeling good and wanting more."
—Hearts on Fire

Outlast the Night

"Ariel Tachna does it again. Beautiful installment to a beautiful series."
—multitaskingmommas Book Reviews

Conquer the Flames

"A great book, one of the best in this series."
—MM Good Book Reviews

"Thanks, Ariel, for a great return visit to Lang Downs. I'm looking forward to the next story in the series."
—Rainbow Book Reviews

By ARIEL TACHNA

Best Ideas
Château d'Eternité
With Nessa L. Warin: Dance Off
Fallout
Her Two Dads
Highland Lover
Home for Chirappu
In Search of Fireworks
The Inventor's Companion
The Matelot
Music of the Heart
Once in a Lifetime
Out of the Fire
Overdrive
The Path
Rediscovery
Revelations in the Dark
Rose Among the Ruins
Seducing C.C.
Stolen Moments
A Summer Place
With Madeline Urban: Sutcliffe Cove
Testament to Love
Why Nileas Loved the Sea

GAMES LOVERS PLAY
Amorous Liaison • Best Behavior • Ride 'em Cowboy

HOT CARGO
Healing in His Wings
With Nicki Bennett: Hot Cargo • Something About Harry

LANG DOWNS
Inherit the Sky • Chase the Stars • Outlast the Night • Conquer the Flames • Cherish the Land

PARTNERSHIP IN BLOOD
Alliance in Blood • Covenant in Blood • Conflict in Blood • Reparation in Blood
Perilous Partnership • Reluctant Partnerships • Lycan Partnership • Partnership Reborn
Partnership Reforged

With Nicki Bennett
All For One • Checkmate • Under the Skin

THE EXPLORING LIMITS SERIES
Exploring Limits • Stretching Limits • Refining Limits
Breaking Limits • Transcending Limits • No Limits

Published by DREAMSPINNER PRESS
http://www.dreamspinnerpress.com

To everyone who asked for more.

CHARACTER LIST

Caine Neiheisel – owner of Lang Downs (*Inherit the Sky*)

Macklin Armstrong – co-owner of Lang Downs, Caine's partner (*Inherit the Sky*)

Seth Simms – Chris's brother, moved to Sydney to get an engineering degree, Jason's best friend

Jason Thompson – Seth's best friend, Patrick and Carley's son, just finished vet school

Chris Simms – Seth's brother, year-rounder on Lang Downs (*Chase the Stars*)

Jesse Harris – Chris's partner, year-rounder, mechanic (*Chase the Stars*)

Sam Emery – business manager for Lang Downs (*Outlast the Night*)

Jeremy Taylor – year-rounder on Lang Downs, Sam's partner (*Outlast the Night*)

Thorne Lachlan – year-rounder on Lang Downs, former Commando (*Conquer the Flames*)

Ian Duncan – year-rounder on Lang Downs, Thorne's partner (*Conquer the Flames*)

Patrick and Carley Thompson – year-rounders on Lang Downs, Jason's parents. Patrick is head mechanic

Neil Emery – foreman on Lang Downs, Sam's brother, married to Molly, father of Dani and Liam, Ian's best friend

Kami Lang – station cook

Sarah Lang – Macklin's mother, now married to Kami

Devlin Taylor – owner of Taylor Peak, the neighboring station, Jeremy's brother

Nick Walker – former Commando, Thorne's best friend

Kyle and Linda – year-rounders. Linda has a daughter Laura from a previous marriage.

Charlie White – year-rounder at Taylor Peak

Michael Lang – deceased founder of Lang Downs, Caine's great-uncle

PROLOGUE

SETH SIMMS tossed his lunch bag on the counter as he walked into his apartment. Ilene would fuss if he left it there, but he needed a shower to get the grease off his hands and out of his hair first. He'd deal with his lunch bag after he was clean. She wasn't due home for another hour anyway.

As he stood under the hot water, Seth wondered, not for the first time, what he was still doing in Sydney now that he'd finished his degree. The job at the local mechanic shop paid the bills and let him root around under the bonnet of as many cars as he wanted, but it was work he could have done when he was sixteen without any of what he'd learned in his mechanical engineering courses. He and Ilene argued about it at least once a month, but looking for anything else would feel too much like making a commitment to stay in Sydney. He didn't hate Sydney the way he'd hated some of the other places he'd lived growing up, before he and his brother Chris moved to Lang Downs, but it wasn't home either. Lang Downs was the only place to ever have earned that designation.

He stepped out of the shower and started drying off. He'd given in to Ilene's demands and spent last Christmas with her family, so it had been more than a year since he'd last visited Lang Downs. He and Chris e-mailed regularly, sometimes even daily, but it wasn't the same. Maybe he should think about using a little of his vacation and going down to visit. Chris and his partner Jesse would make up his old room for him, and Caine, the station owner, wouldn't mind having an extra mouth to feed for a few days, especially if Seth pitched in around the station. That would certainly be easy enough to do. Patrick, the station's head mechanic, never changed anything. Seth bet he could find every tool he needed in the shed blindfolded.

"Seth! How many times do I have to tell you not to leave your lunch bag on the counter?" Ilene's shriek echoed through the apartment, grating on Seth's nerves. Sometimes he didn't know why he was with her in the first place. It hadn't always been like this, although he couldn't have said when it changed. When they first met, three years ago, she'd been fun to be with, always laughing, always happy. She hadn't cared then that even with his engineering degree, he was working as a mechanic. She'd told him the right job would come along in time. She wasn't nearly as forgiving now. Hell, given his track record, it was probably his fault she'd turned into a screeching harpy.

He pulled on shorts and a singlet and walked out of the bathroom. "I was coming to put it away, but you'd have been more upset if I got grease everywhere. I was covered in it today."

She frowned at him but didn't continue her harangue, for which Seth was grateful.

"I was thinking about going back to Lang Downs for a few days to see my brother. Do you want to come with me?"

Ilene's expression was all the answer Seth needed. Lang Downs held no interest for her and never would. It had been the one strike against her when they first started dating, but he'd hoped she would see how important it was to him and learn to love it as he did, or even to tolerate it for his sake. It hadn't happened.

"When are you going?" she asked, her voice so cold and disapproving Seth almost asked her to leave right then. She'd moved in with him. His name was the only one on the lease. He could make her go and she wouldn't be able to do anything to stop him.

"I haven't decided yet. I have to talk to Chris, see when it would suit and all that. Not to mention ask for time off at work."

"You couldn't just go for a weekend?" Ilene wheedled. "I've been looking at cruises for vacation this year. If you use your holidays now, we'll have to wait until next year."

"Ilene, I hate boats. You know that. Why would you even think about a cruise? I'd spend the whole time miserable."

"You hate small boats," Ilene said. "You've never been on a cruise ship. You'll never know you're on a boat if you stay away from the outer decks. It's more of a floating city than a boat."

It was still a boat.

"I'm going to e-mail Chris. I'll see what he has to say and then we can talk about our holiday plans for this year. But no boats."

She humphed but left it at that. Seth unpacked his lunch bag and put it under the sink so she wouldn't have that to harp on when he came back out later. Then he went to the extra room they used as an office and booted up the computer. He could hear her flouncing around in the living room and kitchen, fussing over things that didn't need fussing over just to make her annoyance clear, but he tuned it out. When his in-box opened, he smiled to see a note from Chris at the very top. He clicked it and froze when he read the first line:

Jason is home.

JASON THOMPSON stood on the veranda of the bunkhouse, staring at the night sky. His parents had offered him his childhood room again, but he didn't want to come back as a visitor or as a child. He wanted to come back as one of the men, whether he spent his time as a jackaroo or as the vet, and the only way the year-rounders—and maybe even the seasonal jackaroos—would see him as one of them was if he stayed in the bunkhouse.

"You're awful quiet, mate."

Jason looked up to see who had joined him. It took a minute to place the name of the other jackaroo. Cooper something. He didn't remember the last name. He'd met too many new people all at once in the past two days to remember all the details.

"It's strange to be home and yet have it so different," Jason explained. "Before I went away to school, Mum didn't let me come to the bunkhouse very often, and only with someone for a specific reason. I wasn't one of the jackaroos, so I didn't have any business being here as far as she was concerned."

"And now you do," Cooper finished.

"Maybe," Jason said a little bitterly. "Neil gave me the same job he gave one of the blow-ins this morning. He's either afraid something will happen to me and my father will have his hide, or he's forgotten I've been on the station as long as he has. He still sees me as a kid."

Cooper leaned back against the wooden column that supported the roof of the veranda, giving Jason an uninhibited view of his lanky body. For a second, Jason felt bad about ogling him, but Cooper was ogling right back. "Then he's blind. You certainly aren't a kid."

Jason smiled. Cooper wasn't Seth, but he was there, interested, and available—three things Seth would never be. He could think of worse ways to spend a summer. He tipped his beer back and emptied the bottle. "I could use another beer. I have some in my room. Do you want one?"

Cooper's smile spread slowly across his face as he raked Jason with his gaze again. "Depends on what else you're offering."

Jason smiled back. "I'm sure we could come up with something we'd both enjoy."

ONE

THE SOUND of the phone ringing startled Sam Emery, business manager at Lang Downs, out of his concentration on the end-of-quarter accounting he did every three months for the station. He muttered a curse under his breath as he lost track of where he was in the line of numbers, but no one else was in the big house at the moment to answer it.

"Lang Downs, Sam Emery speaking."

"Is Jeremy Taylor available?"

"No, he's out in the paddocks," Sam replied. "Could I take a message?"

"Could you ask him to call Taylor Peak as soon as he can? It's about his brother."

Sam debated for a minute what he should say. He and Jeremy had made no secret of their relationship at Lang Downs, but Jeremy's brother hadn't been at all accepting, which was why they were still on Lang Downs, not on Taylor Peak, the station directly to the west. On the other hand, if there was a problem, Sam might be able to help… if the man on the phone didn't share Devlin Taylor's prejudices and would talk to him.

"I'm Jeremy's partner. Is something wrong with Devlin?"

The man hesitated for so long Sam thought he wasn't going to say anything, but he finally spoke. "There's been an accident. Devlin's been airlifted to the hospital in Canberra. I know he and Jeremy haven't been on the best of terms recently, but I thought he should know."

"What kind of accident?" Sam's heart clenched at the thought of all the things that could go wrong on a station: broken bones, mangled limbs, or worse.

"He was thrown from his horse," the man said. "He lost consciousness an hour or so later, and we couldn't rouse him. It doesn't look good."

"I'll get word to Jeremy," Sam promised. "Do you need him on the station or should we go to Canberra to be with Devlin?"

"The crew bosses can keep things running for a few days. It's not mating season yet. If it drags on that long, though, someone will have to make decisions. We just do what Taylor tells us."

Sam had a few choice things to stay about stubborn stockmen making stupid decisions, but he'd save those for Devlin when the man recovered. Right now, he needed to get Jeremy in from the paddock and headed toward Canberra. Everything else could wait until they knew what Devlin's prognosis was.

"Thanks for letting us know," Sam said. "If you talk to whoever is with Devlin, let him know Jeremy is on his way. We'll be there as quickly as we can."

"I will," the man said before ending the call.

Sam leaned back in his chair and took a deep breath. He had no idea how Jeremy would take the news. Yes, he and Devlin were estranged and had been for a number of years, but they were still brothers. Sam couldn't imagine how he'd feel if it were his own brother in Devlin's place. He'd be gutted if something happened to Neil. Delaying wouldn't change anything, though, and even seconds could make a difference in whether Jeremy got to see Devlin again. Sam took a deep breath and picked up the radio.

He looked up the frequency Jeremy had been assigned that day and switched the transponder to only call his radio. No need to broadcast the situation to the whole station just yet. They could worry about that when they had more news.

"Jeremy? Are you there?"

The radio crackled for a moment, then Jeremy's voice came over the airwaves. "I'm here. What's going on?"

"There's been an accident at Taylor Peak," Sam said.

Jeremy said something that got lost in the static, but Sam suspected it wasn't terribly flattering.

"You need to come back in," he insisted. "We need to go to Canberra."

"Sam, this isn't a good time," Jeremy said.

"Jeremy Taylor, get your arse back to the station now. Your brother is seriously hurt," Sam exclaimed. "Where are you? I can meet you halfway to save time. One of the other jackaroos can bring your horse back in."

Silence greeted his outburst.

"I'll meet you on the road out of the valley in an hour," Jeremy replied finally. "Bring a change of clothes for me? I stink of sheep."

"I'll wait for you at the third gate from the house," Sam said. "See you soon."

He set the radio down and hurried toward the kitchen. He didn't expect anyone to be there except Kami and Sarah, but he could tell them what had happened and they could tell Caine and Macklin. To his surprise, Macklin sat at the little table to the side of the kitchen.

"What's wrong?" Macklin asked as soon as he walked in.

Sam didn't bother asking how Macklin knew. He was sure it was written all over his face. "We got a call from Taylor Peak. Devlin was thrown from his horse. He's been airlifted to Canberra. Jeremy's on his way. We'll leave as soon as I can pack a bag for us. I don't know how long we'll be gone."

"It doesn't matter." Macklin rose to his feet. "Don't let Jeremy rush back because he feels like he's neglecting his job here. Devlin Taylor and I have never been friends, but he's Jeremy's brother. Jeremy should stay as long as Taylor needs him. We're not shorthanded. We can cover for him until he comes back."

"Thanks," Sam said. "I appreciate it even if he doesn't think to say it."

Macklin smiled. "It's understood."

"I only got halfway through the quarterly reports."

"Sam, go," Macklin said. "Caine will figure it out. Let us know if there's anything we can do to help."

Sam nodded and headed for the house he and Jeremy shared. He threw clothes in a suitcase at random. When it was packed, he tossed it into the boot and drove toward the gate where he'd promised to meet Jeremy. He would probably be early, but better that than being late. As soon as Jeremy got there, they could leave and hopefully reach Devlin in time.

SETH WASN'T terribly surprised not to meet anyone as he drove across Taylor Peak toward home. Sometimes he ran into a group of jackaroos from the neighboring station, but more times than not, he only saw sheep scattered here and there in the paddocks. He was somewhat more surprised to pass a car coming down the road from Lang Downs. He pulled to the side to let it pass and caught sight of Sam and Jeremy in the front seat. He waved, but they either didn't see him or didn't recognize him. He shrugged and drove on. They probably forgot today was the day he was arriving. Chris would have told them, but he was hardly the top of their priority list. He wasn't even really at the top of Chris's list anymore, since he'd moved off the station to go to school, but Chris wouldn't have forgotten he was coming. He could always rely on Chris, even when everyone else disappointed him.

He drove the rest of the way to the station with only his music for company. He couldn't help the sense of relief at being able to choose the tracks and turn it up as loud as he wanted instead of having to cater to Ilene's preferences.

When he pulled onto the station proper, he smiled as Carley, Jason's mother, stepped out of the bunkhouse, her arms full of linens. He rolled the window down and leaned out. "Do you need a hand?"

"How many years have I been doing this, boyo?" Carley teased back. "I think I can handle a load of dirty sheets."

"Toss them in the boot," Seth insisted as he pulled the lever to open it. "You can tell me all the gossip on the way to your house."

She rolled her eyes at him but did as he said and climbed in the passenger seat a moment later.

"What's new on the station?" he asked.

Carley's smile faded. "Devlin Taylor had an accident. Jeremy and Sam have gone to Canberra. I don't know much more than that, but Sam looked pretty shaken when he drove out of here, so I'm afraid it's bad."

Seth's stomach clenched at the thought of anyone having to rush to the side of an injured brother. If they'd taken him to Canberra and not to the closer, if smaller, hospital in Yass, it was serious. "That explains why they didn't wave when I passed them on the way in."

"Now you tell me why your boot is so full. Chris said you were coming for a visit."

"I was," Seth said. "And then I realized I wanted to come home. I'm hoping Caine and Macklin could use another set of hands around here."

"If they say no, I'll set them straight," Carley said, her expression as fierce as Seth had ever seen it. "Patrick isn't a young man anymore, no matter what he thinks. His hands bother him more than he'll admit. His pride won't let him ask Caine and Macklin for help, but he won't say no to you hanging around the tractor shed and doing the heavier work."

"You should have called me sooner," Seth exclaimed. "I would have come right away."

"Patrick would never have forgiven me. You had a life in Sydney—a job, a girlfriend. He wouldn't take you away from that. He's always thought of you as his son too. He wanted you to be happy, and if Sydney was where that could happen, then he wouldn't interfere."

"It doesn't matter now," Seth said. "I'm home for as long as Caine and Macklin will have me. Whether I work in the tractor shed or ride out with one of the crews, I'm here to stay."

"What about your girlfriend? Irene, was it?"

"Ilene," Seth said with a moue of disgust as he parked the car in front of Carley and Patrick's house—*Jason's house*, his traitorous mind supplied. "She wasn't interested in moving back here with me, and I wasn't interested in keeping things going enough to stay. She took over the lease on my apartment. I put the few things I wanted to keep but couldn't get in the car in storage until I have a place for them. Everything else, I left for her. Most of it wasn't worth fighting over anyway."

"Oh, love, I'm sorry." Carley pulled him into a gentle hug.

Seth let himself cling. After his mother died when he was fourteen, Carley had come closest to filling that role in his life. He wouldn't have asked for her mothering—at twenty-six he didn't need to be coddled like a child—but enough of the neglected child remained inside him that he would never turn it away. Ilene wasn't much of a loss, he'd come to realize, but his poor judgment in choosing her and then in waiting so long to break up with her still stung.

"I'm just glad to be home," Seth said eventually.

"Come inside. I'll make you a cup of tea and we can talk while I get the laundry started. Chris had planned to stay close to home today so he'd be here when you arrived, but he rode out to take Jeremy's place after we heard about Taylor. He knew you'd understand."

Seth did understand. He'd have done the same thing if the situation had been reversed, but he still felt his brother's absence. He didn't want to sit in Chris and Jesse's living room with nothing to do until the jackaroos came back in for dinner. "As long as you let me help."

"Fine, you can carry the sheets in, but once they're in the wash, there's really nothing to do but wait."

Seth grabbed the pile of sheets from the boot and followed Carley into the house. He'd spent almost as much time in this kitchen as he had in Chris and Jesse's when he was younger. He and Jason had done their schoolwork together at the table for most of three years. If he'd pretended to have more trouble with math than he really did, it just gave Jason time to catch up with him so they finished their HSCs at the same time. Of course, then Jason had to go and spoil things by going away to vet school.

Seth had applied to the engineering program the morning after Jason got his acceptance letter. And now, seven years later, he had finally come home.

He carried the sheets into the laundry room and put them in the washing machine.

Carley got it started and herded him back into the kitchen. "Sit," she ordered as she began filling the electric teakettle. "Tell me what happened."

Seth shrugged. He couldn't exactly tell Carley he'd come home because Jason had. He wasn't worried about Carley's reaction to him being bi—she'd never batted an eyelash at any of the gay couples on the station—but she might have something to say about him having designs on her son. And even if she didn't, Jason wouldn't appreciate his mother knowing before he did. "We wanted different things out of life. And I realized a couple of weeks ago that I didn't love her enough to give in on everything when she didn't care enough to try to compromise on even the most basic things."

"It sounds like you're better off without her." Carley set the tea chest in front of him along with a mug. "You're not going to meet a lot of girls out here, though. We only have three jillaroos this summer. It seems like we have fewer every year."

"What do you expect? Most of them are looking for a husband as much as they are a job. They think Lang Downs is full of nothing but gay men. Not the best hunting grounds."

Carley snickered. "So ten men constitutes 'full of' these days? We have a larger crew than that."

Seth paused for a moment to count. Caine, Macklin, Chris, Jesse, Sam, Jeremy, Thorne, Ian… that was eight, but Carley said ten. "Do we have a new couple on the station since I was home last?"

"Just because they're gay doesn't mean they're with someone or planning on staying," Carley chided. "We've had gay jackaroos who only stayed a season or two. You know that."

She was right, of course, but Seth never counted them because they came and went with the seasons and often without making any lasting impact on the station or its inhabitants. Seth had always viewed the seasonal jackaroos as a sea of featureless faces unless they showed a particular interest in mechanics.

It wasn't like it mattered anyway. Seth had never managed to be with another man because his heart was too tied up in Jason to go beyond appreciating a handsome face or a nice arse if he saw one. He wasn't going chasing after a gay jackaroo just because he was single now.

"At the moment, I've sworn off girls. After dealing with Ilene for three years, I'm done for a while. It'll be nice just to be home with no pressure or anything." And it would be nice to see Jason again, but that would have to wait until dinner.

"It's good to have you home," Carley said as she poured the hot water into the mug. "I've missed having my boys around. Caine will put you to work just like he did Jason, but I still expect you to come over for Sunday dinner, even if you eat in the canteen the rest of the time."

"Yes, Mum." He'd intended to tease her, but the joy on her face made him promise silently to call her that more often. His own mother had barely deserved the title, but Carley had been a pillar of support and had faith in him almost from the moment he'd arrived on the station.

"What's Caine working on now?" Seth asked to change the subject. "He's always got one project or another going."

"He's been researching solar panels and windmills," Carley replied. "He wants to get electricity in the drover's huts. A fire is fine for most things, but actually having electricity in the huts would be useful if the weather is especially cold or wet. Hypothermia is dangerous."

"I'll talk to him at dinner," Seth said. "Electrical engineering isn't my specialty, but I know enough about it to help out. I'm always happy to poke around in engines, but if I can use my fancy degree, it'll be worth the effort I put into getting it."

"I never did understand why you decided to go for the degree when you already knew almost as much about engines as Patrick did and could have learnt the rest from him."

Seth flushed. "Chris wanted me to have choices, and it seemed like a good idea at the time."

"And now?"

"Now it gives me a set of skills to offer Lang Downs I wouldn't have had otherwise," Seth said. "That makes it worth it."

TWO

JASON PATTED his horse's neck and whistled for Polly to come in. They'd spent the entire day moving the mob from one paddock to another, and Jason was tired, dirty, and ready to go home. He'd feel that way no matter what, but Seth was supposed to arrive today. Jason didn't know how long he'd be staying—besides not long enough—so it grated to lose even a minute of the time they could be spending together because he was out in the paddocks. If he were here visiting too, it wouldn't matter as much—he could tell Caine or Macklin he didn't want to ride out today. But he wasn't a kid or a guest anymore. He'd come home to work and that meant going where Macklin or Neil assigned him. They hadn't needed his skills as a vet near home this morning, so he'd ridden out as a jackaroo instead, like he'd always said he would do.

"That's the last one, mates," Ian called as he closed the gate behind him. "Time to head in. Jason, we can make sure Polly makes it back if you want to ride on ahead."

"Are you sure?" Jason asked. He'd had Polly since she was a puppy, and she'd ridden draped across the saddle in front of him plenty of times, but he wasn't riding Titan today. He didn't know how this horse would react if Polly suddenly jumped up in the saddle.

"Go on," Ian said. "Your mind's been back at the station all day. Might as well get your body there as quickly as possible too. Maybe then you'll stop with the long face."

"I haven't been that bad, have I?" he asked Thorne.

"You really have, lad," Thorne said. "You sure you're not setting yourself up for disappointment?"

"My best friend has come home for a visit," Jason said. "How could that possibly be disappointing?"

Thorne's expression said Jason wasn't deluding anyone, but Seth was straight. Jason had always known that. He even accepted it. Seth couldn't choose to be gay any more than Jason could choose to be straight. It didn't stop Jason from loving him, though. He didn't suppose anything ever would. He'd accepted that too. He hadn't managed to make things work with Riley in Adelaide during vet school, but he blamed that on them wanting different things in life. Jason wanted to go home. Riley wanted to buy into a small-animal clinic in a city somewhere. Jason hoped things would be different now that he was back on the station. Cooper wasn't Seth, but he was a career jackaroo who valued life in the outback. That gave them more in common than Jason had ever had with anyone else.

Except Seth, but Seth wasn't gay. He had that girlfriend in Sydney. Never mind that she was awful for him. She was a complete harpy, always screeching at him for one thing or another. Jason had heard her enough times when he and Seth were chatting on Skype. In person, she'd been even worse. Jason hoped she was a good lay. Seth deserved to get something positive out of their relationship.

Thorne guided his horse a little closer to Jason's. "I'm not trying to run your life for you, but if you'll take a bit of advice from someone who's been around the block a couple of times, try to tone down your enthusiasm for Seth's visit a little if you really want to keep Cooper's interest. A man could start to question where he stood in his lover's life if his lover paid more attention to another man than he did to him."

"Seth'll be here for a few days, a week at the most," Jason said, "and even if he stayed longer, he'd never be interested in me. I don't have the right equipment. But he *is* my best friend. I'm not going to pass up a chance to spend time with him while he's here. He'll leave and I'll give Cooper my undivided attention again."

Thorne looked skeptical, but Jason ignored him and spurred his horse toward the station. If he only had a few days with Seth, he wanted to make the most of it.

Even at a fast canter, it took half an hour to get back to the station. Seth's car wasn't in front of Chris and Jesse's house, but then neither was Chris and Jesse's car, so that could just mean Seth had parked behind the tractor shed in the gravel area they used as a car park. He stripped the tack off his horse and rubbed him down quickly before turning him out into a paddock to graze. He considered the bunkhouse for a moment, but the shower block was probably already full. It would be faster to go to his parents' house and use their shower. Then he could go looking for Seth.

Seth wouldn't notice if he was freshly showered or still sweaty and dusty from the day, but Jason would know. Maybe Seth wouldn't ever care for Jason the way Jason cared for him, but Jason would keep making the effort. If that made him a fool, so be it.

He dashed up the steps of his parents' house and stopped to take off his boots on the veranda. He might not live there anymore, but his mother was no less strict because of it.

"Hi, Mum," he called as he stepped inside. "Can I borrow your shower?"

"You may, but come in and say hello to Seth first. He's been keeping me company this afternoon."

Jason froze. Seth was sitting in his mother's kitchen instead of at Chris and Jesse's or in the canteen or wherever else he could have been. Jason wasn't ready for this. He took a deep breath and reminded himself Seth was his best friend. Nothing else mattered.

He detoured toward the kitchen, working up a smile, but the moment he saw Seth, his nerves disappeared. Seth looked as wonderful as always, tawny blond hair tousled like he'd had the window open while he was driving (or like someone had been running their fingers through it, but that image was too unsettling to dwell on, even if they were Seth's fingers) and green eyes sparkling with laughter. He'd always thought Seth's eyes were his best feature. Alight like they were now, they grabbed Jason's attention and captivated him.

"Welcome home," Jason said, crossing the kitchen to give Seth a hug. "How long are you home for?"

Seth rose to meet Jason's hug so that the quick clasp turned into a full-body embrace. Jason prayed his cock wouldn't act up.

"I'm back for good," Seth said when he pulled away. "I got tired of Sydney."

Jason studied Seth's face, looking for any sign of doubt or hesitation, but he found none. Whatever had finally pushed Seth to come home, he was fully committed to it.

"Then welcome home for real. We're glad you're here." He swallowed hard. "I'm glad you're here."

"Yeah, your mum said your dad's hands are getting arthritic. I'll take as much off him as he'll let me. And maybe I'll be able to get some of Caine's projects going too."

That wasn't why Jason was glad Seth was home, but he'd let Seth believe it. "Just don't mention Dad's hands where he can hear you. He's still in complete denial about how bad they are."

"I won't," Seth said. "I haven't actually seen Caine and Macklin to let them know I'm here for more than a visit. I should probably do that now that everyone's coming back in from the paddocks. I'll see you at dinner?"

"Of course," Jason said. "After years of cafeteria cooking at uni, Kami's cooking tastes even better than it did growing up. You've been getting home-cooked meals at least."

"Such as they were. Ilene couldn't cook any better than I can."

"Speaking of her…." Jason left the question unspoken.

"She chose to stay in Sydney," Seth said. "I won't tell you exactly what she said, but she made it perfectly clear she had no interest in moving to a sheep station."

That was a relief. Jason would have put up with her for the pleasure of having Seth home, but not having to deal with her—not having her in Seth's life anymore—was even better.

"I'm sorry." It was a lie, but it was the proper thing to say.

"I'm not," Seth admitted. "We weren't right for each other. It just took me this long to realize it."

He gave Jason another quick hug, then gave a longer one to Carley. "I'll see you both at dinner."

When Seth left, Jason slumped into the chair Seth had been sitting in. "I am so fucked."

"Language, young man," his mother scolded. He flinched. He hadn't meant to say that out loud.

"Sorry, Mum. I'm used to living in the bunkhouse."

"That's no excuse for bad language. So why do you think that? You were so excited about his visit."

Jason debated how much to tell his mother, but he'd never been good at lying to her. On the other hand, if he said anything, she'd try to meddle. He loved his mother, but she'd never been good about staying out of his business. He pushed out of the chair and headed toward the door. He'd use the shower at the bunkhouse. He couldn't face his mother and her questions right now. "It's nothing. I'm going to get cleaned up for dinner. I'll talk to you later."

Carley caught his elbow as he passed. "I won't pry, but if you decide you need to talk, I'm here."

"Thanks, Mum."

JEREMY STOOD in the corridor outside the ICU in Canberra. The doctors there had done everything they could to stabilize Devlin, but the nurse hadn't sounded optimistic about his prognosis. She'd promised to send a doctor to explain everything to him as soon as one was available.

"Mr. Taylor?"

"Yes, I'm Taylor," Jeremy said, turning to face the doctor. His worn, tired face did nothing to encourage Jeremy. "How's my brother?"

"Not good," the doctor said. "I'm not going to lie. The fall caused bleeding in the brain. We've drained some to try to take the pressure off and avoid brain damage, but given the amount of time between when he was injured and when we began treatment, some damage is almost inevitable.

We're going to keep him here overnight to make sure he's stable enough to move, but we would recommend transporting him to Sydney to a level 1 trauma center. If nothing else, they'll have more resources to help him adapt to his new situation."

Jeremy shook his head in automatic rejection. "He runs a sheep station. He has men depending on him."

"I'm sorry, Mr. Taylor, but the realities of his life don't change the realities of his current medical condition. We'll do everything we can for him, but it's going to be a long time before he'll be in any shape to run the station again. If he lives."

"Thank you for your time," Jeremy said automatically. He could feel his world crumbling around him. He and Devlin hadn't been on good terms for years, but Devlin was still his brother, still a fixture in his life. He couldn't.... Life without Devlin would be.... If he died, Jeremy would lose all chance of reconciliation with his brother.

"Jeremy?"

Jeremy turned toward Sam's voice. Sam took Jeremy's hand and led him away from the window of Devlin's room. They found—Sam found, Jeremy was just following where Sam led—a quiet waiting room. The plastic chairs were hardly comfortable, but it was better than standing.

"Did you talk to the doctor?"

Jeremy nodded, still trying to put some order to his thoughts.

"It doesn't look—" His voice broke before he could finish the sentence. He swallowed hard around the lump in his throat and forced back his tears. Devlin wouldn't cry if their situations were reversed. He'd probably be glad of one less pillow biter in the world. "It doesn't look good. He's alive, but they aren't sure he'll stay that way. And even if he does, he won't be able to run the station again for a while. I don't even know who's in charge to let them know what's going on."

"So we'll call the house and see who answers," Sam said. "And if no one does, we'll call Lang Downs and ask Caine to send someone over with the message to call us. We'll figure out a way to get through this. One step at a time, right?"

Jeremy nodded again, grateful for Sam's steady presence. He could do anything as long as he had Sam in his corner. He just had to remember that.

"Do you want me to call?"

Jeremy shrugged, incapable of making a decision. All of his mental energy was centered on Devlin's room, where his brother was fighting for his life. Oh, God....

"Easy," Sam said, rubbing his back as he doubled over. "Just breathe. I'll take care of everything else. You just concentrate on making your lungs work. In and out, nice and easy."

Jeremy timed his breaths to the movement of Sam's hand across his back. Inhale every time Sam stroked to the right, exhale as he stroked to the left. Inhale, exhale, slow and steady, like Sam's movements. Strong and comforting like Sam's hand. He grabbed Sam's other hand where it rested on his knee and clung to it like a lifeline. The panic faded bit by bit until he could sit up, but he didn't relinquish his grip on Sam's hand. He wasn't sure he could keep it together if he did.

Sam transferred Jeremy's grip to his other hand. "Keep breathing. I'm going to call Taylor Peak."

Jeremy tuned out the conversation and focused on Sam's hand in his. When he felt steady enough, he rose and headed back toward Devlin's room. He wouldn't be allowed inside, but he'd be able to watch the rise and fall of Devlin's chest and console himself with the knowledge that Devlin was still alive. As long as he kept breathing, they could deal with the rest.

Sam joined him a few minutes later, but Jeremy didn't ask whether he'd reached anyone. Sam was nothing if not efficient. If he hadn't reached anyone at Taylor Peak, he'd called Caine and someone from Lang Downs was now on his way to Taylor Peak to apprise them of the situation or to have them get in touch with Sam.

"He'll make it," Sam said. "He's too bloody stubborn to die."

"I hope you're right," Jeremy said. If Devlin died, Taylor Peak would pass to Jeremy, and that was the last thing Jeremy wanted. Once, maybe, but Lang Downs was home now.

SAM HELD vigil with Jeremy, offering silent support with his presence. He wished he could do more, but they were playing a waiting game now. Wait for Devlin to wake up. Wait for the doctors to perform more tests. Wait to see what the long-term prognosis would be. His heart went out to Jeremy. He couldn't imagine how he'd feel if Neil was the one in that hospital room, unconscious. The mere thought of it was enough to make him panicky.

His phone rang, the buzz loud in the silent hall. Sam glanced down at the screen. "It's Taylor Peak. Do you want to talk to them?" Jeremy shook his head. Sam hadn't expected any other answer, but he still had to ask. "Would you rather I go elsewhere to talk to them?"

"No, stay here. They might need me to...." He waved his hand helplessly.

Sam grabbed Jeremy's hand and held tight as he answered the phone. He couldn't do much else, but he could remind Jeremy he wasn't alone.

"Hello?"

"Is this Sam Emery?"

"It is."

"This is Tim Perkins from Taylor Peak. I got a message to call you about the boss."

"Thank you for calling me back, Tim. Mr. Taylor is still unconscious, and the doctors say he has bleeding in the brain. They don't know when or if he'll recover. Are you the foreman?"

"Ain't no foreman on Taylor Peak. Hasn't been since Williams retired a couple years ago. Taylor runs everything himself."

Sam frowned. He knew how much work running a station was. Caine, Macklin, and Neil divided just the outdoor work between them and the other crew bosses, and Sam still worked full-time in the office taking care of the books. If Devlin had tried to do all that himself, it was no wonder he had an accident. "Who's the senior crew boss, then? Taylor isn't in any position to give orders right now, and until he is, someone will have to keep things running."

"Taylor Peak doesn't work that way, mate. Everything's in the boss's head. The rest of us just do as we're told."

Sam wanted to beat his head against a wall, but doing that wouldn't help Jeremy or Taylor Peak. He had no idea if Jeremy cared about the station, but for now, Sam would take care of it as best he could. "Who's been there the longest? I know he didn't hire an entirely new crew this spring."

"Probably Charlie White. I don't know how long he's been here, but he was already here when I got here."

"Then let me talk to him," Sam snapped. Someone on the station had to have enough sense to keep things going for a day or two until they had a better idea of what would happen and could get more specific orders from Devlin. He glanced at Jeremy to see how he was taking the conversation, but Jeremy didn't appear to be paying attention to him at all. He still clung to Sam's hand, but his attention was focused entirely on Devlin.

Sam could hear grumbling as Perkins went in search of the other jackaroo, then "Hello?"

"Do you have enough experience on Taylor Peak and the way Taylor runs things to take charge for a couple of days until we know more about his condition?" he asked bluntly.

"For a few days," White said. "I'm not going to start rotating the mobs between paddocks or anything big like that, but I can make sure chores are done and the animals cared for."

"Good enough," Sam said. "You're in charge until we hear more. If you need decisions made that you can't make by yourself, call me back. I'll talk to Taylor's brother, but I don't want to hear about day-to-day stuff. Just big decisions."

"For a few days," White repeated. "Much beyond a week and it's decisions I can't make."

Sam rolled his eyes and thanked any listening deity that he'd ended up on Lang Downs where Caine and Macklin respected and nurtured their crew bosses' intelligence and independence. "Hopefully by then Taylor will be giving orders again, even if it's from his hospital bed."

White hung up, and Sam resisted the urge to throw his phone down the hall. It wouldn't change anything about the situation on Taylor Peak, but it might make him feel better. It wouldn't help Jeremy, though, so Sam refrained, slipping his phone back into the case on his belt.

"How bad is it?" Jeremy asked after a moment.

"Your brother apparently hasn't allowed his employees any input in how or when things are done," Sam said as diplomatically as he could. "The first person I talked to shut down the minute I suggested he should take charge of things for a few days. The second person was willing to take care of day-to-day stuff but nothing more than basic chores and the like. Nothing that would require a decision. You wouldn't think twice on Lang Downs about rotating a mob between paddocks if they needed it, would you?"

"I'd run it by Macklin first," Jeremy said, "but if he was unavailable for some reason, I'd do what needed to be done. Devlin was always tight with control, though. He listened to Williams because he'd been on the station since we were kids, but he never really listened to anyone else. It's not that much of a stretch to think he wouldn't hire a new foreman after Williams retired."

Sam remembered Williams vaguely from the grassfires four years ago that had brought Thorne to them, but it didn't go much beyond the impression of a weathered man with a shock of white hair. Sam wouldn't be able to pick him out of a crowd now. "Is Williams still on the station? Or somewhere nearby? Could we get him to come back and run things until Devlin's well enough to appoint a new foreman or give the orders himself again?"

"I don't know where he went after he retired," Jeremy said. "We could try to find out, but I don't know if he'd come back."

"I'll see if I can track him down," Sam said. "Even if it just buys us a few weeks to get Devlin sorted a bit, it's better than having to try to run Taylor Peak from here and keep an eye on Devlin too."

"Thank you." Jeremy's voice cracked as he spoke, and Sam gave up trying to be discreet. Jeremy needed him. He pulled Jeremy into his arms and held on tight, relaying with his body what he couldn't put into words. Whatever happened—with Devlin, with Taylor Peak, with anything—Sam wouldn't leave him to face it alone.

THREE

SETH SAT with Chris and Jesse at dinner out of habit. He didn't know any of the seasonal jackaroos yet and hadn't managed to corner Caine and Macklin to ask about staying on, so he didn't feel like he could go around introducing himself. Catching up with everyone he knew was more important than meeting the new men anyway.

Patrick joined them when he came in. "Welcome home, son. Carley tells me you're hoping to stay."

"I'm hoping you'll let me back in the tractor shed," Seth replied with a grin. "I know a bit more than I did ten years ago."

"You knew enough to put more experienced men to shame then," Patrick retorted. "You're welcome in the tractor shed anytime."

"Tell Caine and Macklin that," Seth said. "I want to stay."

"You know they wouldn't turn you away. They've taken in complete strangers. They'll always have a place for family."

The words warmed Seth all the way through. He hadn't had many constants in his life besides Chris, but Lang Downs was the one place he could always come back to—for comfort, to lick his wounds, or simply to come home. "I know."

Neil climbed over the bench next to Seth with a frown on his face.

"No news from Sam?" Patrick asked.

Neil shook his head. "No, and the longer we go with no news, the worse it will be when we hear. They should have made it to Canberra now, so either he's in surgery or he's been moved on to Sydney."

"If there's anything we can do...."

"Same here," Seth added when Patrick trailed off.

"Nothing we can do until we hear what's going on," Neil said. "Jeremy doesn't have the authority to ask us to help without Taylor's consent, assuming he wants to help the no-good—"

"Don't finish that sentence, Neil Emery," Molly, Neil's wife, said as she sat down across from him. "Dani is around somewhere, and I won't have her picking up your bad habits."

Seth repressed a snicker. Neil was as henpecked as ever, and the worst was when it came to their daughter picking up what Molly considered Neil's bad habits. It reassured him in an odd way. Nothing ever changed at Lang Downs.

"Welcome home, Seth," Molly continued. "I didn't get a chance to say that earlier. How long are you here for?"

"For as long as Caine and Macklin will let me stay," Seth said. "I signed over my lease in Sydney. It was time to come home."

"Then welcome home even more. We'll be glad to have your hands around here."

"Just my hands?" Seth teased.

"Of course not," Molly said with a laugh. "But your hands will be particularly useful in all Caine's projects. I think he's been waiting for you to come home so he could get started."

"I'll talk to him after dinner or in the morning. I'm eager to get started on whatever he has planned."

"You should head over to the bunkhouse after dinner and get to know the jackaroos," Neil said. "Talking to Caine can wait until morning, and depending on what he has you doing, knowing the men will be good."

"He's not going to make me a crew boss, is he?" Seth asked. "I was nineteen when I left. I don't know enough to be in charge of anything."

"We aren't short on crew bosses," Neil assured him, "but if he has you putting in windmills or solar panels and running electrical wires, you're going to need more hands than just your own. Molly wasn't kidding about his plans. He wants to put a generator in each of the drover's huts and he's talked about trying to make the main buildings less dependent on outside power too. And that's only the beginning."

"It sounds like there's plenty for me to do, then." He hadn't let himself worry Caine wouldn't have any use for his degree. He'd told himself he could always work in the tractor shed maintaining the station's equipment and be perfectly happy. But what Neil was describing was so much better.

The canteen door burst open and a crowd of jackaroos tumbled inside, laughing and carrying on. Seth shared a familiar eye roll with the others at his table at the ruckus. "It is Friday night," Seth said.

"Then they should have gone to town as soon as they got in tonight," Neil said. "That's what we did."

"Once or twice a season," Patrick corrected. "Most weekend nights, you were partying in the bunkhouse just like those boys will be tonight."

"As long as all the ones on duty tomorrow can do their jobs," Neil grumbled.

"One or two of them might not be happy on horseback in the morning, but other than that, they'll be fine. They don't have enough booze in the bunkhouse to get so drunk they can't work," Jesse said.

Chris chortled while Patrick rolled his eyes and Neil covered his ears. Seth relaxed into the easy familiarity of it. Neil was Caine and Macklin's staunchest supporter and wouldn't tolerate even a hint of homophobic bullshit from the men under his command, but the thought of any of them having sex was the fastest way to send him running. Neil had stood up for Chris when the chips were down, though, and that put him at the top of Seth's list of favorite people.

The sound of Jason's laughter caught Seth's ear. He looked around the canteen and found Jason sitting with the jackaroos who had just come in. That stung a little, but he pushed the hurt aside. They were Jason's friends too. He didn't have to drop everything because Seth had come home. One of the jackaroos slung an arm around Jason's shoulder with what seemed like too much familiarity.

"Who's that sitting with Jason?" he asked Jesse before he could think better of it.

"Cooper Samuels, one of the new seasonal staff," Jesse said. "He's mostly been on Kyle's crew, but he seems like a solid worker. He and Jason have hit it off."

It looked like a whole lot more than that from where Seth was sitting, especially when Cooper stood up and trailed his fingers across Jason's nape as he walked away. Dinner soured in his stomach. "I'm going to bed. I'm still worn out from the trip."

"Seth!"

He ignored Chris calling his name and stalked out of the canteen.

He wasn't sure where he was going. It didn't matter as long as it was far enough from the canteen to escape the vision of another man's hands on Jason's body and far enough from the bunkhouse that he wouldn't have to hear whatever they got up to after dinner. He had no claim on Jason's affections. They were friends, best friends even, but Jason had never given Seth the slightest hint it might go beyond that.

Seth had always known his feelings for Jason were hopeless. He'd figured that out when Jason went away to uni without a backward glance. They'd still been kids then, and Seth had tried to chalk his feelings up to youthful infatuation, but that only got him seven years of dating people he didn't love, most recently Ilene. And if that didn't sum up the sorry state of his life, he didn't know what would. Hearing Jason had come home had made him hope again. He should have known better. He didn't get good things in life. Those were reserved for people like Caine and Macklin. Seth just got the leftovers no one else wanted.

He'd thought Jason was different, but obviously not. He reached the tractor shed and punched the wall as hard as he could. The wood could withstand the abuse and maybe if he let out some of the turmoil inside him now, he could hide it from everyone tomorrow. Pain shot up his arm, but he reveled in it. It served him right, coveting something he couldn't have. His mother hadn't been strict about much of anything, but he'd learned one lesson while he and Chris lived with their stepfather. Taking things that belonged to his stepsiblings guaranteed retribution from both them and his stepfather. He'd learned how to get them back in ways his stepfather wouldn't notice or couldn't pin on him, but that wouldn't help him now, because even if he managed to get Samuels back for stealing Jason, Jason would never forgive him for messing things up for him.

He slammed his fist into the wall again. The sickening crunch turned his stomach. He fought down the bile that rose in his throat. He had to stop or he'd hurt his hand too badly to hide it. He had to be able to work tomorrow. Neil had said as much at dinner. He cradled his hand to his chest and leaned against the wall, his breath sawing in and out of his lungs. He gulped down bile again and stared up at the darkening sky as he tried to control his body's reactions to the pain in his hand and the turmoil in his mind. He focused on his hand, letting it ground him to physical reality rather than the nebulous muck in his head.

When he could do more than just hold himself together by force of will alone, he looked down at his hand. The skin of his knuckles was broken and bleeding. He flexed his fist until the pain subsided a little. He could move all his fingers and make a fist, so hopefully he hadn't broken anything. He'd wrap it so it wouldn't get dirt in it, and he'd get to the shed early in the morning. Mechanics always had scrapes and bruises on their hands. He'd tell everyone he'd fought with a stuck bolt and lost. No one would know about the meltdown, and if things got to be too much, he'd press on the sore spots until his mind settled again. He didn't know what he'd do when they healed, but he'd worry about that later. For now, he could cope.

He had to.

CHRIS'S VOICE caught Jason's attention in time to see Seth barrel out of the canteen and into the deepening twilight. He waited the space of two heartbeats to see if Chris would go after his brother, but when he didn't, Jason excused himself from the table. He'd hear it from Kami later about letting his food get cold, but Seth mattered more. Whatever had upset him, Jason needed to set it right.

He looked up and down the road from the veranda outside the canteen, but he couldn't see Seth in either direction. He frowned as he considered where Seth might have gone.

"Looking for me?"

Jason focused on the voice to his left. Cooper lounged against the veranda support, an unlit cigarette between his full lips.

"I was looking for Seth," Jason said honestly. Cooper's face fell, reminding Jason of Thorne's comment earlier in the day. He pushed his concern for Seth aside. Seth had Chris and Jesse to look out for him if something was really wrong. "But finding you is even better."

Cooper's expression brightened. He pulled the cigarette from his mouth. "And what are you going to do now that you've found me?"

"Depends on what you're offering." Jason relaxed into the easy flirting, reminiscent of their first night together. He had the next day off, specifically arranged so he could spend the day with Seth. Cooper had to work. Jason could spend the evening with his lover and the next day with his best friend. Even Seth couldn't blame him for that.

NOT LOOKING good. Bleeding in the brain. Probable brain damage. Even if he lives, he may never work the station again.

Neil stared down at Sam's text. Bloody fucking hell. He didn't need that kind of news, even about a no-good son of a bitch like Devlin Taylor. He excused himself from the table. He had to tell Caine and Macklin.

"Got a few minutes, boss?" Neil asked as he approached the table where they were sitting.

"Of course," Caine said. "What's going on?"

"Sam just texted me." He handed the phone to Caine and Macklin so they could read the message. "I haven't talked to him, so I don't know what Jeremy's planning, if he's even gotten that far, but this is a game changer."

"So it is," Caine replied. "We can move people around, maybe promote one of the jackaroos who's been here more than one season. I can pick up the slack in the office until we can hire a new office manager."

"Are you firing Sam?" Neil asked sharply.

"You know I'd never do that." Neil flinched at the gentle reproof in Caine's voice. He hated letting Caine down in even the smallest ways.

"Sorry," Neil said. "This has thrown me off."

"I know. I don't have a brother, but it's unsettling for all of us. If Jeremy goes to Taylor Peak to help his brother, or to run the station if Taylor dies, Sam will go with him, and we'd be selfish to expect anything else. Sam could potentially come here a couple of times a week to keep up with some of the business side of things, but Jeremy will need help on Taylor Peak too, and his degree is in animal husbandry, not in business. It wouldn't be fair to Sam to have to juggle both stations. I may spend most of my time outdoors these days, but I do have a business degree. I can manage the office until we find someone new."

"And if Taylor won't let them help?" Neil asked.

"Then we'll go on as we always have," Macklin said. "What happens on Taylor Peak is only our business as it affects Jeremy or if they try to start something again. Taylor's personal opinions aside, things have been peaceful for the past few years. We won't be the ones to rock that boat."

"What should I tell Sam?" Neil asked.

"Tell him we're all thinking about them and to let us know how we can help," Caine said. "And then tell him he and Jeremy are officially on leave of absence for as long as they need. They have enough to worry about without adding their jobs here to the list. We'll make do without them until things settle enough for them to come home."

"Thanks, boss. I'll let them know."

Neil texted Sam back as he walked out of the canteen. The message had barely finished sending when his phone vibrated again.

Don't ever do something stupid enough for this to be you.

I won't, Neil texted back, even if he couldn't realistically make that promise. Even the best riders got thrown sometimes. He paused for a moment, then added, *If I can help, I will. Even if it means making nice with Taylor.*

Thanks.

Neil had expected more than that, some sort of quip about him growing up or learning to control his temper or any of the hundred things Sam and Molly teased him about. Sam's silence worried Neil. Not that it was the right time for teasing, but Neil would give them another couple of hours and then he'd call Sam. If things took a turn for the worse, he wanted to know about it. He didn't give a shit about Taylor, but he did care what happened to Jeremy.

JASON STIRRED in Cooper's arms. Every muscle in his body was lax with postorgasmic bliss, but his mind wouldn't settle. He kept seeing Seth run from the canteen. "I should go back to my own room. You have to work tomorrow, and I don't want to disturb you."

"You don't 'disturb' me." Cooper nuzzled Jason's neck. Jason resisted the urge to push Cooper away. He didn't want to fight with Cooper over it, but he *was* going back to his own room tonight.

"Then I should go back so you don't wake me up in the morning." He kissed Cooper to soften his insistence on leaving. Cooper tried to deepen the kiss, but Jason pulled away and sat up. His shirt and jeans were near the door, so Cooper would get a show when he walked over to get them. That would have to hold Cooper for a while.

Cooper grumbled a little, but he didn't sound too upset, so Jason winked at him before he bent over to pick up his clothes. Cooper grinned at that and leered comically at him. Jason breathed a sigh of relief. He really didn't want a fight. He just wanted his own bed and a few hours to sort out what having Seth home for good would mean for his peace of mind. Once he'd figured that out and put everything in its proper perspective, he could spend Saturday with Seth, find his balance again, and relax into his relationship with Cooper. He'd be fine by tomorrow night. He simply needed a little time and space right now.

When Jason was dressed, he turned back to Cooper. "Be careful out there tomorrow. I don't know exactly what happened on Taylor Peak, but falling off a horse could happen to anybody. I don't want you to be rushed to the hospital."

"I'm always careful," Cooper said with easy confidence. Jason hadn't seen anything to refute that, so he accepted the assertion. Cooper rose and strode across the room completely naked. Jason took a moment to admire his wiry build and the way the light and shadow played across his muscles. Cooper slid his arms around Jason's waist, resting his hands on the curve of Jason's arse, so Jason took that as permission to fondle Cooper's arse in return. Jason kissed him softly. Cooper squeezed his handful again as he returned the kiss. "Sure I can't convince you to stay?"

"Not tonight." Jason gave Cooper's bare skin a light swat. "Get some sleep. I meant what I said about being careful, and you can't do that if you're falling asleep in the saddle."

"Fine, but tomorrow night, I'm not taking no for an answer."

They'd see about that tomorrow night. Jason enjoyed Cooper's company—and the sex was a nice bonus—but if he spent too many nights in Cooper's bed, the year-rounders would have them paired off and moving into a house of their own before he could blink, and he couldn't picture that at the moment. Maybe someday, but not yet.

Or at least not with Cooper, his traitorous mind supplied. He could all too easily imagine it with Seth. Except for the one small detail of Seth being straight.

"I'll see you tomorrow night," Jason replied. He gave Cooper one more quick kiss and pulled out of the embrace. He checked the hallway and slipped down to his room. He hadn't made his relationship with Cooper a secret, but he didn't want to listen to the teasing if anyone saw him coming out of Cooper's room either.

Safely ensconced in his own room, Jason stripped back down to his underwear. He needed a shower to get rid of the sweat and lube, but if he headed to the shower block, he ran the risk of running into Cooper. They'd shared the shower, both before and after becoming lovers, but Jason wasn't in the mood for it tonight. He'd wait and shower in the morning, when everyone was already out in the paddocks. He could just be sweaty until then.

He crawled between the sheets and tried to relax. Usually he had no trouble falling asleep after sex, even if he got up before going to sleep, but sleep wouldn't come. He kept seeing Seth tearing out of the canteen. He rolled over and looked at the clock by his bed: 10:08. Too late to go knocking on Chris and Jesse's door, asking to talk to Seth. Chris had agreed to take Jeremy's crew again the next day, giving up his day off. Jason probably should have offered in Chris's place, but he wasn't technically a crew boss, even if he knew as much about the station as anyone else did.

He didn't regret having the day to spend with Seth. E-mails, Skype, and the like were better than nothing, but they couldn't compare to a day spent together in person. He'd volunteer to cover for Chris on Sunday so Chris could spend some time with Seth too.

FOUR

"HOW IS he this morning?" Jeremy asked Devlin's floor nurse when they arrived at the hospital. Visiting hours didn't start for another two hours, but he couldn't stare at the walls of the hotel where they'd spent the night for one more minute. Even if he paced the waiting room instead of the hotel room, he'd be close if anything happened, good or bad. He wanted to believe it would be good, but either way, he'd be here.

"No change. The doctors are doing rounds now, so maybe they'll have more news for you after they've seen him this morning." She sounded tired, but that could just as easily be because she was at the end of a night shift as because no change was bad news. Sam rubbed the small of Jeremy's back, making his stomach fall. If Sam felt the need to comfort Jeremy, he thought the news was discouraging.

"Thank you," Jeremy said. "I'll talk to the doctors in a bit, then."

She gave him a forced smile and went back to her duties.

"No change is better than a change for the worse," Jeremy said doggedly when he turned back to look at Sam.

"It is, but it's not good news. I just don't want you to get your hopes up too much."

"What I am supposed to do?" Jeremy demanded. "Just give up on him?"

"Of course not," Sam said as he led Jeremy to the row of chairs lining the wall near the window. "But the longer he stays unconscious, the harder his recovery will be when he wakes up."

Jeremy hated the unspoken thought at the end of Sam's sentence. "If he wakes up. You might as well say it. Not talking about it doesn't make it less of a possible outcome."

"I'm trying to stay positive."

"So am I, but it's hard. Even if he wakes up right now, he's not going back to running the station tomorrow," Jeremy said. "And that means fighting with him over who's going to run the station in his place, not to mention listening to him go on about how if he had a 'real' brother, it wouldn't be an issue because he could just ask his brother to cover for him. But since he's stuck with a pillow biter who'd rather fuck around on Lang Downs than live up to his family name, he'll just have to make do on his own."

"This is not your fault," Sam said so fiercely Jeremy could almost believe him. "Even when you tried to be who he wanted you to be, he made your life miserable. No one could expect you to live with that kind of abuse. And you didn't tell him not to hire a new foreman after Williams retired. He could have found someone to help him, even if it wasn't you. This was an accident, nothing more, nothing less."

"Maybe," Jeremy said, "but you know he won't see it that way."

"That's his problem, not yours," Sam insisted.

If only that were true, but as strained as their relationship had been since Jeremy grew old enough to see Devlin's prejudices, enough of the adoring younger brother still lived in his psyche for Devlin's words to hurt. He made himself smile at Sam as he reached for his hand. "Don't ever take Neil for granted. I know we haven't always seen eye to eye, but you're lucky to have him for a brother."

"You know he thinks of you as his brother-in-law," Sam said. "Even if the worst happens with Devlin, you'll still have a family."

Jeremy blinked hard, fighting tears. He couldn't cry here, not while Devlin still held on by a thread. He had to be strong. "You don't know how much that means to me."

"I do," Sam said. "I thought I'd lose Neil if he found out I was gay. To have him accept me... I know how lucky I am. I came to Lang Downs with next to nothing, expecting to lose what little I had left, and instead I found a new family, a new home, a new relationship with my brother, and you. If I could change Devlin's mind, I would do it because I know how much it tears at you every time he rejects you because of me."

"Not because of you," Jeremy said, "or not only because of you. He'd reject me for being gay even if I was still single. Having you is what makes his rejection bearable."

Sam pulled Jeremy into a tight hug. Jeremy clung to him. Without Sam's support.... He burrowed deeper into the curve of Sam's neck. That thought didn't bear consideration. He had Sam's support, and no matter what happened with Devlin and Taylor Peak, that wouldn't change. Sam might not be a stockman, born and bred in the tablelands, but he was Jeremy's bedrock as completely as the land that rooted him.

Sam let him cling, waiting patiently until Jeremy no longer felt like he'd shatter into a million pieces without Sam to hold him together. Eventually his stomach rumbled, breaking the weight of the moment.

"I guess we should find food while we wait for the doctors," Jeremy said.

"I can find something if you want to stay here," Sam offered.

It would be so easy to agree, but staying wouldn't change anything or speed up how quickly the doctors came out to talk to them. If nothing else, going to get breakfast would make the time pass faster. "No, I'll come with you. It'll do me good to walk around a bit. I'm not used to sitting still."

"MACKLIN, DO you have a minute?" Seth said when he caught the station owner after breakfast.

"I can spare one or two." Ten years ago, the expression—or lack thereof—on Macklin's face would have sent Seth running for the hills, but he'd learned to see beneath the stoicism and recognize when Macklin really didn't have time for an interruption.

"Somewhere private?"

Macklin looked surprised but led Seth out of the canteen and into the big house. "What's on your mind?"

"I… um… I want to come home," Seth blurted out. "Not just for a visit, but to stay." Macklin cocked an eyebrow at him and waited, so Seth took a deep breath and plowed on. "I hate Sydney. I mean, I don't hate it, but it's big and noisy and people expect things, and it's not home."

"People will expect things here too," Macklin said. "That's part of being an adult."

"I know that, but the expectations here are that I'll work hard and pull my own weight, and that if I fuck up, I'll admit it and get help to fix it," Seth said. "I can live with those expectations. It's all the other ones I hate."

Macklin nodded, his expression suggesting he understood exactly what Seth was talking about. As far as Seth knew, Macklin hadn't lived anywhere but Lang Downs since he was a kid, but from the stories he'd heard, Macklin had hidden in plain sight until Caine came along and dragged him out into the open, changing the complexion of Lang Downs for good.

"Carley said Patrick's hands were starting to bother him. I could take some of that work off him, and anything else you need me to do, I'll learn if I don't already know it," Seth said. "Please? I… *need* to come home."

"Why?" Macklin asked. "I'm not saying no. I won't say no, but I need to understand. I can't help you if I don't understand."

"You won't tell anyone?"

"Have you ever heard me telling tales?" Macklin countered.

Seth hadn't. He'd heard plenty of gossip when he lived here before, even with the jackaroos trying to protect his "innocent ears," but none of it had ever come from Macklin's lips.

"I broke up with Ilene," he said, trying to decide where to start. "It wasn't working between us. There's… someone else. There always has been, but I can't…. He'll never look at me. I know it's hopeless. He's with someone else, but at least if I'm here…. Bloody hell, I'm making a complete arse of myself."

"Love has a way of doing that to a man," Macklin agreed. "Here's the deal. You can stay. This is your home as much as it is his." Seth grimaced. He hadn't meant to be that transparent. "But it can't interfere with your work. Either of your work. If that means you don't work on the same crew as him, that's fine. I can assign you to different crew bosses. If that means coordinating your days off so you aren't off at the same time, I can do that. But it's up to you to handle the times when you can't avoid him. In the canteen, in the bunkhouse—unless you're staying with Chris and Jesse?" Seth had been tempted to do that, but that would be too much like admitting defeat. He shook his head. "Then we'll need to find you a room in the bunkhouse too. And you're going to have to deal with the bunkhouse gossip. Neil won't let them talk about Caine and me, he shuts them down almost as fast when they talk about Jeremy and Sam, and they're all too scared of Thorne to talk about him and Ian. That leaves Chris and Jesse—who are too domesticated to be interesting most of the time—and whoever might have paired off out there."

Seth had heard enough gossip about Chris and Jesse when they were still in the getting-together stage to know exactly what to expect. He'd have to sit there with a smile pasted on and pretend it didn't kill him every time Jason's name was paired with Cooper's. He'd have to tease Jason the same way he'd tease any other jackaroo once he couldn't pretend not to hear the gossip. He'd have to put on the façade he'd perfected while living with his stepfather and act like everything was fine when nothing was fine at all. And he'd have to do it so well that his best friend didn't suspect.

He clenched his fist, pulling the torn skin over his knuckles. The bite of pain settled him. He could handle it. "It'll be worth it to be home."

"You could try telling him," Macklin said. "You might be surprised."

"He's with someone else," Seth repeated. "I don't poach. If it doesn't work out for them, I'll think about it, but I won't be the other guy in this story."

"Your choice," Macklin said. "Now, if you're staying, we need to talk about duties. I doubt you want to spend all your time following the mob around."

"Carley mentioned Caine had plans," Seth said. "Might as well use my fancy degree for something."

JEREMY GLANCED down at his watch again. Ten o'clock. How long did it take for the doctors to do their rounds? He'd expected someone to come talk to them an hour ago at least.

"Checking your watch every two minutes isn't going to make them come any sooner," Sam said.

"I know, but it's been hours already."

"Only because we got here so early. Ten o'clock isn't that early unless you work on a sheep station, love."

Jeremy sighed and looked at his watch again: 10:02. "If I have to watch any more bad telly, I'm going to scream."

"Don't do that. My ears wouldn't survive."

Jeremy spun around at the unexpected voice.

"Neil! What are you doing here?"

Neil shrugged in the way Jeremy had learned to expect when Neil had done something nice and then tried to pretend it didn't matter. "I hadn't heard anything this morning, so I figured I'd come check on you."

"So you got up at the crack of dawn to get here?" Sam snarked. "Even if we had news this morning, you left before we could have got it to you."

"My brothers needed me," Neil said in such a matter-of-fact tone that Jeremy had to fight back tears again.

"We're glad you're here." Jeremy's cheeks burned at the sound of his voice breaking, but he needed Neil to understand how much his presence meant. "I'm glad you're here."

"What did Caine say about you coming?" Sam asked.

"He said if I wanted to spend my day off in the car, that was my business," Neil replied. "As long as I leave by dinner, I can get home tonight. It'll be a long day, but it'll be worth it."

"It wasn't your day off," Jeremy said with a frown. He was out of it, yes, but he knew Neil's day off was always Sunday, not Saturday.

"Caine seemed to think it was when he made that comment last night," Neil replied with a shrug. Gratitude surged through Jeremy again. Whatever happened with Devlin, Jeremy would still have a family, one far more reliable than his brother had ever been.

"Mr. Taylor?"

Jeremy took a deep breath and steeled himself to face the doctor.

"Yes, I'm Taylor."

"We did another CT scan on your brother this morning. That's why it's taken me so long to come talk to you." The doctor's tone was kind, overly so.

"It's bad news, isn't it?" Jeremy said. He shivered despite the room being warm. Sam and Neil flanked him, the heat from their bodies steadying him. He wasn't facing this alone.

"It's not good news," the doctor agreed. "We drained the blood that was putting pressure on your brother's brain in the hope of reducing the risk of brain damage, but the bleeding hasn't stopped despite the medication he's on, and the pressure is building back up. We've scheduled another procedure to relieve the pressure, but the longer this goes on, the harder his recovery will be."

"Will he recover?" Jeremy asked. "Don't give me platitudes. I don't want to hold on to false hope. If you do this procedure and relieve the pressure, does he have a chance of recovering?"

"I don't have an answer to that," the doctor said. "The brain is an unpredictable organ at best, and so many factors can influence the situation. Factors we can't account for right now. If the bleeding stops and we only have to relieve the pressure, his chances are better than if we relieve the pressure but the bleeding continues. We aren't equipped to do the kind of surgery your brother needs. He needs to go to Sydney. Normally we wouldn't transfer a patient as unstable as he is, but I'm afraid if we don't, we'll lose him anyway."

"What do you need me to sign so you can transfer him?" Jeremy said hoarsely. "I'll take full responsibility if it's what it takes to save his life."

"I'll have a nurse prepare the paperwork," the doctor said. "We'll see how he does through the second procedure. It could be his vital signs will stabilize once the pressure on his brain goes down again. If that happens, we can transfer him with no problem. We have a few minutes still before we start the procedure. Would you like to see him?"

Jeremy almost said no. He had too few good memories of Devlin and more than enough of him lying unconscious in a hospital bed. If he didn't go and Devlin died, though, he'd always regret it. He'd go in for a moment, tell Devlin to get better, and come back out to wait. "If it won't delay the procedure."

"They're still prepping the room. I'll show you back."

Jeremy nodded and followed the doctor. Sam and Neil stayed right next to him, buoying his flagging spirits with their silent support. Maybe they wouldn't be allowed into Devlin's room with him—he didn't know how strict the hospital would be about visitors—but they'd be waiting for him right outside when he finished. He might be the only one in the room with Devlin, but he wouldn't have to face it alone.

The doctor led them to the same room as the night before—not that Jeremy expected it to be a different one, except the way things were going, he wouldn't have been surprised—and stood aside to let them enter. Neil hesitated on the threshold, but Jeremy grabbed his arm and pulled him inside too. If the doctor would let them all in, Jeremy wanted his whole family with him. Sam slipped his hand into Jeremy's on the other side, surrounding him in their support.

Devlin's skin looked sallow in the bright light despite the tan from a life spent outdoors. It hadn't even been a day since his accident, but his cheeks had taken on a sunken appearance. His chest rose and fell in time with the hiss of the respirator, and a machine beeped in time with his pulse. If the bursts of sound were less steady than Jeremy's own pulse, that was to be expected, given the state Devlin was in.

"Go talk to him," Sam urged. "Maybe he can't respond, but that doesn't mean he can't hear you. We can step outside if you don't want us listening in."

Jeremy shook his head. Sam and Neil knew how badly his relationship with Devlin had deteriorated since he'd moved to Lang Downs. Nothing he could say now would come as a shock to them. If only he knew what to say....

"Bloody hell, Devlin," he muttered finally. "Why'd you have to get yourself in this mess? You couldn't have hired a new foreman and shared the load a little? How am I supposed to run things on Taylor Peak when I live on Lang Downs? And don't say I'm not supposed to. I can't very well leave it to go to hell in a handbasket while you're in here getting better. I'd never forgive myself, even if you forgave me. Of course you'd probably hate me more for doing things my own way while you weren't there to stop me." He choked back a sob. "I'll even try to do things your way for once if you'll just get well so I can turn it back over to you. I'll stay out of your hair and stop trying to change your mind about Sam and me and about Lang Downs and everything. I'll disappear completely if that's what you want. Just don't die on me."

Sam wrapped his arm around Jeremy's waist and Neil put a hand on Jeremy's shoulder, and that did in his control. He turned into Sam's embrace, buried his face against Sam's neck, and cried.

FIVE

JASON WALKED into the canteen well after breakfast was over on Saturday morning, but Kami and Sarah always left extra food warming on the weekends for the jackaroos who had the day off. He'd find something to eat and then he'd find Seth, since Seth wasn't in the canteen like Jason had hoped he'd be. That didn't matter. He had time. Seth was back to stay, so they didn't have to hoard every hour like a dragon with its treasure. They could miss each other now and then and still have plenty of time to spend together.

So why did it feel like Seth was slipping through his fingers?

He ran his hand through his hair. It was getting long. He'd have to ask his mother to cut it when he went to Sunday dinner. He filled a plate with eggs and toast and sat down to eat, grimacing as his arse came into contact with the hard bench. Normally that would bring a smile to his face, a reminder of a thorough fucking the night before, but this morning it just annoyed him. He could already hear Seth teasing him.

"What did my eggs do to make you scowl at them like that?"

"Morning, Sarah," Jason said, summoning a smile for Macklin's mother. "Nothing. I just have a lot on my mind."

"Anything you want to talk about?" she asked as she sat down across from him.

"Not really," he replied. He knew Sarah wouldn't be bothered by him being gay—she certainly didn't love Macklin any less because he was gay—but he didn't feel comfortable talking to her about his current conundrum. It was all in his head anyway. He got tired of reminding his errant heart that Seth was straight and only interested in Jason's friendship. It didn't do any good anyway.

"Did you and your young man have a spat?"

"Something like that," Jason said. It looked like he'd be talking about it even if he didn't want to. "I like him, but I'm not sure I'm in love with him. It's too soon for that. He doesn't seem to share those concerns."

"I'm going to tell you two things," Sarah said, "and it's going to sound like I'm contradicting myself, but hear me out. First, time runs differently here on the station than it does elsewhere. You spend far more time with people here than you would in the city. You only have one group of people here, so work, your social life, and your downtime all include the same people. You can get to know someone pretty fast out here. Second, don't let him rush you into something you aren't ready for. I know what it's like to feel trapped into something, and I wouldn't wish that on my worst enemy, much less on a sweet lad like you. I guess what I'm saying is if it's right, time isn't a reason to delay, but if it's wrong, it's wrong no matter what. And if you don't know which it is yet, then don't make promises you might not want to keep."

"Thanks, Sarah," Jason said. "I really just want to spend a day with Seth. That always puts things back in perspective for me."

"You'll have to hurry if you want to catch him," Sarah said. "He was heading to the tractor shed to do a little maintenance and then out to check on some of the drover's huts. Macklin put him to work right away."

Jason grabbed a piece of toast and bolted for the door. "Thanks again, Sarah. I'll see you at dinner."

She shook her head at him even as she waved him off. He stuffed the toast in his mouth and headed toward the tractor shed. Seth's car was still outside Chris and Jesse's house, but Seth would probably take one of the utes if he was heading out into the tablelands.

"Seth?" he called as he neared the tractor shed. "Are you in there?"

No one answered, but Jason could hear the sound of muffled cursing and of tools clanging against metal. His dad didn't usually curse that way when he worked, so either the problem was worse than usual or Seth was still there.

"Chris never did manage to break you of that habit, did he?" Jason asked as he stepped into the tractor shed.

Seth spun around, wrench in hand, then slumped against the tire of the tractor. "Bloody hell, Jase, don't scare me that way."

"Sorry, I didn't mean to sneak up on you," Jason said. "Did something break?"

"No, just regular maintenance." Seth's voice sounded odd. "I figured I'd better get familiar with the machines again if I was going to be partially in charge of them."

"Oh." Jason tried to keep his disappointment from showing. "I was hoping we could spend the day together since we haven't seen each other in so long. E-mails aren't the same."

"I wish I could," Seth said, "but I won't have a day off until next week. Unless you want to hang out in here with me while I finish this up? Then I have to head out to the drover's huts."

The hopeful tone of Seth's voice decided Jason. "Of course I'll hang out with you. I don't know if I'll be any help, but I'll keep you company. I can hand you tools like I did for my dad when I was a kid."

"I thought he knew where every tool was in his toolbox blindfolded," Seth said with a smirk. Jason shouldn't have been so susceptible to that expression, given they were talking about his father, but the subject matter didn't change the way his gut lurched in reaction to Seth's teasing. He had no defenses where Seth was concerned.

"He does, but he still managed to make me feel absolutely essential to the smooth running of the shed until I was about ten and started wondering what he did when I wasn't around to help him." Jason came deeper into the tractor shed and took a seat on one of the bales of hay, much like he had always done with Patrick.

"You're lucky to have a dad like that."

"And I know it," Jason replied. "I've listened to too many stories from the other jackaroos not to know it. Sometimes I think Caine and I are the only two with normal childhoods, and Caine had the stutter to contend with. Everyone else had one issue or another growing up."

"Not all of us had the chance to grow up here," Seth said. "Those of us with sense just got here as soon as we could."

Jason smiled, as Seth had intended, even as he remembered the sullen, defensive teenager who'd arrived on Lang Downs in his brother's wake. The only things Seth had cared about when he first came to the station were his brother and machines. Jason liked to think he had a part in making the years Seth spent here before going off to uni better than the years before he arrived. If only he hadn't fallen in love with his straight best friend in the process.

"So what are you working on?" Jason asked. "I might not have your fancy degree, but I learnt a few things growing up with my dad."

"MR. TAYLOR?"

Jeremy looked up to see a different doctor standing at the door to the waiting room.

"Yes?"

"Walk with me."

Sam squeezed his hand. "Want me to come with you?"

"Both of you," Jeremy said, looking at Neil. "If it's good news, we'll celebrate together, and if it isn't, I'll need your support."

They followed the doctor back to Devlin's room. The bed stood empty, the machines silent. "Is Devlin still in recovery?"

"I'm sorry, Mr. Taylor. He went into cardiac arrest during the procedure. We couldn't get his heart started again. The bleeding in his brain put too much pressure on his brain stem."

Jeremy stared at the doctor blankly, trying to make his brain process the words. Sam and Neil flanked him in an instant, an arm around him from each side. His knees trembled as he struggled to make sense of this new reality. He couldn't force his mind to work. Devlin couldn't be gone. He'd always been there, even when Jeremy wished he wasn't. Everything else in Jeremy's life had changed—for better or worse—but not Devlin. And now he was gone.

He bent double beneath the pain, only Sam's and Neil's arms keeping him from falling. "I can't...," he gasped. "He can't be gone."

"I'm sorry for your loss," the doctor repeated.

Jeremy forced himself upright. "Can I see him?"

"In a few minutes," the doctor said. "They're cleaning him up. You can wait here. An orderly will come get you when they're ready for you."

Jeremy nodded and the doctor withdrew.

"I'm so sorry," Sam whispered as he pulled Jeremy into his arms.

Jeremy shuddered, trying to hold back his sobs. He'd already cried once today. He could hear Devlin sneering at him for his tears. *Real men don't cry.* Once had been bad enough. Twice in one day would be too much.

"Don't hold it in," Sam ordered. "He's your brother. You're allowed to cry for him."

"He'd disown me," Jeremy said around a hiccough.

"I'll disown you if you don't," Neil muttered.

Jeremy tried not to laugh, but he couldn't stop it. Tears streamed down his face as he cried and laughed and cried some more. "Bloody hell, Emery," he said between sobs. "You can't say shit like that. You're the only brother I have left."

"Pretty sure there's a few more men on Lang Downs who would give you that title," Neil replied, "but I'll claim you."

Jeremy's laughter quieted, his grief getting the better of him again. Tears continued to leak from his eyes unhindered as he sat on the empty bed. Sam sat next to him, a bedrock of support.

"Did Devlin have a will?" Sam asked. "Or anything to tell us what kind of arrangements he wanted?"

"There's a family plot on the station," Jeremy said. "He'll be buried there. Everyone in the family has been for a hundred fifty years."

He and Devlin would be the last ones.

"That takes care of funeral arrangement, then," Sam said, "but we'll still need to find his will and insurance policies, if he had them."

"If he did, they'd be in the safe in his office. I know what Dad's combination was. I hope Devlin didn't change it."

"Can you tell me where the safe is?" Neil asked. "I can see if Molly will drive to Taylor Peak to look for it. She's sort of family."

"She's family," Jeremy said firmly.

"Not in a way most of them will recognize," Neil reminded him, "but the jackaroos are still less likely to challenge her than they would be to challenge any of the men. And it'll be faster than you driving all the way there and then having to come back to deal with everything here."

"The station…. There's no foreman."

"So assign one," Sam said. "Perkins or White or someone. Even if it's just for a few days, until we can get there and see what's what."

"You can worry about that tomorrow," Neil interrupted. "Tell me where Molly should look. Everything else can wait a day or two."

Jeremy closed his eyes and tried to picture Devlin's office. He hadn't been in there since he moved to Lang Downs almost ten years ago. Even when he went to Taylor Peak to torture himself with Devlin's continuing rejection, he never got past the living room—if he even got that far. Half the time Devlin ran him off before he reached the veranda.

"The office is in the back of the house, to the left off the living room," Jeremy said. "If Devlin didn't move anything around, the safe will be in the closet. If he moved it, it could be anywhere in the house. Dad's combination was twelve, twenty-nine, three."

"I'll tell Molly," Neil said. "Do you need anything from home? She can pick it up before she goes to Taylor Peak."

And wasn't that the kicker? His home was the house he and Sam had helped build and had lived in for years, but Taylor Peak was his family legacy. Unless Devlin had written Jeremy completely out of his will—they did have a distant cousin Devlin might have given it to out of spite—Taylor Peak, with all the associated responsibilities, would be his now.

He was going to be sick.

"Jeremy?"

"No, I don't need anything from home," Jeremy said as he struggled to swallow down the bile that rose in his throat. "Tell Molly I'm sorry she has to come all the way here."

"Don't be daft. Under the circumstances, she'll be glad to do it," Neil said. "I'll go call now. Twelve, twenty-nine, three, right?"

Jeremy nodded, and Neil left.

"I can't do this," Jeremy said to Sam when they were alone.

"Do what?" Sam scooted closer to Jeremy.

"Give up the life we built together, take the station, step into Devlin's shoes—any of it. Even if I wanted to, I wouldn't know where to start."

"At the beginning," Sam said, "and going to Taylor Peak doesn't mean giving up our life together. I can work remotely part of the time and drive to Lang Downs the rest of the time. Caine will find a way to make it work for us. You know that."

"That assumes I want it to work," Jeremy said. "What if I want to say forget the whole bloody thing and just go home?"

"Then that's what we'll do," Sam said, "but you still have to figure out what to do with Taylor Peak. If nothing else, Devlin hired men to work the station for a season and you have livestock you can't abandon. If you want to get through the season, sell off the whole mob and let the land go unused, you can, but then you'll continue to have the yearly taxes and everything to deal with without any income."

"I could sell it," Jeremy said. "Hell, I'll give it away. Or maybe I got lucky and Devlin left it to someone else. Then I won't have to worry about it."

"We'll worry about that when Molly gets here," Sam said. "But whatever you decide, we're in it together. Nothing can change that."

CAINE LOOKED up when Molly walked into the office. The look on her face told him all he needed to know. "It's bad, isn't it?"

Molly nodded. "Taylor died this morning. Neil asked me to go to Taylor Peak to see if I could find the will and then to take it to them in Canberra. Linda said she'd watch the kids for the day, but I don't know if I'll make it back tonight."

"Macklin and I can keep an eye on them tonight if Linda can't," Caine said. Kyle's wife Linda frequently exchanged child-care services with Molly and Neil, although Linda's daughter was old enough now to be the one watching Molly's young children. "Give Jeremy our condolences and let me know if there's anything we can do. In Canberra or on the station."

"I will," Molly said. "I'll call when I get to Canberra or if I hear anything else from them before then."

She left the office, and Caine leaned back in his chair with a heavy sigh. He'd barely known Devlin Taylor and hadn't particularly liked what little he knew, but his death still left Caine shaken. For better or worse, he'd been a fixture in the local landscape.

He'd been an experienced grazier and a competent horseman, and he'd still been thrown and hurt so badly the fall killed him. Caine shuddered. How easy it would be for the same thing to happen to any of the jackaroos on Lang Downs.

To Macklin.

Rationally he knew Macklin was fine. He was spending the day working around the main buildings of the station, repairing tack, checking fences, and any other regular maintenance that he could find to do. He'd chosen those tasks specifically so he would be nearby if they got news from Jeremy. The panic clawing at Caine's throat wasn't rational. He grabbed his hat and headed outside. He had to see for himself that Macklin was fine.

He found Macklin a few minutes later outside the shearing shed with a hammer in his hand and a handful of nails between his teeth. Relief flooded through him.

Macklin finished sinking the nail on the repair he was making, set the hammer down, and grabbed the nails. "Caine? What's wrong?"

"Molly's gone to Taylor Peak. Devlin died this morning. And I might have freaked out a little thinking how easily it could have been you or someone else on the station."

Macklin pulled him into a hug—he always knew exactly what Caine needed—and held him tight. "We take precautions. We never ride out alone. We train the horses not to spook at unexpected noises or movement in the bush. We do everything we can to make sure everyone will come home at the end of the day. And sometimes accidents happen anyway." He tipped Caine's chin up so their gazes met. "But the same thing is true anywhere. Car accidents, house fires, you name it. Accidents happen no matter how careful people are. How's Jeremy holding up?"

Caine swallowed hard. "I didn't talk to him, and I don't think Molly did either. I told her to let us know if we could help, but I don't know what that would be."

"It might be as simple as sending a couple of men to Taylor Peak to keep things running until Jeremy can get his feet under him," Macklin said. "Devlin never asked for help, but I remember Michael sending people to help out when old man Taylor was still running the place and had a lot of damage from a tornado that hit Taylor Peak but missed us."

"I'll text Sam and offer," Caine said. "I don't even know if they've let the jackaroos at Taylor Peak know."

"I know you want to help, but don't overstep your bounds," Macklin cautioned. "Jeremy will have to find his own footing with the Taylor Peak jackaroos, just like you did when you arrived. We can't undermine that by stepping in too quickly or too often."

"At least he knows what he's doing," Caine said. "I couldn't have been any more of a blow-in if I'd tried when Uncle Michael died and I came to see if I could run a station."

"True, but he'll be fighting the same distrust you did, with the disadvantage of everyone knowing from the start that he's gay. It wouldn't surprise me if he lost people the same way we did the second summer. He'll recover if he can stick it out, but he's in for a rough road."

"You tell me that, and then you tell me not to step in?" Caine said. "You don't really expect me to sit by and do nothing, do you?"

"No, but I expect you to let Jeremy decide what kind of help we give and how often," Macklin said. "We run as much of a risk of making things worse by helping too much as by not helping enough."

Caine wasn't convinced, but arguing with Macklin was pointless, especially since he couldn't do anything until Jeremy came back to the station and they saw what the situation really was. Maybe they were all worrying for nothing and Jeremy would step into Devlin's shoes seamlessly.

SIX

SETH LAUGHED at Jason's joke and pushed his hair out of his eyes. With his bruised and battered hand.

"What did you do to yourself?" Jason asked, grabbing his wrist.

"Nothing," Seth said, heart pounding at the thought of Jason finding out what he'd done. He wouldn't understand. No one did. The pain steadied him, but that didn't make sense in anyone else's head. Just in Seth's. "Just skinned my knuckles fighting with a stuck bolt this morning."

It was a flimsy excuse at best, but he hadn't been able to come up with a better one. In school, before he came to Lang Downs, he'd been able to excuse it away by saying someone had picked a fight with him—a fight he'd always provoked, but subtly enough no one attributed it to anything more than hotheaded adolescence. He couldn't use that excuse now. He was no longer an adolescent who could get away with stunts like that. He had responsibilities, and that meant finding other ways to steady himself when the noise in his head became too much to bear.

"Did you get someone to look at it?" Jason asked. "You don't want it to get infected."

"I cleaned it out when it happened," Seth said. He'd learned more than enough first aid in his attempts to hide his injuries to keep the scrapes clean. He hadn't covered them because it would have made working this morning difficult, but he'd do that before dinner. People would notice the gauze more than a few scrapes, but if they couldn't see the marks, they couldn't question his story.

"That must have been one hell of a bolt," Jason remarked. "So what else is on the agenda today?"

"I have to drive out to a couple of the drover's huts to get the lay of the land. I heard a rumor about solar generators and windmills. It's not my area of expertise, but I had a couple of classes on green energy, so I should be able to get an idea of what might work. But for that I need to see the huts, because each one will be different. You don't have to go with me if you don't want to. It won't be particularly interesting work."

"It's not about the work," Jason said. "It's about spending the day with you. We haven't had a day together in a long time. Even if you have to spend this one working, at least we can be together. I can take notes for you, if nothing else."

Take the bloody excuse not to come, Seth thought miserably. He craved spending the day with Jason, but having him there and yet so far away was salt in the wounds on Seth's heart. He could deal with physical pain, but the pain in his heart made him want to run for the nearest knife. "Sure. You got something to write with?"

"No, but I'll get something from Mum. Give me five minutes and I'll be good to go."

Seth nodded as Jason walked out of the tractor shed. The minute Jason was out of sight, Seth slumped against the tractor. Fuck, he was a glutton for punishment. Why had he decided to come home again?

As easy as it was to wish he'd stayed in Sydney, he'd been miserable there too. Maybe not the cutting kind of miserable, but more a numb, dead inside kind of miserable. The kind cutting couldn't fix. As hard as it would be to see Jason every day and know he went off with Cooper every night, at least he was home.

Jason hadn't said anything, of course. He was too discreet for that. But Seth had seen the way he sat carefully, the way he'd winced when he shifted on the hay bale from time to time. Seth might not have any personal experience with it, but he recognized the lingering signs of a good fuck when he saw them. He just wished he'd been the one to leave Jason feeling that way.

Far too quickly, Jason popped back into the tractor shed. "I have a notebook and pencil. I'm ready to go when you are."

"Let's go."

They headed toward the gravel car park where they kept the station's utes when they weren't in use. Seth climbed in and found the keys in the ignition. "Ready?" he asked Jason.

"I was born ready," Jason retorted.

The familiar comeback made Seth smile. How many times had they had that exact exchange before a test for School of the Air? God, it was so easy to fall back into all the old habits with Jason, but they weren't teenagers anymore, and Seth knew a little more about himself than he had then. Would things be different if he'd been able to put a name to the warmth in his chest when he was sixteen or eighteen? He doubted it. He was Jason's best friend, the buddy he joked around with, studied with, played tricks with, but not the lover Jason took to his bed. No, someone else had that privilege. Seth wanted to be happy for Jason. Really, he did. If only Jason's happiness didn't come at such a price.

He's worth it, he told himself. *And boyfriends come and go. Best friends are forever.*

He just had to keep reminding himself of that until he believed it. He'd dated more than one person while he was in Sydney, and Jason had more than one relationship during vet school, but nothing had shaken the core of their friendship. Not even Jason leaving him to go away to school could weaken that foundation. Seth just had to cling to that and let the rest alone. If he stopped obsessing over Jason, maybe he'd even find a jackaroo of his own.

The thought turned his stomach. He could imagine being with Jason in every way known to man, but the minute he tried to replace Jason's face with another, he felt sick. He didn't trust any other man the way he trusted Jason.

"You're awfully quiet," Jason said, breaking Seth's train of thought.

"Sorry, just trying to remember what I learnt about orienting solar panels. It's been a while since I took that class."

"Yeah, I feel that way about some of the small-animal stuff I learnt in my first year of vet school," Jason said. "I learnt it well enough to pass the class, but I always knew it wasn't what I was going to do with my life, so I didn't bother trying to retain it beyond that."

"Except that you really don't need it, and now I do," Seth said.

Jason shrugged. "That's what the Internet is for. You can use Mum's computer if you don't have one of your own and look up anything you've forgotten or didn't learn in school. That's what I do if I need to check something."

"I have a laptop," Seth said. "And I will double-check everything before I start installing anything. I'd do that even if it was my field rather than something I studied for a semester on a whim."

"Aren't you glad now that you did?"

"Caine has a way of making you glad for everything you do for him."

Jason laughed. "Isn't that the truth! So what are we looking for?"

Seth settled into an explanation of storage capacities, panel angles, relative exposure, and cost versus output ratios. From the look on Jason's face, more than a little of it went over his head, but he asked questions occasionally that pushed Seth to consider things from a different perspective. By the time they reached the first hut, the sick tension in Seth's gut had faded and their easy camaraderie had returned. Maybe the afternoon wouldn't be all torture.

BY THE time they drove back into the valley for dinner, Seth had managed to forget most of his worries and bask in the warmth of Jason's presence. They'd only visited two of the dozen or more drover's huts scattered around the station, but Seth had a much better idea of what he'd need to look up and calculate in order to make Caine's dream of a generator in each hut a reality. They didn't need much. Enough for a refrigerator, a lamp, and a space heater, and only the refrigerator would be a constant drain on the stored power. They'd only need the heater in the winter and the lamp on the nights someone was using the hut. The two huts they'd visited that afternoon were both south facing and in full sun most of the day. A couple of solar panels on the roof and a good storage capacity on the associated battery would be plenty. If any of the huts had trees around them that would block the sun for part of the day, they might have to look at different options, but he'd worry about that later. For now, he had something to report for his first day on the job.

"Neil's car still isn't back," Jason said as they parked the ute. "I hope that doesn't mean they've had bad news."

"Yeah, I hope not," Seth agreed. He knew Devlin Taylor by sight, but little else. The grazier had made his opinion of everything about Lang Downs perfectly clear, so Seth didn't have much use for him. He didn't want Jeremy upset, though, and whatever happened with Devlin would affect Jeremy. Seth refused to think of Chris in a similar situation. Chris had been the only stability in his life before they came to Lang Downs, and Chris was still the only person he cared about who hadn't abandoned him at least once. If Chris had an accident like Devlin had… it didn't bear thinking about.

"I'm going to clean up before dinner," Jason said, "and I ought to see what Cooper's plans are for the evening. I shouldn't neglect him too much."

So much for forgetting his worries.

"I'll see you at dinner, maybe," Seth said. "Or not, if you want to spend time with him."

"You could join us in the bunkhouse," Jason offered. "There's a lot of great blokes working the station this summer. You'd enjoy it."

"I'll think about it," Seth said. He'd told Macklin he would take an empty room in the bunkhouse, but the more he thought about it, the more he couldn't stomach the idea. He'd stay with Chris and Jesse for now and make more permanent arrangements later. "I have to work again tomorrow, so I don't want to stay up too late." He didn't want to watch Jason snuggled up with another man.

"I have to work tomorrow too," Jason reminded him. "People come and go as they need to, but it's better than sitting alone in your room."

"I'm not alone. I have Chris and Jesse."

"So you do," Jason agreed. "I guess living with your brother is different than moving back in with your parents. I couldn't get into the bunkhouse fast enough when I came back."

Couldn't get into Cooper's bed fast enough, Seth thought cynically. "It would be hard to take Cooper back to your place if you were still living there."

"Mum and Dad don't care that I'm gay or that I'm seeing Cooper," Jason said. "But the other jackaroos already see me as a kid. Living with my parents would make that worse."

"I guess," Seth said. "You've got more experience than most of them put together, though, so what does it matter what they think?"

Jason shrugged. "It's nice to have friends my own age. I didn't know you were coming home when I moved into the bunkhouse."

Could all this have been avoided if he'd shared his plans with Jason sooner instead of wanting to surprise him with the news? The thought made him sick to his stomach.

"I'll see you at dinner," Seth said. He had to get away from Jason before he said something he'd regret. He didn't poach. As long as Jason was happy with Cooper, Seth couldn't say anything. If he made Jason uncomfortable, he'd lose even their friendship, and that would kill him.

He bolted from the ute, leaving the notes Jason had taken and everything else behind. He'd come back after dinner and make sure everything was ready for whoever took the ute out next, but he had to be alone now. He thought he heard Jason call after him, but he didn't turn around to check. He couldn't deal with Jason right now.

Chris was in the living room when Seth came in. "Hi, how was your day?"

"Fine," Seth said through gritted teeth, "but I really need a shower. We'll talk when I'm done, okay?"

"Sure." Chris looked surprised, but Seth couldn't do explanations right now. Talking to Chris might be easier than talking to Jason, but only marginally. He'd get his balance back, and then he could go back to pretending nothing was wrong.

He grabbed a change of clothes in the bedroom and paused for a moment to consider his razor. He'd always liked the feel of a straight razor when he was shaving, and no one questioned him owning one or having it in the bathroom. He pressed hard against the scrapes on his knuckles, but they'd lost most of their painful sensitivity overnight and with all the work he'd done that day. "Fuck."

He grabbed the razor along with his clothes and headed for the bathroom. He needed to shave anyway. Maybe the shower would help and he could just get rid of his stubble without needing it for anything else.

He stripped down and set the razor on the sink. Less temptation than setting it on the edge of the tub, where he could reach it more easily. The shower would work. Hot water, plenty of steam, to wash all the tension away along with the sweat and dirt from the day. He could do this. He didn't need to cut himself to find his balance.

He scrubbed at his hair, cursing softly when the strands caught on his uneven nails. He either needed a haircut or a pair of nail clippers. He hadn't thought working on the station would be that much harder on his hands than working in the shop in Sydney, but his hands were a mess. He clung to that thought instead of dwelling on Jason going back to the bunkhouse to find Cooper. They wouldn't shower together. The shower block in the bunkhouse didn't offer enough privacy for that.

He scrubbed at his scalp harder. He was focusing on getting clean, not on what Jason might or might not be doing with another man. It wasn't his business anyway, unless Cooper did something to hurt Jason. Then it could be Seth's business as Jason's best friend. But Jason hadn't seemed upset. He seemed happy with Cooper. So Seth couldn't interfere. Jason wouldn't appreciate it, and if Jason was annoyed with Seth, he'd start spending even less time with him.

Seth braced his hand against the wall. He had to stop. He couldn't let his thoughts spiral out of control this way. It wasn't healthy and didn't help anything. He forced himself to rinse his hair and reach for the soap. He lathered the washcloth and scrubbed at the dirt and grease on his skin. The rough nap of the fabric felt good, and the sting of the soap in the cuts on his hands was a breath of fresh air in the blackness of his mind. He took a deep breath and focused on that, scrubbing harder than strictly necessary until his skin smarted from the friction.

He was okay. He didn't need to do anything drastic to deal with this. Jason was happy. Seth could be happy for him. He could be Jason's best friend like he'd always been, and they could laugh at all the same bad jokes and watch all the same old shows on the telly.

Feeling reasonably in control of himself again, Seth turned off the water, dried off, and climbed out of the tub. He would go ahead and shave so it was done and he didn't have to worry about it in the morning. And then he'd dress and go to dinner and maybe take Jason up on his invitation to come to the bunkhouse for a while. He might even find that he liked Cooper if he could get past his instinctive jealousy.

The scrape of the razor over his skin felt good in a normal kind of way, a safe kind of way. He was in control of what it cut, and all it removed was the day's growth of whiskers. No cuts, not even any nicks. Just smooth, freshly shaved skin. Nothing for anyone to worry about. Nothing for anyone to see.

Finished with his ablutions, he dressed, tossed his dirty clothes in the hamper, and rejoined Chris in the living room. "Sorry I was short earlier. It was really hot and dusty out in the paddocks today."

"I thought you were working in the tractor shed," Chris said.

"I did this morning, but this afternoon, Jason and I went out to a couple of the drover's huts. We wanted to check out the lay of the land so I can figure out how to give Caine what he wants."

Chris laughed. "We all spend an awful lot of time figuring out how to give Caine what he wants, don't we?"

Seth smiled. "I haven't forgotten I owe him and Macklin your life. And probably mine, for that matter. I don't know what would have happened to us if they hadn't been there."

"We would have found a way," Chris said, "but that doesn't make me less grateful. We have a safe place to call home, and that's worth a lifetime of loyalty. I'm glad you're home. I don't think I said that yesterday."

"I think I needed to go away," Seth said. "I needed to see what else was out there, but there's nothing out there that can come close to what I have here. Now that I know, I'm here to stay. At least as long as Caine and Macklin will have me."

"Do your job, tell someone if you screw up, and don't pick fights, and they'll have no problem with you staying," Chris said. "You're family to them too."

"I haven't picked a fight since we moved here ten years ago," Seth said. "I outgrew that phase."

"There wasn't anyone here for you to fight," Chris said.

There hadn't been any reason to start a brawl to drown out the chaos of his life with pain. Life on Lang Downs was many things, but it had never tormented him the way his life had before he arrived.

"Maybe not, but I'm not fourteen and out of control anymore," Seth reminded him. "I've had a few years to learn how to deal with my temper." He rubbed at his knuckles, the twinge enough to settle him. "I'm going to head to the canteen. Are you coming or are you waiting for Jesse?"

"Jesse won't be back tonight," Chris said. "He drew an overnight shift in the south paddock. He'll be back tomorrow around lunch. I'll walk over to the canteen with you."

They walked out onto the veranda and Seth paused to take a deep breath. Yes, it was hot and even in the valley, he could smell the dust, but he could also smell the jasmine from Carley's garden. It smelled like home.

"We should plant some flowers around our veranda too," he said. "We're the only house that doesn't have at least a few."

"Be my guest," Chris said. "Jesse and I tried, but we don't have the knack for keeping flowers alive."

"I'll give it a try," Seth said. "It'll be good to have something to look after. Like a pet, only easier."

"If you say so." Chris jostled his shoulder as he walked toward the canteen. "Come on. I'm hungry."

Seth laughed and hurried to catch up with Chris. His good mood lasted until they walked through the door to the canteen. The silence in the room had a weight of its own. Seth looked around, seeking the source of the unease. Everyone sat in their usual groupings except for Dani and Liam, Neil's kids. They sat with Linda and Kyle, two of the year-rounders, instead of with their parents. "I know where Neil went. Where's Molly?" Seth asked.

"I don't know," Chris replied, "but whatever happened, I don't think it's good." He walked toward the table where Thorne and Ian sat. Seth trailed behind him. The last thing he wanted was bad news, but pretending nothing was wrong wouldn't change anything.

"What's going on?" Chris asked as he sat down.

"Taylor didn't make it," Thorne said. "I didn't get all the details, but I had enough field training in the Commandos to guess the fall caused bleeding in his brain. It doesn't have to be fatal, but it can be, all too easily."

Seth shuddered. How many times had he seen jackaroos come back into the station dusty from a fall? It didn't happen weekly, not even monthly, but often enough that no one considered it outside the realm of possibility. And that kind of a tumble had just killed a man.

"What's going to happen at Taylor Peak? Did Caine say anything?" Chris asked.

Thorne shook his head. "Everyone's still in shock. I figure it'll be Monday before they release the body to the mortuary and then Tuesday or Wednesday before they can have the funeral. After that, it'll depend on how Jeremy's feeling. It's not an easy thing to lose the only family you have."

"No, it isn't," Chris agreed.

"When my family was killed, it took me weeks before I could think straight," Thorne said. "Of course some people would say enlisting in the army and going fast-track into the Commandos was proof I still wasn't thinking straight even when I felt capable of making a decision."

Seth stood up abruptly. He couldn't listen to any more or he'd lose it right there. "I'm going to get some tucker. I'll be back."

He grabbed a plate and nodded to Kami, the station's cook and Sarah's new husband. The old man wasn't talkative on the best of days. His silence was exactly what Seth needed right now. He almost asked if he could eat in the kitchen, but that would give too much away, so he filled his plate and struggled to maintain his composure. Chris being bashed had sent him running headlong looking for help. He'd stumbled into the Yass Hotel, where he'd found Caine and Macklin, who had stopped him from losing the one thing he had left. Still, he'd lost enough to know how it felt to have the rug pulled out from under his feet. He'd lost his mother and his home in a matter of days when his stepfather kicked him and Chris out the night of her funeral. If it hadn't been for Chris…. That didn't even bear thinking about.

At least Jeremy wouldn't have to worry about losing the roof over his head.

Seth pushed the thought aside and returned to the table. He'd eat as quickly as he could and then go somewhere where the conversation wouldn't center on Taylor's death. Surely someone would have something else on their mind.

SEVEN

SETH LASTED all of half an hour in the bunkhouse before the conversation got to be too much for him. He'd hoped none of the seasonal jackaroos would know Taylor well enough to dwell on his death beyond the appropriate somberness at the news, but he wasn't that lucky. It had been all they could talk about, whether it was speculating on what had killed him or discussing if taking him to the hospital sooner could have saved him. Seth didn't have an answer to either of the questions, but the discussion itself left him reeling. It could so easily have been Chris or Caine or any of the men Seth had come to count on at Lang Downs. Taylor's lifetime of experience hadn't been enough to keep him from having an accident. Caine and Chris had far fewer years under their belts.

"I'm beat," he told the jackaroo next to him—he hadn't even managed to catch the man's name. "I'm going to bed."

"G'night," the jackaroo said without even looking away from the rest of the room.

Yeah, that was exactly how important Seth was to anyone in the bunkhouse. Even Jason didn't look in his direction as he wended his way toward the door. The cherry on the cake of his already fucked-up day.

The temperature had dropped with sunset, giving the air a hint of freshness it hadn't had earlier, but Seth didn't linger to enjoy it. He was holding on to his composure by his fingernails. All he cared about was getting somewhere private so he could melt down without anyone seeing him. He'd pull it together by morning and no one would be any wiser, but for that, he had to get to his bedroom without Chris waylaying him. Normally he'd rely on Jesse to hold Chris's attention, but Jesse wouldn't be home, and with the news of Taylor's death, Chris would want the comfort of Seth's presence.

Seth briefly considered trying to sneak in the window, but he wasn't sure it was unlocked. Even if it was, he wasn't fourteen and trying to get away from his stepfather Tony anymore. He could tell Chris he was tired and didn't feel like talking tonight. Chris wouldn't say that was back talk and greet it with the back of his hand. Chris would accept it, give him a hug, and tell him to sleep well.

Right now, he'd prefer the backhand. It would jerk him out of the bog his thoughts had become. Chris's kindness would only reinforce how much he had to lose.

God, he was so fucked up, but knowing it didn't change anything. He had learned to cope with life in Sydney most of the time, but nothing had prepared him for the turmoil being back at home had caused.

"Seth? What are you doing standing outside?"

Chris's voice broke through Seth's thoughts. "Nothing. Just looking at the stars."

"Jesse's not here to point everything out to you, and I still don't know everything he does. I can show you the Southern Cross, but that's about it."

"Anyone with eyes can see the Southern Cross," Seth snarked. "Come on, you haven't learnt more than that in ten years? What kind of boyfriend are you?"

Chris laughed. "I'm telling Jesse you said that. You didn't used to want to hear his answer to that kind of question."

Seth had been young and clueless back then, with no paradigm for bisexuality and no time to think about it between school and trying to help Chris keep a roof over their heads. He hadn't wanted to talk about anything related to sex, especially his brother's sex life. Ten years had changed his outlook on sex in general, but not where his brother was concerned.

"Just don't expect me to stick around for his answer."

"Come on. It's late and we both have to work tomorrow. I don't know when Jeremy and Sam will be back, but it won't be in the morning, so we'll have to keep covering for them."

"If there's anything I can help with, let me know," Seth said as they went inside. "I did all the routine maintenance this morning, so unless something breaks, I can fill in wherever. Caine's new projects can wait a few days if they need to."

"That'll be for Macklin to decide, since Neil is still in Canberra with Jeremy, but I know he'll appreciate the offer even if he doesn't take you up on it."

"Anything I can do," Seth repeated. "I learnt enough before I went off to uni to do pretty much anything for a day or two."

"I'll let him know," Chris said. "Sleep well. You doing okay in your old room?"

"I'm fine." It was a bald-faced lie, but the problem wasn't in the room or in anything Chris could change. The problem was in his head, and nothing could fix that.

"Let me know if you need anything. G'night."

Seth waved in reply and fled toward his room. He'd have to be quiet until he was sure Chris was asleep, but Chris had never come into his room without permission. Even if he came knocking, Seth could ask to be left alone and Chris would respect that.

He shut the door and leaned back against the solid wood barrier. He could flip the lock and keep the world away, but it wouldn't do anything against the nightmare he carried inside him. His razor glistened on his dresser, drawing his attention. His gaze flitted around the room as he tried to find something else to focus on. He'd already busted his knuckles yesterday. He didn't need to do anything else today. It had only been twenty-four hours. He'd never had it happen that fast. He was an adult now, not some kid without enough sense to cope with life normally.

The razor beckoned, a siren's lure he didn't know how to resist. He could pick it up and make one or two little cuts where no one would notice. It would settle him enough to sleep tonight and to get back up tomorrow and do whatever Caine and Macklin asked him to. Or he could stand here and pretend he wasn't falling apart at the seams for the next eight hours and be so tired tomorrow he ended up getting injured.

He couldn't do that to Chris. He had to get it together so he didn't get hurt. It didn't matter what it took. A few slices to his skin were a small price to pay to protect Chris's sanity.

Before he could talk himself out of it again, he grabbed the razor, his towel, and the first-aid kit. Fortunately the towel was black. Chris had bought it saying it wouldn't show the dirt stains. It wouldn't show blood either if Seth cut a little deeper than he meant to. He hadn't lost control like that in years. He wouldn't start now.

He spread the towel out on the bed with the razor on top, set the first-aid kit next to it, and stripped down to his underwear. The question now was where to cut. It was too hot for long sleeves—even if Ian always wore them no matter how hot it got—so his arms were out. He didn't know what Macklin would need him to do in the morning, so he couldn't cut the inside of his thighs because he might have to ride. He'd have to cut along the top of his leg and bandage it tightly in the morning so it wouldn't bleed through if he spent the day on horseback. It would be unpleasant, but having someone see the marks would be worse.

He tested the razor with his thumb, even though he'd shaved with it a few hours earlier. Then he hadn't wanted to cut himself. Now he did. Satisfied it was sharp, he wiped the razor and his leg with an alcohol pad. He'd had a cut get infected from a dirty blade once, and only some quick talking had kept the nurse from figuring out what he'd done. He didn't intend that to happen again, because Chris wouldn't be mollified with weak excuses and him walking out the moment he had medicine for it.

The rhythm of his preparations lulled him enough that he considered setting the razor aside and seeing if that would be enough, but he wouldn't get another chance before tomorrow night if it wasn't, and he couldn't crack in front of the others. He hadn't known Taylor well enough to use that as an excuse, and while he could pass off some of his unease as worry for his own brother, it wouldn't be enough to fool anyone for long.

He took a deep breath and slid the razor across his skin, a paper-thin slice a couple of millimeters deep. He hissed as the familiar, welcome pain arced through his system. He controlled this, not anyone else. He decided when it hurt and when it stopped. And he determined the placement, depth, and number of cuts. The knot of tension inside him uncoiled a little as he focused on the blood that welled up ruby red against his white skin. His face, hands, and arms were brown with the time he spent working outside, but his legs never saw the sun, encased in dungarees to protect them from sharp tools and anything else he encountered in the tractor shed or out in the paddocks. The contrast pleased him in a twisted sort of way. He ran his finger along the cut, smearing the blood beyond its borders. He winced at the sting but didn't stop. Instead he pressed a little harder, letting the alcohol that lingered on his fingers add to the discomfort. He'd have to clean the cut again when he was done, and that final burn would push him all the way back to sanity again for a while. He could do it now, and then if it wasn't enough, he could do a second cut and have double the burn when he cleaned both of them at the end. Yes, that would be better than making the second cut right away. If he could find his balance with just one cut, it would be better than having two.

He wiped the blood away with sterile gauze and reached for the bottle of rubbing alcohol. He could use an alcohol pad, but it wouldn't go as deep or burn the same. He bit his lip to smother the yelp he inevitably let loose when alcohol hit an open cut.

He let it sit as long as he could stand, burning its way into his bloodstream, down to his very marrow. The first time he'd done this, he could barely stand to wipe the cut with an alcohol pad, but now he relished the waves of pain. They whited out all the noise in his head until he could breathe again. Only then did he use the gauze to dab up the alcohol. He put a couple of butterfly bandages along the length of the cut to hold it closed and taped a gauze pad over it to keep it free of dust the next day. He'd been careful and not cut too deeply, so the bleeding would stop quickly and it would be mostly closed in the morning probably, but better safe than sorry.

He cleaned and sterilized the razor and put everything away. He blew his nose and hid the bloody gauze inside the used tissue so Chris wouldn't see if it he emptied the trash. Seth didn't think Chris would stoop to poking through his garbage, but this way he didn't have to worry. Everyone had used tissues in their trash can. Chris wouldn't think anything of that. Bloody gauze would be a different story entirely.

He lay down on the bed and let the throbbing in his leg lull him into sleep.

JEREMY LAY in the hotel bed staring at the ceiling as the light filtering in around the curtains grew brighter. Sam slept on next to him, undisturbed by Jeremy's wakefulness. At least one of them had gotten a good night's sleep. Jeremy had fallen asleep quickly, wrung out from the emotionally trying day and the relief of knowing he hadn't so alienated his brother that Devlin had written him out of the will. For better or worse, Taylor Peak was his now.

The alarm on Sam's phone went off. He rolled over and turned it off. "How are you feeling this morning?" he asked as he rolled back toward Jeremy.

"Tired," Jeremy admitted. "I've been awake for a while."

"I'm sorry." Sam pushed up on one elbow so he could peer down at Jeremy's face in the low light. "Do you want to talk about it?"

Jeremy shrugged. "Nothing to talk about. Devlin is gone, and Taylor Peak is mine. Neil and Molly will be waiting for us to have breakfast. We should get ready."

"Pretending nothing has happened won't make it easier to deal with." Sam stroked Jeremy's face as he spoke.

Jeremy pulled away and sat up. "I'm not pretending." His voice sounded harsher than he'd intended, but sometimes Sam drove him crazy. "My brother is dead. I inherited his station, something I never wanted, and especially not in these circumstances. All the talking in the world won't change that. I'm doing the only thing I can—trying to figure out how to do the job he left to me. I'm going to take a shower."

Sam didn't call him back, making Jeremy hope he'd gotten the message. He went into the hotel bathroom and turned the water up to scalding. He stripped down and climbed into the tub. The hot water stung his skin, but he didn't step back. He needed something to penetrate the fog that hung around him. If the hot water could do that, he'd relish it for as long as he could stand it. A rush of cool air into the tub signaled the door opening. Jeremy rested his head against the ceramic tiles for a moment, praying for the patience not to snap at Sam for invading the few moments of privacy he'd managed to get since they heard about Devlin's accident.

He heard rustling and then Sam climbed into the tub behind him. Jeremy braced himself for more questions, but Sam didn't say anything. He just wrapped his arms around Jeremy and held him tight. Jeremy relaxed into the embrace and let Sam support him. After a moment Sam reached for the shampoo and poured some into his hand. Jeremy tilted his head and let Sam wash his hair. Sam massaged his scalp as he worked the gel into a lather. Jeremy leaned into the caress—because he had no other word for it despite the practicality of the gesture—and let Sam's care for him surround him, insulating him from the world outside the tub. Everything could go to hell for all he cared. He had Sam in the tub with him, taking care of him despite his surliness. Nothing else mattered.

"Rinse off," Sam murmured. Jeremy stepped completely under the spray and let the water wash away the suds and some of his tension. When the water ran clear, he stepped back toward Sam, intending to return the favor, but Sam shook his head. "Nope, not done with you yet."

Jeremy subsided and let Sam continue as he pleased. Sam ran a soapy washrag over Jeremy's chest and shoulders and then down his torso to his hips, legs, and feet. "Turn around."

Jeremy did as he was told, but he couldn't stop from looking over his shoulder with a grin. "You missed a spot."

"I'm not done yet," Sam replied with a matching grin.

Devlin was probably rolling in his grave, but Jeremy found he didn't care. Devlin was gone, and Jeremy was still here... with Sam. And Sam's love was the only thing keeping his shit together right now. If flirting with Sam was wrong, Jeremy would gladly be damned.

Sam worked his way up Jeremy's legs to his back and then his shoulders and neck. He stepped in close behind Jeremy, fitting their bodies together perfectly. Jeremy closed his eyes and leaned back against him, enjoying the way they complemented each other. The plop of the washcloth was his only warning before Sam reached around and stroked his cock with soapy hands. Jeremy moaned softly. They didn't have time for shower sex, but fuck, it felt good to have Sam's hands on him. Maybe they could just jerk each other off before they met Neil and Molly for breakfast. Surely they had time for that.

"Stop thinking and relax." Sam's breath tickled his ear and sent shivers down his spine. Jeremy tried to do as he was told and block out everything but the sensations evoked by Sam's hands. Warmth pervaded his body, warmth that had nothing to do with the water still running over them both or with the lust Sam's hands usually evoked. No, this was different, tender and compassionate and supportive, more about affirming the soul-deep bond between them than about either of them getting off. Jeremy wasn't even fully hard, but he didn't need to be. He just needed for Sam to keep touching him and loving him. He could deal with everything else as long as he had Sam to keep him steady.

He gave Sam his full weight, knowing Sam wouldn't let him fall.

"That's better," Sam murmured. "Think you can face the day now?"

Jeremy nodded. "What about you?"

"My brother is meeting us for breakfast. I'm not the one we need to worry about today." Sam kissed the side of Jeremy's neck. "If you're feeling steady enough to go meet him, then I have what I need."

The reminder of Devlin's death—not that Jeremy really needed reminding—stung, but he wasn't alone. Neil and Molly were as close to family as the law would allow and closer in their hearts. If he said the word, any of the year-rounders at Lang Downs would do everything in their power to help him. He wasn't facing this alone, whatever "this" turned out to be.

"I'm ready."

Sam turned him around so they could kiss properly. When he pulled back, he turned off the water and threw a towel at Jeremy's head. "Dry off. I'm not your personal servant."

Jeremy chuckled. "Could have fooled me when you were washing me."

"Just keeping you on your toes," Sam retorted.

Jeremy smiled all the way through drying off and getting dressed. "Let's go eat and figure out what happens now."

Sam reached for Jeremy's hand and together they left the hotel room to go in search of Neil and Molly.

They found them in the hotel restaurant, looking over the menus.

"About time you got here," Neil said. From the way he winced, Molly had kicked him under the table. The thought made Jeremy smile.

"I took a long shower," Jeremy said. "After two days at the hospital, I felt grimy."

"You're entitled," Molly said with a pointed look at Neil. "And if you decide what you want to do today is go back upstairs and sleep, no one will blame you."

Jeremy shook his head. "There's too much to be done. I have to arrange for transportation to take Devlin home. I have to find someone to have the funeral. I think he still went to church in Boorowa, so maybe the minister there would be willing to come say a few words in his memory. And then I have to figure out how I'm going to run a station as large as Taylor Peak with no time to learn the ropes. I can sleep later."

"I can't do much about the transportation or the minister," Neil said, "but if Taylor didn't have a coffin or anything picked out, Ian could make you one. He made Michael's when he died. It wouldn't be anything fancy, but it would be personal in a way a purchased one never could be. And as far as the station is concerned, you know all you have to do is ask. I can be there in a couple of hours. Hell, if you asked, I'm pretty sure Macklin would come take a look at things for you and help you get everything sorted. You can't ask for better advice than he'd give you."

"I know," Jeremy said. "And I appreciate it, but Devlin had his own way of doing things. I didn't do a lot right as far as he was concerned, but I'd like to try to do right by his legacy."

Sam frowned. "You were always complaining about how badly he ran things. Are you sure you want to keep doing things the way he did them?"

"I don't want to make mistakes, but I need to understand what he was doing and why before I just go changing things left and right. Devlin ran Taylor Peak for a long time, and he learnt from our father who learnt from his father. There must be some wisdom in the choices he made, even if I can't see it from where I'm sitting now. It's all I have left of him. I have to try."

"Whatever you need," Neil said. "Even if that's for us to leave you alone to do it. We're here to support you, not to make your life more difficult."

EIGHT

JASON LOOKED up when Caine walked to the front of the canteen and whistled to get everyone's attention.

"I spoke with Jeremy this morning," he said. "The funeral will be on Tuesday at Taylor Peak, and Devlin will be interred in the family plot immediately after. I've made adjustments to the shift rosters in order to allow those closest to Jeremy to attend. I realize this means some of you will sacrifice your day off this week, but we will add an extra day's pay to this week's payroll to make up for it if you're in that situation. We appreciate everyone's hard work in keeping things running despite the uncertainty of the past few days."

He posted the new shift rosters on the bulletin board and then returned to his seat. Some of the seasonal jackaroos rose to look at it, but none of the year-rounders bothered. Caine would have arranged for them to be free to support Jeremy. Jason would check on his way out, not sure if he counted as a year-rounder as far as this was concerned. He'd spent enough time with Sam and Jeremy to want to go to the funeral, but he also understood the reality of running a station, and he hadn't been here for the past seven years. If Caine needed him to stay, he would, and he'd find another time to go down to Taylor Peak to speak with Jeremy and Sam.

"I'd better get started tonight, then," Ian said, bringing Jason out of his thoughts.

"Started on what?"

"On the casket," Ian said. "Sam texted to ask if I'd make it, but they didn't know when the funeral would be. It's the least I can do for Jeremy after everything he's done for us. I just wish it weren't necessary."

"Don't we all," Chris said from next to Jason. "I wish I had something that concrete I could do for him. I'll have to settle for offering to help them move whatever they want to take with them."

"Are they really going to move to Taylor Peak?" Seth asked.

Jason could sympathize. Sure, he'd gone away to uni, but the idea of leaving Lang Downs for good didn't sit well with him.

"They haven't said," Chris replied, "but how else is Jeremy supposed to run the station? It's an hour and a half in ideal conditions to get to the main house at Taylor Peak. If the weather's bad, some days you can't get there at all. I don't see how they can live here and work there. It's just not feasible."

"I can't imagine them not being here," Jesse said. "Who will ruffle Neil's feathers if Sam isn't around to tease him?"

"I'm sure we can take up the slack," Ian replied, "but you're right. They're as much a part of the station now as any of us. Bloody hell, why did Taylor have to get himself killed? Bad enough when Michael died, but at least he was old and had lived a full life. We're losing two year-rounders in one blow because Taylor was careless."

"We're not losing them," Linda, Kyle's wife, insisted. "No, they won't be here every day, but you don't lose friends like that just because they don't live as close anymore. You all have days off, even if you only take them half the time. You could spend your days off at Taylor Peak helping out if Jeremy needs it, or just visiting if he doesn't. Maybe not every week if he doesn't need help, but often enough that you'd still see him. We all know Taylor had an odd way of running things. Jeremy may get in there and realize the whole system needs an overhaul, and if that's the case, he'll need all the help he can get. And who better to give it to him than the men who understand the way he's lived since he got here? If anyone knows how to run a station, it's the lot of you. If you alternated your days right, you could each give him a day a week and he'd have an extra set of hands he trusts and someone who thinks the way he does every day. Think what a difference that could make to him."

"I guess we'd better talk to Caine and Macklin about the schedule for days off," Jesse said. "He's tried to arrange it so couples are off together, but that only covers five days, six if they go down to help too."

"I can take a day," Jason offered. "If nothing else, he probably needs a vet to take a look at the mob and make sure they're healthy, and I'd always intended to offer my vet services to Taylor. I just hadn't got around to it yet."

"I can go too," Seth said. "I don't know if they have a mechanic, but even if they do, I can ride out with a crew."

"And there's the week covered," Linda said. "See? That wasn't so hard."

Jason smiled at her. Kyle had done a good thing when he married Linda and brought her and her daughter to the station. He didn't know if Laura had plans after high school, but she'd already made a place for herself on Lang Downs. "Now we just have to convince Sam and Jeremy to accept."

"That's easy," Thorne said. "We don't ask them. We just show up and get to work. They can't say no to that."

JEREMY WATCHED in stony silence as Devlin's casket was lowered into the ground. He didn't even know the men holding the ropes. Sam had asked for volunteers and had arranged it without Jeremy's input. That was the way most of his life felt at the moment. Probably just as well, since he didn't feel capable of making even the most basic decisions. Life just kept eddying around him, but he was too numb to feel it.

The minister had spoken words of comfort and praise for a life well lived, but they hadn't been enough to break through the ice that had settled in Jeremy's chest since they'd returned to Taylor Peak Sunday night. Neil had taken charge of the jackaroos, making sure the station kept running, and Sam had taken charge of the arrangements for the funeral.

"Jeremy."

He blinked a couple of times at the sound of his name, trying to pull himself together enough to respond. Sam stood next to him holding a shovel. Jeremy took it and stepped toward the gaping hole that held Devlin's remains. He swallowed hard and filled the shovel with dirt. Shuddering against the thought of the cold, hard earth covering the casket Ian had so quickly and beautifully crafted, Jeremy did as expected and tossed his spadeful into the grave.

All around the site, men and women stood with heads bowed, hats held respectfully over their hearts. Molly had tears in her eyes, he noticed. So did Linda.

Linda was here? He didn't remember her arriving, but as he looked around the small crowd, he saw other familiar faces mixed in with the Taylor Peak jackaroos. Ian and Thorne stood next to Neil and Molly. Caine and Macklin stood in the back with Seth and Jason. He remembered Jason coming back to the station, but he'd thought Seth was just coming for a visit. Kyle stood with Linda and Laura, his arm around Laura's shoulders. Chris and Jesse were there too. All his friends from Lang Downs had come to support him. He shouldn't have been surprised. If the situation had been reversed, he would have gone to their sides in a heartbeat, but the days at the hospital had created a gulf he didn't know how to bridge. He wasn't a Lang Downs crew boss anymore. He was the grazier at Taylor Peak, and everyone knew the two crews didn't mix.

The minister finished the final prayer and people began milling around. Some of the jackaroos left almost immediately. Jeremy didn't blame them. He'd leave too if he could, but a hundred fifty years of family history tied him to the station, and he couldn't slough that off.

Molly came up to him first, enclosing him in a gentle embrace. He leaned against her soft shoulder and let the contact steady him. She wouldn't ask more of him than he could give. Everyone else needed something from him, even Sam and Neil to some extent, but Molly was just there for him.

She'd gone through Devlin's closets and boxed up his clothes. She'd organized the kitchen and taken care of the week's order from Boorowa. She'd cleaned the main house from top to bottom so Sam and Jeremy would have a fresh start. And she'd done all of it without asking Jeremy a single question. He hadn't had to decide if this or that was worth keeping or where to put a single pot or pan or photograph. And when the weight of his responsibilities became more than he could bear, she'd set aside what she was working on and held him until he could go out and face the world again.

"I'm so sorry," she said against his hair. "I know I've said it a dozen times, but it's still true."

Jeremy nodded, not able to speak. He wanted to thank her for everything, but if he opened his mouth, he'd start crying. It wouldn't matter if Molly saw him cry, but he'd lose all credibility with the jackaroos at Taylor Peak if he broke down in front of them. He had little enough to begin with. Neil hadn't given any explanation for the three jackaroos who had quit in the past two days, but Jeremy didn't need one. They'd taken one look at Jeremy and Sam and seen all they needed to see. He was only surprised it wasn't more. If he wanted to keep running the station, he'd have to be ten times tougher than anyone else or they'd never listen to him.

Neil joined Molly and put a comforting hand on Jeremy's shoulder as he wrapped his other arm around Molly's waist. "I talked to Caine before the funeral started. We're going to stay for at least another week, until you get your feet under you. Caine says Macklin is enjoying getting to be the foreman again. I think he just likes scaring the shit out of the blow-ins who don't know one end of a horse from the other."

An entirely inappropriate snort of laughter escaped at that. "I might have to sneak back up to Lang Downs to watch," Jeremy said. "Watching my dad and Williams with the blow-ins was always a good start to any season. You don't take their crap either, but you're not scary the way Macklin or my dad were."

"Just watch me," Neil said. "Even the blow-ins at Lang Downs don't need to be taken down a peg or two. The idiots your brother hired, on the other hand… I have some arse to kick before I turn them over to whoever you pick to be your foreman."

"Can any of them be the foreman?" Jeremy asked. "I haven't seen enough gumption in the lot."

"If not, find one as fast as you can," Neil said. "You don't want to do this by yourself. You're a bloody good crew boss, and you'll be fine as the grazier, but trying to do it all himself is what got Devlin killed. You're not allowed to make the same mistake."

"I won't," Jeremy said. "If you hear of anyone looking for work, send them my way? I doubt we're done with men leaving because of Sam and me. I'm going to need all the help I can get."

"I'm setting that straight too," Neil said. "They'll learn to watch their mouths or they'll be docked pay or out of a job. Most of them aren't stupid enough to badmouth the boss directly, but there's a few I'm not so sure about."

"Thank you," Jeremy said. "I think Sam said something about food. You should go eat."

"Sarah and Kami outdid themselves with some help from your cook," Molly said. "But that can wait until you're ready."

"I'll come," Jeremy promised, "but I need to speak to everyone first."

"You can speak to them while we're eating," Sam insisted. "It'll be easier than standing out here in the heat of the day."

Jeremy let Sam and Molly lead him away from the family plot back toward the main house. He didn't want to go in the canteen and face the jackaroos, but as he drew closer, he saw that someone had set up tables under the trees behind the house, and Sarah and Kami had all the food set out buffet-style on the veranda.

He looked around for Neil, but he was talking with Thorne and Ian. At Molly's urging, Jeremy filled a plate and took a seat at one of the tables. He'd taken three bites when Thorne joined him.

"My condolences," Thorne said. "I know what it's like to lose your family, so I know words don't help. If I can help in any other way, please let me know."

"I don't suppose you know an out-of-work foreman," Jeremy quipped. "Neil can only stay so long, and I need someone to whip my jackaroos into shape."

"Actually," Thorne said, "I might. You remember my friend Nick Walker who came to visit last time he was on leave?"

Jeremy nodded. Walker had spent a week on Lang Downs, and Jeremy had wondered at the time how long it would be before the man became a permanent fixture on the station.

"He retired from the Commandos about a month ago. He wasn't looking for a job right away. He said he wanted to relax and travel a bit before he decided what to do next. Anyway, he's back in Wagga Wagga and looking for a job. He grew up on a sheep station in Western Australia. He's never worked as a foreman, but he knows how a station runs, and if he can lead a Commando team, he can handle a group of jackaroos with bad attitudes. Do you want me to see if he's interested?"

"If he's interested, he sounds about perfect," Jeremy said. Walker was nearly as big as Thorne, six-foot-something and built like a brick shithouse.

He pitied any of the jackaroos who thought they could mouth off with him around.

"I'll call him tonight," Thorne promised. "If he's interested, I'll bring his number by in the morning."

"You don't need to make a trip just for that," Jeremy protested.

"It's not for that. Tomorrow's my day off. I figured I'd pitch in around here, help you get your feet under you. I may not have Walker's childhood of experience, but I've learnt enough since I got to Lang Downs to take a crew out and evaluate them for you. And Ian said he'd help out too. Neil's already assigned us to crews for the day."

"I…. You didn't have to," Jeremy stuttered. "Thank you."

"No thanks necessary," Thorne said. "If our situations were reversed, you'd do the same. Now, enjoy your meal before it goes cold."

Jeremy smiled weakly and turned back to his plate. He wasn't hungry— hadn't been for days—but if he didn't eat, Sarah would make Molly's mothering look like child's play. He loved that about her, but not today, so he put another bite of potato salad in his mouth and pretended it didn't taste like dust to him.

"Hey, Jeremy."

Jeremy swallowed so he could answer Seth. "Hi, Seth. I didn't expect you to still be here. I thought you'd be on your way back to Sydney by now."

"No, I'm back for good," Seth said. "There's no place like home and all that shit. Caine's got me helping out Patrick and looking into improvements for the drover's huts, but I still get a day off a week. Do you have someone maintaining your equipment?"

"No one who hired on just for that," Sam answered when Jeremy turned to look at him. "Devlin didn't appear to believe in specialization. I haven't finished talking to all the jackaroos to see if any of them have enough of a background or interest to take on the job."

"Then I'll see you on Friday," Seth declared. "I don't know if I can check everything out in one day, but I'll get through what I can. I'll be more help to you that way than out with a crew."

"Wait," Jeremy said as Seth started to stand up. "Why are you coming on Friday?"

"It's my day off," Seth said like it was the most obvious thing in the world. Maybe it would have been at any other time. "I might as well do something useful with that time. Tuning up your machinery will be fun."

"Fun," Jeremy repeated. "I guess that's one word for it."

Seth grinned. "You forget. Engines were the only thing I was good at before I moved to Lang Downs. Even now, I'm happier with grease up to my elbows from cleaning out a dirty engine than doing anything else."

"We need to find you a girl, mate, if that's what makes you happiest," Jeremy said with a shake of his head.

"I had one," Seth said. "I left her in Sydney where she belongs. We're both happier this way."

"If you say so," Jeremy replied. "I don't know if I can pay you. We haven't even made a dent in the station's finances—"

"Who said anything about paying me?" Seth interrupted. "Family helps each other. You might be living here instead of on Lang Downs now, but you're still one of us."

Jeremy took a deep breath to steady himself. "Thank you. That means a lot."

"Cheers," Seth said as he stood up. "I'm sorry about your brother. I can't imagine what it would be like if Chris weren't there. I can't bring him back, but I'll help any way I can."

Jeremy summoned a smile and sent Seth off with a nod.

"How are you holding up?" Sam asked.

Jeremy shrugged. "I haven't broken down today."

"I'm not sure if that's good or bad," Sam said. "At least we'll have plenty of extra help if we need it. Hiring Walker is a good idea if he will come."

"Can we afford it?" Jeremy asked.

"We've had three men quit in the past two days," Sam reminded him. "We can take Walker's salary out of that."

NINE

SETH STOOD to the side of the gathering. He'd spoken to Jeremy and made his offer. He had to stay until everyone else was ready because he'd ridden over with them and so had no way to get home quicker, but he'd about had his fill of Taylor Peak for a while. No one said anything in Jeremy's hearing—or even in Neil's—but Seth had overheard some of the comments the jackaroos had made.

"Poofter" was the nicest word he'd heard them use to describe their new bosses. Most of them had gone straight for "shirt lifter" or "pillow biter." On Lang Downs, that kind of language got a man a warning and then his walking papers, but after eleven years of Caine and Macklin's benevolent guidance, most people never even went that far. The year-rounders and the repeat seasonal staff made their opinions clear, and anyone who didn't like it could leave. They had enough hands to cover the shifts. Seth feared Jeremy wouldn't be so lucky. If he kept them, he'd have to listen to their insults for the rest of the season. If he fired them, he'd be shorthanded in a matter of days. All the year-rounders at Lang Downs had offered to help on their days off, but that only came to fourteen extra hands total, and Jeremy would rarely have more than two of them at a time. They couldn't run a station this size with a crew that small.

"Seth? You okay, mate?"

Seth looked up as Jason ambled toward him. "Yeah, just worried about Jeremy and Sam."

"It'll be hard, but they'll manage. They know how to run a station."

"All the knowing in the world doesn't do any good if they don't have the men to do the work."

"What are you talking about?"

"I've been listening to the Taylor Peak jackaroos, and I've heard a lot of language that would get them thrown off Lang Downs," Seth said. "It makes me nervous for Jeremy."

"Bloody hell," Jason said. "It'll be like the summer you came to Lang Downs all over again. The worst summer I can remember the station ever having."

"Hey, I thought it was a good summer," Seth protested.

"It was, for me, but having you there was its only redeeming feature. You didn't see it, I guess, since you didn't know how things were before, but almost all the seasonal jackaroos were blow-ins, new to the work as well as to the station. We had enough bodies but not enough knowledge to really run the station right. I've never seen Neil or Macklin as run-down as they were that summer. All the crew bosses worked extra shifts, trying to teach the blow-ins what to do and keep the station running at the same time. They kept it together, but it was close."

"I'm scared it'll go even farther than that," Seth said. "It wouldn't be the first time a mob mentality took hold and someone got hurt. They attacked Chris in broad daylight in town. What's to stop them from attacking Sam and Jeremy? Or even Neil and Molly, since they're helping out?"

"You think it'll come to that?"

"God, I hope not, but I didn't believe it would happen in Yass either."

"We should say something to Thorne. He's got the most training."

"I didn't hear any actual threats," Seth said. "Just grumbling. I hope they'll take their attitudes and just quit. Even if we have to work double to help Jeremy through the season, it's better than someone getting hurt."

"Yes, but let's not borrow trouble if we can help it," Jason said. "A little grumbling isn't the same as quitting or even being disrespectful to Jeremy and Sam directly. Maybe they'll get it out of their systems and settle back in to work. Jeremy *is* a Taylor, and he *does* know what he's doing, so if they stay more than a few days, they'll see it's still a good place to work."

"I guess it depends on how much of Devlin's feud with Lang Downs carried over to his jackaroos. Caine never let us—even Neil—get away with bad-mouthing Taylor Peak, but from what Sam and Jeremy have said, Devlin had no qualms about talking shit about us. Do you know why he hated Lang Downs so much?"

"Not really," Jason said. "His dad died fairly young too, and Michael—Caine's uncle—tried to help him, but Devlin wouldn't ever accept. Maybe he suspected Michael was gay and hated him for that, or maybe he just hated him for being successful while Taylor Peak struggled. I know he wanted to buy Lang Downs when Caine's mother inherited. He figured she wouldn't know what she had and would sell it cheap. Caine came instead, which ended his hope of acquiring the station. Then Jeremy left Taylor Peak for Lang Downs, and that was the end of any hope of reconciliation."

"Will we make things worse by coming to help?"

"That's Jeremy's call. If he decides it's doing that, he'll tell us, and if he does, we'll listen. I'm going to catch Thorne. You want to come with me?"

"Yeah. I'm the one who heard the comments, after all."

They headed toward where Thorne sat. Seth wondered where Ian was, but maybe he'd gone to get something else to eat or drink. "Ready to go, lads?" Thorne asked as they approached.

"I was ready an hour ago," Seth said, "but before we go, I figured you ought to hear what's being muttered by the hands."

"Some combination of working for poofters and Lang Downs taking over?"

"So you heard it too?"

"Hard not to unless you're so caught up in grief that you don't hear anything not said to your face," Thorne replied. "I'll call Walker when we get home. You didn't meet him when he came for a visit, but he's one of my mates from the Commandos. He just got out and is looking for a job. Even if he just fills in for the summer until Jeremy can find a full-time foreman, he'll keep the jackaroos in line."

"And they'll think twice about attacking Sam and Jeremy if they have to get through someone like your friend," Jason said.

Thorne sat up straighter. "Did you hear someone making threats?"

"No," Seth admitted, "but the blokes who attacked Chris before we came to Lang Downs never made threats either. They just jumped him one day. In town, in broad daylight. If it could happen there, how much more easily could it happen out here in the middle of nowhere?"

"I'll call Walker as soon as we get back to Lang Downs," Thorne repeated, "and I'll put a word in Neil's ear. Sam might not be much of a fighter, but I've heard enough tales of Neil's misspent youth. They won't catch him off guard."

"Thanks, Thorne," Seth said. "I'll feel better knowing they have someone looking out for them. If it were different circumstances, I wouldn't worry about Jeremy. I know he can take care of himself, but like you said, he's too caught up in his grief to hear what's going on around him right now."

"We'll watch out for him until he can look after himself again," Thorne promised. "None of us want to see anything happen to either of them. We're ready to go if you want to head toward the car. I'll find Ian and Neil and meet you there."

"NEIL. CAN I speak with you for a minute?"

Neil looked up when Thorne called his name. "Yeah, what's going on?"

Thorne tipped his head at Jeremy and started walking away. Neil frowned and followed him until they were out of Sam and Jeremy's earshot. "What's going on?" he repeated.

"You've probably heard, if not today then earlier, that not all the jackaroos are happy with Jeremy inheriting the station and bringing Sam with him," Thorne began.

Neil snorted. "I've had three men quit already and I expect a dozen more to leave once the funeral is over. I'm hoping we still have a skeleton crew by the time the week is out. I don't think the year-rounders will leave. They've got a certain loyalty to the station and to the Taylor family that will hopefully keep them around long enough to see that Jeremy's a good man despite his 'faults,' but it's going to be a rough summer."

"I already told Jeremy I'd see if Walker wanted a job, but I was just talking to Seth and Jason. I think Seth is overreacting, but he's worried some of the jackaroos will do more than just talk and we'll have a mob on our hands—and not of the animal variety. I told him I'd warn you, just to be safe, and I'll tell Walker as well. It's probably his memories of Chris being bashed instead of anything based on the current situation, but forewarned is forearmed, and all that."

"I'll keep an eye out," Neil said. "I haven't heard any threats, just complaints, but they know where I stand on the matter so they'd be stupid to let me hear them making threats. Molly had talked about staying a few more days, but I'll send her home with someone today. I can use the kids as an excuse so she won't worry."

"Just don't do anything stupid," Thorne said. "I've heard stories."

Neil grinned, the hothead he'd left behind rising to the surface at the thought of a threat to his brothers. "I won't start anything because that wouldn't help Sam and Jeremy, but I damn well will finish anything they start."

"HEY, LACHLAN, I didn't expect to hear from you today. Didn't you tell me you had a funeral to attend?" Walker's voice was a balm to Thorne's nerves. Only Ian could settle him more quickly than Walker, but Thorne didn't want Ian anywhere near the current situation. He didn't want Ian getting hurt.

"That's kind of what I was calling about," Thorne said. "You remember Sam and Jeremy from when you were here?"

"Yeah, big blond stockman with the blue-eyed dog and the accountant with the cat that followed him around like a puppy," Walker said.

"Yeah, that would be them. Jeremy's brother owned Taylor Peak, the station next to Lang Downs—"

"Owned?" Walker interrupted.

"It was his funeral. He had an accident and didn't recover. Jeremy's brother wasn't known for his tolerance, and Jeremy's already lost a few men. More than that, his brother was a bit of a control freak and didn't have a foreman, but Jeremy needs one. He has enough issues as it is without trying to do everything himself. You still looking for a job?"

"Does he know you're offering me one?" Walker countered.

"I told him I'd call you," Thorne said. "He seemed grateful. And just between you and me, things are really tense right now. It wouldn't hurt for Sam and Jeremy to have a little protection."

"Is this your gut talking or do you know something?" Walker asked.

From anyone else, Thorne would have taken offense at the question, but Walker knew him better than anyone else alive. "A little of both. We heard a lot of grumbling, and one of the kids is worried it'll turn into more. My first reaction was to dismiss it. His brother was bashed before he came to Lang Downs, so it's a sensitive topic for him. But then I got to thinking, and it's not as far-fetched as I want it to be. The more immediate concern is keeping half the crew from quitting so they have enough men to keep the station afloat for the season. They can advertise for more men, but this time of year, jackaroos with any experience are in short supply."

"And the ones who don't have jobs usually are unemployed for a reason," Walker agreed. "Does he have a house for me? What do I need to bring with me?"

"I don't know. The funeral wasn't the time to talk details," Thorne said. "I'll call Sam and give him your number. He was the office manager at Lang Downs before all of this. He'll be on top of the details. And, Walker?"

"Yeah?"

"Thanks. You didn't have to agree."

"I can count on one hand the things you've asked me to do in more than twenty years that weren't related to the job," Walker said. "You saved my life. I think I got the better end of this bargain."

"That's not the way it works."

"The hell it isn't. I'll call you when I get to Taylor Peak. You can come visit and we'll scare the shit out of some know-it-all jackaroos. It'll be just like the first day of basic training with all the rookies. Bring Ian with you. They'll know you're gay and have to shut their traps and deal with it because you're too much of a scary bastard for them to say anything. It'll be fun."

Thorne laughed. He would bring Ian with him. It would be worth the constipated looks on the faces of the Taylor Peak jackaroos to watch Walker tear them a new one. "It's a date."

JEREMY PICKED mechanically at his food. After the funeral ended and everyone left, it had been back to the usual business of running a station, except Jeremy still didn't feel like he knew where to start. Sure, he knew the mechanics of all the tasks required to run a station. He could do the job of any man he employed, with the possible exception of fixing a broken engine. But he'd never been the one to keep track of all those tasks—who needed to do what and when and with whom and schedule rotations—and just thinking about it made his head hurt. He was a capable crew boss. He might even go so far as to say a bloody good crew boss. But he didn't even know where to start when it came to being a grazier.

Thank God for Neil. He'd have gone under a dozen times already without his support.

The sound of someone clearing his throat drew his attention from his morose thoughts and neglected plate. One of his jackaroos—he didn't know their names yet, although he needed to learn—stood in front of him, hat in hand. "Yes?"

"No disrespect, Taylor, but I signed on to work for Devlin Taylor, not his brother. And I sure as hell didn't sign up to work on Lang Downs." The glare he sent in Neil's direction shocked Jeremy with its venom. He'd known Devlin hated the Lang Downs jackaroos, but he'd hoped it hadn't carried over to the rest of the men on Taylor Peak. It appeared he'd hoped in vain. "I'll pack my things and be off the property first thing in the morning."

Jeremy nodded—because what else was he supposed to do?—and gestured toward Sam. "Leave an address with Sam for where you want your last paycheck to be sent. We'll post it on Friday along with everyone else's."

"I don't want your money," the man said. "It's as tainted as everything else you poofters touch."

Neil was on his feet and in the man's face before Jeremy could blink. "Be glad you already quit, mate." The bite in his voice broke Jeremy out of his stupor. It wouldn't help anything if a fight broke out. "Because that's the kind of comment that'll get a man fired. Forget about tomorrow. Pack your bag tonight. You have half an hour to get out before I throw you out."

"You and what army, Emery?" the man spat back.

Jeremy rose from his seat and moved to separate them. Sam got there before he could. "I'd hate to have to dock your pay for damages," he said coldly. "I suggest you take Neil's advice."

The jackaroo glared at all three of them and stormed out of the canteen.

"Anyone else feel that way?" Jeremy asked the men left in the canteen. "Because if you do, now's the time to get out. No harm, no foul, no hard feelings. Your paycheck will be in the post on Friday. If you stay and I have to fire you because of your attitude, you won't get even that much."

Half a dozen more men stood and followed the other jackaroo out of the canteen.

"Good riddance to them," Charlie White, a year-rounder Jeremy had known since he was a teenager, said after they'd left. "They were lazy sons of bitches anyway. You're a Taylor, lad, and that's all that matters to most of us."

"Thanks, Charlie," Jeremy said. He looked around the room, taking the time to meet the gaze of each man in the room. "Just so we're clear here.... Yes, I'm gay. Yes, Sam is going to be here helping me run the station. No, I don't expect you to like it, but I do expect you to respect it." He waited for the murmurs to die down. No one else had walked out yet—a good sign. "Yes, Neil is the foreman on Lang Downs. He's also my brother-in-law, which means he's going to be around. Devlin had a bone to pick with Lang Downs, a lot of it because of me. I never wanted anything to happen to him, but he's gone now and I'm running things. Unlike my brother, I don't have a bone to pick with Lang Downs. If that's going to be a problem, the door is right there."

More grumbling, from different quarters, Jeremy noted. Interesting that the men who had issues with Lang Downs weren't all the same as the ones who had issues with him being gay. Had he missed a reason for the tension between the stations? He'd have to ask Charlie about it later. "Chances are, Neil won't be the only one either. The closest vet lives on Lang Downs. The best damn mechanic I've ever met lives there too. They've both offered their help in their areas or anywhere else I need it. I intend to take them up on it. And finally, I don't have the same attitude toward how to run a station that Devlin did, which means there will be some changes. I'm willing to discuss them if people have questions or concerns, but I expect everyone to respect the final decisions I make. If that doesn't work for you, now's the time to leave."

No one moved, although that could have been because no one wanted to do anything with him watching. He gave one last nod and grabbed his hat from next to his plate. He'd lost his appetite.

"Sam, Neil, let's leave them to their dinner."

Neil looked like he wanted to argue, but Sam herded him toward the door. As they walked toward Devlin's house, Jeremy wondered how many men he'd have left come morning.

TEN

JASON JUMPED out of the ute as soon as he reached the big barn on Taylor
Peak. His heart pounded as he grabbed his bag of supplies and hurried inside.
Jeremy's call had been terse, bordering on frantic. They needed a vet and they
needed one now. Jason had torn out of Lang Downs as fast as he could safely
drive. He hadn't been back to Taylor Peak in the two weeks since Devlin's
funeral, and this was not how he'd wanted his first return visit to go.

"What happened?" he asked when he saw Jeremy.

"Who are you?" one of the jackaroos asked.

"Jason, thank you for getting here so quickly," Jeremy said before Jason
could answer.

"I'm the vet," Jason told the jackaroo.

"You're not Dr. Nelson."

"No," Jeremy agreed, "but he is a vet, and he was closer than having
Dr. Nelson come out from Boorowa. Back here, Jason. We were moving the
mob between paddocks and my horse got tangled up in barbed wire. We cut
him loose as best we could and brought him back in, but he's a mess. He's…
bloody hell, he was my horse before I came to Lang Downs, and he's the
horse Devlin used almost exclusively. I don't want to lose him. He's covered
in blood."

Jason's gut clenched. Bad enough for his first emergency to be on
Taylor Peak where he would have to deal with their distrust of everything
related to Lang Downs. Having it be Jeremy's one link to his brother only
made it worse. If it had been a sheep, he could have assessed the situation and
told them it would a better choice to butcher it than treat it. He couldn't do
that with this horse unless he had no other choice. It didn't look that serious,
but horses were fickle creatures. He'd seen vets do everything right and the
horse just up and die on them anyway. And he'd seen others so badly hurt no
one expected them to survive and they just had.

He approached the jittery horse carefully. The animal wasn't fighting the crossties holding it in place, but Jason could see the way its muscles jumped in pain and protest. "Take a deep breath, Jeremy. Horses bleed. It doesn't have to be a bad thing. Let me take a look at him before we panic. What's his name?"

"Misfit," Jeremy replied.

Bloody hell, Jason thought. If that wasn't a biting commentary on Jeremy's life before coming to Lang Downs, Jason didn't know what would be.

"Okay, Misfit," he crooned to the horse, "let's take a look at you. You did a number on yourself, didn't you?"

He held his hand out so Misfit could sniff it. He hadn't sterilized them yet because he wanted the horse to smell him, not antiseptic. The time for sterilization would come later. Misfit snuffled at his hand like he was looking for a treat.

"I don't have anything for you just yet, mate, but let me take care of you and I'll give you the apple I was going to eat for lunch," Jason promised. He ran a soothing hand down Misfit's neck as he stepped to the side away from Jeremy to assess the injuries. Someone had removed the barbed wire, but the damage the braided metal had left behind on the horse's skin was obvious. Mostly around its back legs, fortunately, with no injuries he could see on Misfit's chest or belly, but the chestnut coat would hide small amounts of blood. He'd look more closely as he worked, but Misfit was still standing, so he doubted anything critical had been torn open. *Suture him up, give him antibiotics, something for the pain.* He could handle this.

"Okay, I'm going to give him a sedative for the pain and to keep him calm while we treat him." Jason rummaged in his bag for a syringe and filled it with the sedative. It would take a few minutes for it to work, but he could use that time to scrub up and find out what had happened. Misfit shivered all over when Jason injected the sedative, but he calmed to Jeremy's touch.

"Is there a sink I can use to clean up before we start? I don't want to make him worse because I have dirty hands."

"Over here," Jeremy said.

Jason scrubbed his hands and arms thoroughly. "Where'd the barbed wire come from?" he asked while he waited for the sedative to take effect.

"It was lying in the scrub," Jeremy muttered. "The more I find out about the way Devlin ran things the past couple of years, the less I like. I've found more than one pile of scrap from fences just lying around in the paddocks. I've ordered it cleaned up, but I only have so many men and that isn't our only chore."

A jackaroo joined them as Jason was washing up.

"Who's the kid?" he asked.

"Jason Thompson, from Lang Downs," Jeremy replied. "He just finished vet school and came home to work. Jason, this is Tim Perkins, one of my crew bosses."

Perkins made a noncommittal noise and went to stand by Misfit's head, stroking his forelock soothingly.

When Misfit's head began to drop and he started looking drowsy instead of frantic, Jason grabbed his clippers. "I'll be as gentle as I can, but if he moves around, he runs the risk of getting hurt worse. Keep him as calm as you can. I'd rather not twitch him unless we have to."

Jeremy joined the other man at Misfit's head. Jason could feel them watching him. He did his best not to squirm under Perkins's assessing gaze, but he could feel the weight of judgment from every jackaroo in the station in that look. Jason knew how gossip spread on a station. By now, all the hands not in the barn would have heard all about how the new vet—a kid—had come instead of the usual vet. And every one of them would judge him based on how well he treated Misfit.

He couldn't focus on that. He had to pay attention to what he was doing or he could make matters worse, and that wouldn't do anything to help his reputation.

He turned the clipper on and waited to see how Misfit would react to the noise. He twitched his ears a little but didn't seem overly bothered. Jason set the base against Misfit's shoulder so he could see that the vibration wouldn't hurt him. When that got no more of a reaction than the noise had, Jason breathed a sigh of relief. He headed to Misfit's back legs, where the wire had done the most damage, and started shaving around the injuries he found. Most of the marks were puncture wounds rather than lacerations. He clipped the hair back from them so he could clean them, but they would heal without any extra repair. The lacerations would require more work.

He finished the first leg without finding anything serious, but he didn't hope for his luck to hold. When he moved to Misfit's other hind leg, he grimaced. The barbed wire had cut deep, tearing the muscle and exposing the flexor tendon. If it was ruptured, he didn't know if he'd be able to save the horse. "Bring me my bag?" Jason asked Jeremy.

Jeremy brought it to him and hissed when he saw the wound. "That looks bad."

"Don't panic yet," Jason said, trying to keep himself from doing just that. "It's exposed. That doesn't mean it's compromised." He filled a new syringe with a local anesthetic and injected it in Misfit's hindquarters, just above the injury. "I'm going to give that a moment to work so I can clip around it and clean it without him trying to kick the shit out of me, and then we'll see if it's as bad as it looks."

"Perkins, hold him steady," Jeremy ordered.

"Keep a close eye on him," Jason added. "He's sedated and I've numbed the area as well, but that doesn't mean he won't react when I start working on him. If he starts acting like he's in distress, tell me."

Perkins's disgusted glare told Jason exactly what he thought about a "kid" telling him how to do his job, but Jason didn't fancy getting kicked in the head while he worked.

While Jason waited for the lidocaine to kick in around the laceration, he grabbed the antiseptic wash and started rinsing the areas he'd already prepared. With the blood washed away, most of them weren't as serious as he'd feared, which was a good sign, but that exposed tendon haunted him. He didn't want to put down an animal the first time he was called out, especially when it was Jeremy's horse. Not just a Taylor Peak horse, but Jeremy's horse. Jason could all too easily imagine how he'd feel if someone told him he had to put his dog Polly down. He didn't want to be the one to say those words to Jeremy. A couple of the other lacerations, though not as serious as the one on Misfit's flexor tendon, would need sutures as well, so he injected them with lidocaine too. When he thought it had been long enough, he went back to where Jeremy was still standing, staring at the injured leg.

"Go stand at his head again," he told Jeremy. "You'll steady him like no one else can." And if it would keep Jeremy from hovering over Jason while he worked, all the better. Jason didn't want anyone to see the way his hands trembled as he shaved the area around the gash and poured antiseptic into it. Once the worst of the gore was out of the way, he examined the tendon for any visible damage. He couldn't see any, which was a good sign. At the very least, it wasn't ruptured, and any more minor damage would heal, given time. Testing it would have told him that if he'd been thinking when he started. He cursed under his breath. He should have had them walk Misfit around to see if he was limping before he sedated him and numbed the area. Then he would have had a better idea of any damage. Too late now, though. He'd have to suture the wound and hope for the best.

He sutured that one up and sprayed it to keep the flies off, then moved back to the others he'd numbed. Everything else was easy in comparison— serious enough to need cleaning and suturing, but not serious enough to worry about beyond that unless they got infected.

And then he was back at Misfit's head, with Jeremy watching him worriedly. "The tendon looked intact. He'll be stiff and sore, and that one will take the longest to heal, but he should recover. I'll give him an antibiotic and tetanus shot booster now and leave bute sachets to put in his food for the next few days, but unless he takes a bad turn, all he needs now is time and restricted activity to heal. Keep the sutures clean and call me if you see anything that concerns you."

Perkins took that as his cue to leave. Jason frowned after him. Macklin would've had a few words to say to the man about deserting his post, but Macklin wasn't here, and Jason didn't have the authority now that the emergency had passed.

"Thank you," Jeremy said. "What do I owe you?"

Jason shrugged. "Let me replace the supplies I used and I'll send you a bill."

"No," Jeremy protested. "You do a vet's work, you earn a vet's pay."

Jason smiled. "Pretty sure I decide what to charge for my own time. I'll send Sam the bill. You just take good care of this old boy and get that barbed wire cleaned up so it doesn't happen again."

"I'm doing the best I know how," Jeremy said, "but it hasn't been easy, even with Walker throwing his support behind me 100 percent."

"Have you asked Neil about lending you a crew for a day? You could send them out to do nothing but check for trash like this. It would be better than animals getting caught in it unexpectedly."

Jeremy shook his head. "Neil would send one in a heartbeat, but things are tense enough around here without me making it worse by turning to Lang Downs every time I need something. I'm pretty sure Charlie White, one of my year-rounders, is the only one who actually believes I can do this."

"Sam believes it."

"Sam loves me. He has to believe it."

"I believe it," Jason said, "and I like and admire you, but I'm sure not in love with you. So there."

"You don't live here," Jeremy countered. "It's not the same thing."

"I'm sorry. I wish there was more I could do."

"You've done plenty," Jeremy said. "You patched up Misfit. The rest will sort itself out eventually. Say hello to everyone on the station for me."

"I will," Jason promised. "And you call me if there's anything else I can do, as a vet or just as a jackaroo. You aren't in this alone, no matter how much it feels that way."

"Thanks," Jeremy said. "I'm going to get Misfit settled. I'll call if anything changes."

Jason knew a dismissal when he heard one, so he gathered up his equipment and headed back to the ute. No one was standing around staring when he left the barn, but he knew better than to think no one was watching. He stowed his bag, climbed in the ute, and headed toward home. He only hoped he got there before he collapsed. His heart was still trying to pound its way out of his chest. It would be too late to ride out to help rotate the mobs like he'd originally planned to do that afternoon, but he'd still have an hour or so to kill before everyone came in to clean up before dinner. He'd do what he always did when he had time to kill—he'd head to the tractor shed. As a child, his father had always been there. As a teen, it was the likeliest place to find Seth. Jason hadn't asked Seth what he planned to work on today, but if he wasn't scoping out drover's huts, he would be there. The smell of engine oil and petrol relaxed him like nothing else could.

"SETH?"

The sound of Jason's voice calling his name broke Seth's focus on the plans he was drawing for the windmill installation at one of the drover's huts. It had too much tree cover for him to feel comfortable relying on solar panels for the generator, but the ridge above it was the ideal spot for a windmill.

"Hey, Jase, you're back. Is everything okay down at Taylor Peak? I saw you tear out of here earlier." He set his pencil on the table where he'd been working and joined Jason toward the back of the shed on the pile of hay bales that had been their frequent hideaway when they were younger.

"I'm not sure 'okay' is the word I'd use, but I did my best," Jason said. "Jeremy's horse tangled with some barbed wire that had been left in one of the outer paddocks, and you know how that goes."

Seth knew exactly how that went. Caine and Macklin were careful, so it didn't happen often, but he'd seen what barbed wire could do to an animal. They'd had to butcher a couple of sheep that got scared by a storm and bolted into a fence. "The horse lost. Is it going to make it?"

"He was still standing when I got there, and the bleeding had stopped. He had some deep punctures and lacerations, but only one of them was serious by itself. It was right near his flexor tendon, and if it had ruptured the tendon, I couldn't have saved him."

"But it hadn't," Seth said. "You didn't have to put him down." He wasn't even an animal lover the way so many of the jackaroos were, but he hated it when they had to put an animal down. The sheep didn't bother him— that's what they were there for—but the death of the working animals on the station left a pall for weeks. Taylor Peak had enough grief right now. They didn't need the death of a horse—Jeremy's horse—on top of it.

"No, the tendon looked intact, so as long as none of the wounds get infected, he should be fine in a few weeks. That wasn't the problem."

"Then what was?"

"Why would anyone in their right mind trust me to take care of an injured animal?" Jason asked.

Now there was a stupid question if Seth had ever heard one. For as long as he'd known him, Jason was the one to take in strays—okay, not Little Bit, but only because Sam got there first—or to trail along behind the vet or even to offer to deal with minor injuries so they wouldn't have to call the vet. Maybe he hadn't ever dealt with anything this serious, but he'd certainly proven his competence more than once. "Because you're a vet? What makes you ask that question? Did something go wrong?"

"I have a fancy diploma to put on my wall," Jason corrected. "It's not the same thing."

It was so much more than a bloody diploma, but Seth had done enough questioning of his own credentials to recognize the look on Jason's face. "It looks like it from where I'm sitting."

"I spent the entire time I was down there convinced I was going to do something wrong," Jason admitted.

"But did you actually do something wrong?" Self-doubt was Seth's status quo, but it had never been Jason's default when they were kids. Had something gone wrong in vet school to shake Jason's confidence so much?

"One thing. I didn't see the bad laceration before I sedated the horse so I couldn't walk him around to see how much damage he'd done to it like I should have."

"But did that keep you from treating him and will it keep him from making a full recovery?" Seth pressed. He hated seeing the dejected look on Jason's face, but the greedy part of him was gleeful that Jason had come to him with those fears, not his boyfriend. Cooper might be the one he slept with—Seth resolutely pushed that thought aside—but Seth was the one he came to for comfort. He didn't know a lot where relationships were concerned, but comfort surely lasted longer than sex.

"It shouldn't, but you never know with horses. I like sheep. Sheep are easy. Horses are a pain in the arse."

"Horses are a part of life on the station," Seth said with a shrug. He'd even learned to ride one, mechanic that he was. He only rode them when he had no other choice, but sometimes the weather got so bad the roads were impassable, and then knowing how to ride could save someone's life. He'd heard the stories about Caine saving Neil, and since he owed Chris's life in part to Neil's loyalty, he hadn't refused. He'd never be the stockman the others were, but he could keep his arse in the saddle well enough. "You knew that when you decided to come back here instead of opening a clinic in town, where you wouldn't have to deal with them."

"It wasn't home," Jason said. "This is what I've always wanted to do. I just have to figure out how to do it."

It wasn't home. How many times had Seth thought that exact thing when he was in Sydney? They were a pair of dropkicks, but they'd both learned their lesson and come home. The rest would come in time.

"One day at a time," Seth replied. "Isn't that how we do everything?"

Jason laughed. "Yeah, I guess it is. Enough of my whinging. How was your day?"

"Don't change the subject," Seth said. Jason had talked about what happened, but he wasn't feeling any better, and nothing he'd said explained why he was upset. Seth knew how much pent-up emotions could hurt. He wouldn't let Jason do that to himself. "I can tell you're upset, but what you're saying doesn't line up with that. So tell me what's really going on."

Jason sighed. "It was just…. The whole time I was working, I felt like a fraud, you know? Like that fancy diploma wasn't worth the paper it was printed on. And then there were the jackaroos. Jeremy was there, so Perkins didn't say anything, but it felt like the whole station was watching and judging me. They don't know me from Adam, but I'm young and I'm not Dr. Nelson, and I came in from Lang Downs. I could have performed a miracle and they would have found a way to turn it against me."

"Why do you care what they think?" Seth asked. "Jeremy trusts you enough to call you, and from what you said, his trust wasn't misplaced. Caine trusts you enough to keep an eye on everything here, even with all the regulations about treatment in order to keep the station's organic certification."

"I'd be willing to bet I know a lot more about treatment options on organic outfits than Dr. Nelson does," Jason said.

"See?" Seth said. "Nothing to worry about. So why do you care what the Taylor Peak jackaroos think of you?"

"Because it's hard not to care," Jason said. "Yes, I'm the one Jeremy called, but there was this weight hanging over the barn, and I guess it got to me."

"I know the solution to that," Seth said.

"What's that?" Jason asked.

"A beer. Chris has Tooheys at the house, but we could probably find something else if you don't want that."

"Tooheys is fine," Jason said. "And yeah, a beer sounds good. Maybe I'll be able to relax then."

"Are you that much of a lightweight?" Seth teased. "Come on. We'll go sit on the veranda and drink a beer or two and you'll feel better."

Jason smiled. "You always make me feel better. That's why I came in here."

Seth's heart bloomed beneath the words. Let Cooper chew on that for a while. Seth was still Jason's source of solace when he needed it, and he'd be damned if he'd let anyone take that away from him.

ELEVEN

JASON WALKED into the canteen with Seth, all but doubled over with laughter. He never stopped marveling at how Seth could put everything back in perspective for him. His first solo experience as a vet was under his belt now. Misfit would be fine in time. He could do this.

"Where are you sitting tonight?" Jason asked. "You're welcome to join me if you want."

"Or you could join me," Seth said. "I know you're sleeping in the bunkhouse, but you're a year-rounder too."

"Yeah, but I haven't seen Cooper all day. I should probably sit with him. There's no reason you can't join us, though."

"If you're going to spend all your time flirting with him, I'd rather sit with the year-rounders," Seth said. "Less painful than your pathetic attempts at being subtle."

Jason elbowed Seth in the side. "At least I have someone to flirt with. You're never going to meet anyone way out here. Laura's too young for you, and all the other girls are married or seeing someone back home."

"I don't need someone to flirt with," Seth replied. "I just got rid of a ball and chain. Why would I want a new one?"

"I said flirt, I didn't say marry," Jason replied. "There is a difference."

Seth shrugged. "Go see your jackaroo. I've had you for the afternoon. I can give him a little of your time at dinner."

What was that supposed to mean? It wasn't the first odd comment Seth had made since he'd been home, but Jason hadn't managed to string enough of them together to figure out what Seth's problem was. Deciding he'd worry about it later, he grabbed a plate and sat down next to Cooper.

"Hi, how was your day?" Cooper asked.

"Rough," Jason admitted, "but I found Seth in the tractor shed when I got back, and he helped me get my head on straight again."

"Straight?" Cooper asked. "Should I be worried?"

Jason rolled his eyes. "Not that kind of straight. He talked me down from overreacting. I can always rely on him to calm me down when I'm upset."

"You should have come to find me," Cooper said. "I was working in the valley today. I told you that this morning."

He could have done that, Jason supposed, but he hadn't even thought about it. His only thought had been finding Seth. "Sometimes a bloke just needs his best mate. Today was one of those days."

"It kinda seems like he's all you need these days," Cooper muttered.

Jason ran a hand through his hair. He didn't really want to do this right now. He'd already had a shitty day, only somewhat redeemed by the time spent with Seth. He didn't want to argue with Cooper on top of it. "Look, he's been my best friend since I was fifteen. I've known you for a few weeks. I like you. I enjoy the time we spend together. But I needed Seth today. Maybe someday I'll know you the way I know him, but if you can't deal with Seth and me being friends, that isn't going to happen."

Cooper's jaw tightened and lines formed around his mouth as he frowned. "I see. Some of the jackaroos warned me. I should have listened."

"Warned you about what?" Jason asked. He was so through with this conversation, but that had piqued his curiosity.

"Warned me you were too in love with Simms to see anyone else, but he wasn't here and you certainly seemed interested, so I figured I'd see what happened. Turns out they were right. I'm through."

Jason flushed. Was he that transparent to everyone but Seth? "If that's as much patience as you have with me having mates besides you, then yeah, we're through." He grabbed his untouched plate and tossed it in the bin of dirty dishes. He needed to be anywhere other than here. He didn't know what Seth had overheard, but even if Seth hadn't heard it directly, plenty of other people had. Word would get back to him, Seth would come find him, and when he did, Jason would have to tell Seth the truth. He only hoped it didn't cost him Seth's friendship. He could deal with losing Cooper. He had genuinely liked the man and the sex had been good, but he hadn't been in love with him. He could deal with Seth not loving him back. He'd always known that was hopeless anyway. But if Seth decided they couldn't be friends? Yeah, Jason couldn't deal with that.

He paused to take stock of where he was. Without his conscious volition, his feet had taken him back to the tractor shed. And didn't that say everything that could be said about his state of mind? Even when he was running from Seth, he ended up going to their hangout spot for solace.

He let himself inside, leaving the door open in invitation. Maybe Seth wouldn't follow him right away, but if he did, he'd know where Jason was and know he was welcome.

Jason snorted. This was Seth's domain, not his. If anyone should question his welcome here, it was him, not Seth. God, he was so fucking pathetic.

SETH STARED mutely as Jason tossed his plate and stormed out of the bunkhouse. He looked down at his own plate, trying to collect his racing thoughts, and then back at the door to the canteen. A foot connected with his beneath the table. He looked up at Thorne, sitting across from him.

"I don't know you as well as some of the year-rounders do, but take a little advice from someone old enough to be your father. I don't know what you two have been waiting for, but he just handed you the perfect opening. You won't get a better chance than now."

"He didn't say he loved me," Seth replied automatically.

"He also didn't deny it," Thorne said. "You're the only one on this station who hasn't figured it out yet. If you feel the same way—and I think you do—you owe it to both of you to say something."

Seth thought he might be sick. If Thorne was right, he and Jason had wasted so much time. None of it was Jason's fault, of course. The blame lay squarely on Seth's shoulders. Jason didn't even know Seth was bi. Jason wouldn't say anything because he wouldn't want to mess up their friendship by crushing on a straight man. Seth got that part perfectly. No, he'd have to own up to everything he'd never said and hope Jason loved him enough not to hate him for his silence.

Dusk had well and truly arrived when Seth stepped outside the canteen. He looked up and down the valley for some indication of where Jason might have gone, but he'd delayed long enough talking with Thorne that Jason wasn't in sight. That narrowed down his options somewhat, because Jason could only have gone so far in that time. If Seth had to guess, Jason had gone to one of three places: his room in the bunkhouse, his parents' back veranda, or the tractor shed. At the bunkhouse, he could shut his door, but that wouldn't stop people from knocking. The seasonal hands would be less likely to seek Jason out at Patrick and Carley's house—assuming any of them went looking—but at some point his parents would come home and he'd have to talk to them. If he wanted to be alone with no interruptions, the tractor shed was his best bet. Of course if he was hoping to avoid Seth, it would be the last place he went simply because it would be the first place Seth would look.

"Bloody hell, it's hard when you know someone this well," he muttered as he started toward the tractor shed. Maybe Jason didn't want to avoid Seth. Maybe he'd gone there so they'd have somewhere private to talk. Maybe— fuck, he was a fool for even thinking it, but Thorne had planted the idea in his head—Jason was even hoping Seth would follow him so they could be done with secrets for good.

The door to the tractor shed was ajar when Seth distinctly remembered closing it, but the lights were off. Seth pushed it open wider, not that visibility was any better outside than inside. "Jason?"

"Yeah?"

"You okay, mate?" Jason didn't sound okay. He didn't sound okay at all, but Seth was feeling his way here, and the last thing he wanted was to push if Jason just wanted to be left alone. Although he'd left the door open....

"I don't know," Jason said. "I just broke up rather publicly with the bloke I'd been seeing, and he chose to do it by saying some things I didn't really want shared. How am I supposed to be doing?"

Seth made his way to the back of the tractor shed by habit rather than by sight. He and Jason had to talk, but maybe it would be easier to bare his soul if they couldn't see each other. He found the pile of hay bales and sat with his back against it, close to where he thought Jason's legs would be but not touching him.

"I don't know. At least Ilene and I broke up in private, although she hurled an awful lot of the same accusations at me," Seth said into the darkness.

"You could at least tell her how wrong she was," Jason replied.

Seth shook his head before realizing Jason couldn't see him. "She wasn't wrong."

"What the hell, Seth?" Jason said. "You're not gay. Every person you've ever gone out with has been female."

"I'm not gay," Seth agreed. "I like women. I just happen to like men too. Well, one man anyway, except he deserves so much better than a bloody mess like me. And then he went away to school and so did I, and when I came back—"

"Stop," Jason interrupted. "Just fucking stop. Say it or don't, but don't dance around it."

Seth closed his eyes and mustered all his courage. This was it. Jason would either accept it or he'd lose the only good thing in his life. "I've been in love with you since we were both too young and stupid to know what that word meant. But you left, so I did too. And whenever I came back, you were with one bloke or another, so I figured you didn't feel the same. And then I came home—because you were coming home, by the way—but by the time I got here, you were already involved with Cooper. You were entitled. Just because I've always been too wrapped up in you to do more than look at another bloke doesn't mean you have to feel the same. But now it's over with Cooper, and it seemed like maybe you felt the same. Everyone else thinks you do, anyway, so I followed you, hoping maybe they were right."

He heard Jason moving, but he didn't have time to brace himself before Jason straddled his thighs, pinning him to the hay. "You really mean it?"

"I...." Fuck that. In for a penny, in for a pound. "Yes, I really mean it."

"Thank God."

Before Seth could wonder what would happen next, Jason kissed him. He'd imagined this moment more times than he could count—sweet and shy, suave and sophisticated, even hot and heavy on occasion—but he'd never believed it would actually happen. He'd never hoped one day he'd end up sitting on the floor of the tractor shed with Jason in his lap, kissing him. Oh, fuck, Jason was kissing him.

His brain, already on autopilot, short-circuited as the reality of Jason's weight on his legs and Jason's lips against his settled in. Jason was *kissing* him. He reached blindly for Jason, wrapping his arms around his shoulders and holding on for dear life. Jason's stubble caught against his lips, making him intensely aware of not having shaved that morning. Would it bother Jason? Ilene had hated it when he didn't shave. He didn't *seem* bothered, but—

"Stop thinking so hard and kiss me back," Jason said, so close Seth could feel his breath against his mouth. "Or I'm going to start thinking you don't want me after all."

"I want you," Seth assured him, sliding his hands from Jason's shoulders to his neck so he could pull Jason back in. His aim was a little off in the darkness, but Jason moved to meet him, and this time Seth poured everything he had into the kiss—all the years of dreaming and hoping and wanting, all the jealousy every time he heard Jason talk about another man or watched Cooper touch him in all the ways Seth was never allowed, but most of all, all the joy at finally—*finally*—having Jason for himself.

JASON NEARLY wept with relief when Seth finally kissed him back. He'd been so sure he would never get this chance, and then Seth said he loved him, but he hadn't reacted when Jason kissed him, and then—

He forced his brain to stop. If he had to guess, Seth had probably had this same problem. They'd wasted so much time.

No more, though. Seth loved him. He wouldn't have to dream anymore. He could simply reach out and touch. He broke the kiss on a gasp, lack of air or the sheer joy of finally kissing Seth leaving him light-headed. He kept his forehead against Seth's, though. He didn't want Seth to think he was pulling away.

Seth's hands dropped from Jason's shoulders to his hips. Jason smiled and settled more fully on Seth's lap. "Is that what you wanted?"

Seth moaned and Jason echoed him as the movement brought their bodies into greater contact.

"I'll never say no to anything that keeps you close," Seth said.

Jason grinned, high on the euphoria of finally having Seth in his arms. "Just say the word and we can be as close as you want."

"I want that," Seth said, "but…."

"But what?"

"I've had sex before, but never with another bloke. I don't exactly know what I'm doing here."

If that wasn't the biggest turn-on ever, Jason didn't know what could top it. "You're doing just fine from where I'm sitting," Jason said. "I don't imagine it's all that different from sex with a woman. Just do to me what you like done to you. We've got the same parts. It's a pretty good guess the same things will appeal, and if they don't, we'll figure out what does as we go along."

"When I'm with a woman, there's never any question of who's…."

"Pitching and catching?" Jason suggested.

"Yeah, that."

Jason smiled. "Good thing I like it both ways, then. We'll figure it out. The hard part is over."

"And what part was that?" Seth asked as he rocked his hips. "Because I'm feeling some pretty hard parts right now."

"You love me," Jason said. "I never figured I stood a chance, so I never let myself want it. Bloody lot of good it did me. We're here now, together. The rest is just pieces and parts." He ran his hands over Seth's chest, listening for a reaction since he couldn't see anything. Night had fallen completely in the time they'd been talking and kissing. Seth arched into his hands, so Jason kept exploring. They'd spent enough time sleeping in each other's rooms as teens for him to have some idea of Seth's body, but that had been years ago. Once they went away to school, those sleepovers stopped. The body beneath his hands now didn't belong to a teenager. Seth had filled out, no longer as skinny as he'd once been. Jason wanted to see as well as touch, but that would have to wait. He wasn't about to suggest they stop, even if moving meant light and a more comfortable setting. Or condoms and lube, for that matter.

His whole body trembled at the thought of Seth fucking him. He'd come apart at the seams the minute Seth touched him, the way he felt right now. The thought of fucking Seth… no, he wasn't going there even in his mind. That could wait until Seth was more comfortable. And if he never got that comfortable, Jason could live with that too. As long as Seth loved him.

Seth's hands on his chest startled him, but he arched into the touch immediately. Seth moved hesitantly, like he wasn't quite sure what to do with

Jason now that he had him. That was ridiculous. Jason leaned back a bit and stripped his shirt off. There, that would give Seth something to explore.

"Jase," Seth groaned.

Jason grinned as he moved forward to kiss Seth again. He'd never get tired of Seth's mouth. Although he hoped Seth would eventually want to put it elsewhere too.

Seth returned the kiss a lot more aggressively this time, like he'd finally gotten over the shock of everything. Jason parted his lips, offering his mouth for Seth's taking. Seth took him up on it immediately, holding Jason's head in place with a firm hand to his neck as he claimed Jason's mouth with his tongue. Damn, he could kiss when he set his mind to it.

Jason twined his tongue around Seth's, giving back as good as he got. His body hummed with need, every nerve firing at the slightest contact. Seth kept one hand on Jason's neck, holding him into the kiss—like Jason was going anywhere—but he let the other wander over Jason's bare torso. Every touch went straight to Jason's cock, and he moaned into the kiss. Much more of this and he'd embarrass himself.

Voices outside the tractor shed shattered the stillness. Seth tensed beneath Jason's hands, so Jason broke the kiss and rocked back on his heels. "Maybe this isn't the best place to be doing this."

Seth chuckled. "Like we'll have much privacy anywhere on the station." His voice was gratifyingly husky to Jason's ears. "Everyone knows everyone else's business. I don't know how Macklin kept being gay a secret for as long as he did."

"By not getting involved with anyone on the station," Jason replied. He reached blindly for his shirt, hoping he hadn't tossed it too far away in his haste. He found it by touch and checked to make sure it was right side out before he pulled it back on. His stomach rumbled unhappily as he stood up and offered Seth a hand.

"You didn't eat," Seth said.

"No, I didn't get a chance," Jason said. "Although I'll take kissing you over eating any day."

"You don't have to choose," Seth replied. "This isn't an either-or proposition. Let's go see if Kami has anything left. Then we can find someplace actually private and pick up where we left off."

"I like the sound of that."

They walked out of the tractor shed, pausing long enough for Seth to secure the door. Jason started to reach for Seth's hand as they walked toward the canteen, but despite Seth's comment about the lack of privacy on the station, he didn't know if Seth was ready to tell everyone else. Seth answered that by twining his fingers in Jason's.

"Okay?"

"Absolutely," Jason said.

He really should have expected the canteen to still be full of the year-rounders. He and Seth had made enough of a spectacle of themselves that everyone would want to know they'd worked things out. It didn't stop his cheeks from burning at the round of applause or the teasing catcalls when he and Seth walked in together. Seth's cheeks were as red as Jason's felt, but he didn't let go of Jason's hand, and that made any amount of embarrassment worth it.

"About bloody time," Chris said when the noise died down. "I was starting to think you two would never get your act together."

Macklin clapped them on the shoulders, making Jason jump. "Year-rounder or seasonal jackaroo, the same rules apply. I don't care what you do on your own time, but when it's my time, I expect the work to be done." He squeezed a little tighter. "I also expect you to make each other happy."

"We'll do our jobs like always," Seth said.

"Probably better because we won't be distracted," Jason said with a laugh.

Caine joined them with a smirk on his face for Macklin. "I'll talk to Sam and Jeremy this week, but if they're still planning on the move to Taylor Peak being permanent, there will be an empty house for you when you're ready for it. And my record is still perfect."

Jason felt Seth tense next to him. "Give us a few days to get used to the idea, yeah?"

"When you're ready," Caine repeated.

Jason could have moved in there tonight, but he wouldn't pressure Seth into anything he wasn't ready for. They had time. They would figure it out.

TWELVE

JEREMY STARED down at the numbers Sam had set in front of him in disbelief. Every station had a bad season now and then. The weather didn't cooperate, they had fewer lambs born, the price of feed went up, a bad storm wiped out part of the mob or damaged property.... It was part of being a grazier, and Jeremy had grown up listening to his parents save up in the good years so they'd have what they needed to tide them through the lean ones. It wasn't that Devlin had gone through a bad year, or even a couple of bad years. The problem was the cushion—specifically the lack of one. If Sam's calculations were correct—and Jeremy had no doubt Sam had double- and triple-checked them before bringing them to Jeremy—the station was so far in debt Jeremy ran the risk of losing it to the bank if he couldn't come up with a significant chunk of money by the end of the season.

"We'd have to sell off almost the whole mob to come up with that kind of money," Jeremy said, looking up at Sam.

"And if we do that, we won't have anything to earn money next season," Sam finished for him. "I don't know what Devlin intended to do, but he's left you one hell of a mess."

"Any suggestions?" Jeremy asked.

"You could throw yourself on the bank's mercy," Sam said. "We can put together a plan of how we're going to pay off what Devlin owed over a couple of years, but there's no guarantee they'll accept it, and even if they do, we're going to end up hurting because of it, because the only way I can see us coming up with that kind of cash even over a couple of years is to sell off stock. We could build the mob back up eventually, but it's not going to be easy."

"Can I just sell the place and go back to Lang Downs where we belong?" Jeremy asked. He hated it here. Hated the looks he got from most of the jackaroos. Hated the way everyone seemed to be comparing him to Devlin—and how he always came out looking worse. Three people on the entire station believed in him—Sam, Walker, and Charlie. And some days, Jeremy wasn't even sure about Walker. "I'm a crew boss, Sam. That's all I've ever wanted to be. I'm not cut out to be a grazier."

"Could you really sell it?" Sam asked. "If someone walked in here and offered to take it off your hands, could you really walk away?"

"Yes."

"Really?" Sam pressed. "Your childhood home? The plot where your parents and grandparents are buried? A hundred and fifty years of family legacy?"

Jeremy flinched at Sam's words. He hated it when Sam played dirty. "What choice do I have? Even if the bank agreed to a plan of some kind, it will take us years to work our way out of this kind of a hole, and for what? We don't have kids. There aren't any Taylors left, other than some cousins who are all perfectly happy with their lives in the city. They aren't going to want it, and their kids certainly aren't. If it's going to pass out of the family's hands anyway, why should I kill myself trying to save it now? At least if I sell it, I walk away with something. If the bank forecloses, I lose everything."

"All very valid points," Sam agreed. "So answer me this: Who would you sell it to? It's remote enough that I don't see developers being interested. That means you'd have to find a grazier interested in expanding. You know anyone?"

"We could advertise," Jeremy said. "There are trade journals, that kind of thing."

"Before you do that, I have another idea," Sam said. "If you want to hear it. But if you really want to just sell it and walk away, I won't try to stop you."

The last thing he wanted to do was walk away. He just didn't see how he could stay. "I'm listening."

"What we need is an investor," Sam said. "Someone to give us an influx of capital in exchange for a percentage of future profits. If we scratch out the debt for a minute, if we look just at the figures for this year, both current and projected, we're not in bad shape. We'd have to have a significant loss before we have to worry about not breaking even. The only reason we're even having this conversation is because of the debt. And with everything we learnt watching Caine and Macklin run Lang Downs, next year has the potential to actually be profitable, debt aside. So if we have an investor who would pay off the debt, we could assure that person of a return fairly confidently. He wouldn't make his money back in a season, but he would see a return on his investment."

"So this person gives us money now in exchange for some percentage of the profit later," Jeremy said. "What if we don't turn a profit one season? It happens. It happened to Devlin three seasons in a row. It hasn't happened on

Lang Downs recently, but I know there have been bad years there too. Running a station isn't rocket science, but it's also not predictable. Mother Nature can be a bitch."

"We'd need someone who understood that," Sam agreed. "Someone who would be in it for the long haul."

"Like who?" Jeremy asked. "It's a grand idea and all, but where are we going to find such a person?"

"I had a couple of ideas about that too," Sam said. "Walker's made a couple of comments about investing his pension from the army, and he understands how stations work. He's already here and working. It would give him an added incentive to stay and to make the station as successful as possible."

"I don't know what kind of pension you think the army pays, but I don't see it being enough to cover the full debt," Jeremy said.

"It probably wouldn't be," Sam agreed, "although it might be enough to buy us time with the bank even if we didn't get the station completely out of debt, but I said I had a couple of ideas. Walker was just the first one."

"And the other one?"

"We talk to Caine and Macklin," Sam said. "I did the books there long enough to know they could afford it, especially if Walker was also in. I also did the books long enough to know Lang Downs can't grow any more without more land. They talked about adding to the mob a couple of years ago and decided they couldn't support it on the land they have without sacrificing the organic certification. It would take three or four years, since Taylor Peak isn't organic certified, but if we got it there and could run the two stations as one, we could cut down on a lot of overlap in expenses, allow both stations to grow, and increase profitability all around."

Jeremy considered the suggestion. It wasn't ideal, but ideal had flown out the window when he inherited Devlin's debts along with his property. It would allow him to mostly keep his family home and it would take away some degree of the burden of running the station. He might still be the one nominally in charge, but he'd have Caine and Macklin to help him with the big decisions. He'd have Walker to help him run the place, not just temporarily but for good. As they got closer to running the stations as one, he'd have the support of his friends—his family—on a more permanent, planned basis instead of when they had time to come help on their days off. As far as plans went, it was far better than he'd hoped for. Devlin was probably spinning in his grave, but he'd gone and got himself killed. He didn't get a say in the matter anymore.

"What do we need to do?"

"Give me a couple of days and I'll put together a proposal," Sam said. "We can invite Caine and Macklin to dinner, get Walker to join us, and pitch the idea to them then."

"And if they say no?" Jeremy asked.

"Then we'll throw ourselves on the bank's mercy and hope for the best," Sam replied with a shrug. "But they won't say no."

BY THE time Jason had finished his second attempt at dinner, everyone else had wandered off to their own homes for the night, leaving Seth and Jason alone in the canteen. "I don't want to go back to the bunkhouse," Jason admitted as he dealt with his dirty plate.

"So don't," Seth said.

"I have to eventually," Jason replied. "I have to work tomorrow, and that means I have to sleep."

"I do too, but you don't have to sleep in the bunkhouse. You could stay over with me. We've done it before," Seth offered.

Jason looked at him intently.

"Just to sleep," Seth said. "That way you wouldn't have to go back to the bunkhouse."

"I'd like that," Jason said. "As long as it won't make you feel pressured."

Seth couldn't promise it wouldn't, but he owed it to them both to try. They walked to Chris and Jesse's house in silence, shoulders close enough to brush but not otherwise touching. Seth led Jason into his bedroom, the same as he had done a thousand times before. Jason kicked off the sandals he'd put on after he got rid of his boots after work, the same as he'd done a thousand times, and settled on the bed next to Seth… the same as he'd done a thousand times. It felt so incredibly familiar to be here with Jason like this. How many nights had they lain side by side in one room or the other, talking about their days and their dreams? They'd spent the better part of three years sleeping over with each other, and at least half the nights they were home on breaks from uni or just because.

Then Jason tugged on his hand and pulled Seth into his arms.

That was new. Years overdue to hear some of the year-rounders tell it, but definitely new.

Seth wrapped his arms around Jason's chest, tucked his head under Jason's chin, and held on. Now that he had the right to touch this way, he wasn't about to pass up an opportunity.

"You know everyone who saw us walk this way together is going to think we're having sex," Jason observed softly.

Seth tipped his head back so he could look at Jason. "With my brother in the next room?" he said with a shudder. "I don't think I could get it up, knowing he could hear every sound we made."

"You mean you never snuck a girl into your room before you and Chris came to Lang Downs?" Jason teased.

Seth shook his head. "When we lived with Tony, I didn't bring anyone home because I didn't even want to go into that hellhole. Why would I have brought anyone else there? And after Tony kicked us out, I didn't have a room of my own. We were lucky to have a bed in some of the places we stayed. I didn't have my own room again until we moved here."

Jason's arms tightened around Seth. "You never talk about your life before you got here. I always forget growing up wasn't the same for you as it was for me."

Way to go, Simms, Seth thought. *Totally fuck up the mood.*

"Mostly I just want to forget about it too," Seth said. "But no, no sneaking girls into my room. Boys either, for that matter. I slept over with friends a few times, but that never lasted long when I wouldn't reciprocate."

Jason kissed the top of his head. Seth alternated between feeling comforted and patronized. He pushed the second reaction aside. Jason wouldn't patronize him. He needed to change the subject, though, because Jason would feel sorry for him, and Seth hated that. "We talked about Misfit, but I didn't ask how Jeremy was doing."

"Jeremy looked really run-down."

"It's got to be hard," Seth said. "I can't imagine what I would do if something happened to Chris. He was all I had for so long."

Jason's arms tightened around him. "Nothing's going to happen to Chris, but even if it does, you won't be alone. I promise."

Seth would have given anything to believe that, but he knew the value of promises. His mother promised things would get better when she married Tony. She'd promised Tony would take care of him after she died. Hell, Tony even promised her he'd see to her boys. He'd seen to them all right. He'd seen them right out the door. Chris was the only person who had never broken a promise to him, who had never left him. Seth wanted to believe Jason, but he didn't know how to trust anymore.

"I need to get over to Taylor Peak and take a look at Jeremy's machinery," Seth said instead of acknowledging Jason's promise. "It's not much, but if I can take that worry off his mind, he can focus on other things."

"I know he'd appreciate it." Jason scooted down on the bed so he was lying nearly flat and rearranged his arms so one lay across Seth's chest and the other rested between them. He stroked the line of Seth's sternum lazily, the contact more relaxing than arousing. That could change in a heartbeat, but for now, Seth purred under the touch like a lazy kitten. It had been a long time since he'd just basked in someone's presence this way. Ilene hadn't been the relaxing sort, and even then, she'd expected him to take care of her, not the other way around. Seth would happily take care of Jason anytime he needed it, but the casual affection implicit in Jason's light caress soothed rough edges he didn't even know he had.

God, he hoped this meant Jason loved him too. He'd told himself repeatedly that Jason's reaction in the tractor shed was more than enough proof that Jason felt the same way, but a part of him really wanted to hear the words. Asking for them would be admitting how needy Jason made him feel, though, and he couldn't make himself that vulnerable. Not even to Jason. Jason wouldn't hurt him deliberately, but Seth had learned the hard way not to open himself up to being hurt. He could be patient. They had time. Jason would say the words when he was ready and everything would be fine.

If he said it enough times, he might even believe it eventually.

Jason rolled onto his side and kissed Seth hungrily. Seth responded instantly, his body reacting despite his earlier comment about Chris in the next room.

"Think we can come up with an excuse to get Chris and Jesse out of the house for a few hours?" Jason asked. "Because I really want to get naked with you."

The words sent shivers through Seth. He wanted Jason so much it scared him. He leaned in for another kiss to cover his nerves. "They'll see right through any excuse we come up with."

"Does it matter?" Jason asked. "We're both well over the age of consent. There's no reason we shouldn't have sex. I guarantee they do. And probably have since you've been home."

That wasn't an image Seth needed in his head. "Way to kill the mood," he grumbled. "I don't guess the bunkhouse is an option either."

"Those walls are even thinner than the walls here. And… I'd feel like I was rubbing it in Cooper's face, and that seems like a shitty way to thank him for pushing us into getting together, even if that wasn't his intention."

Seth was twisted enough to want to rub it in Cooper's face a little, but Jason was right, and Seth had won the prize, so he could be magnanimous. "Drover's hut?"

Jason laughed. "Why don't we just suggest to Jesse that he should take Chris into town on their next day off? Yes, they'll know, but it'll be worth it to have you to myself."

"You talk to him," Seth said. "I'm not going anywhere near either of them with this. One sex talk with my brother was enough to last for a lifetime."

"Don't think I won't," Jason replied. "Just not right now."

Seth snuggled deeper in Jason's embrace. Jason could worry about that tomorrow. Seth had more important things on his mind. Like keeping Jason there until they fell asleep together. Just like old times, only better.

THIRTEEN

"ARE YOU sure you're okay with this?" Sam asked as he and Jeremy got ready for dinner. It had been a week since Sam had brought up the idea of asking their friends to invest in the station. Caine and Macklin had agreed to come over, and Walker had shrugged and told them he didn't care where he ate as long as he got food. "We can forget about it and just enjoy dinner with friends and our foreman. We can ask Caine and Macklin's advice on all the things we still feel like we're guessing about, and we can explain Walker's presence because he's the one who will help us carry out whatever plans we make."

"No." As much as Jeremy hated admitting he was in over his head, the other option was losing the station to the bank, and that would be even worse. "As hard as this will be, it's still the best alternative we have. If they say no, we'll consider other options, but we have to try." Devlin wouldn't agree, but it was Jeremy's best choice for preserving some part of his family's legacy. "We should go down. They'll be here soon."

"I'll be down in just a minute," Sam said. "I want to look through the numbers one more time, just to make sure I haven't missed anything."

Sam hadn't missed anything. Jeremy knew that as surely as he knew his own name. That was nerves talking. Sam didn't want to do this any more than Jeremy did, but they didn't have a choice. Jeremy gave Sam a quick kiss and headed downstairs to the kitchen. Philippa, the station cook—nowhere near as creative as Kami but still a sight better than the station cook from before Jeremy had moved to Lang Downs—had left dinner warming in the oven so all Jeremy would have to do was serve. The food would be edible and filling, but he wondered what he'd have to bribe Caine with to get her lessons with Kami. Or maybe he could borrow Sarah for a week. She'd picked up all of Kami's recipes by now. Most nights the Lang Downs jackaroos couldn't guess who had actually made the meal anymore.

"Stop stalling," he muttered to himself as he set the table. "Even if they say no, they're still your friends and you can enjoy an evening together."

He heard a car door close and booted feet on the veranda. "They're here, Sam," he called up the stairs as he went to open the door. "Hi, Caine, Macklin. Thanks for coming."

"We're glad to be here," Caine said. "Is everything okay? You said you had something you wanted to talk about."

"Dinner first, business later," Sam said as he joined them in the foyer. "No need to spoil our appetites. We're just waiting for Walker."

"How's he working out as foreman?" Macklin asked.

"Better than I could have hoped," Jeremy replied. In the month Walker had been at Taylor Peak, Jeremy had already come to rely on him as much as he relied on Sam, albeit for different things. "He's not always up to date on the latest trends, but he's smart and willing to learn. Most importantly, though, he put the fear of God in the jackaroos. Some of them still look like they might argue with Sam or me, but they see him coming and get to work without him saying a word. It suddenly doesn't matter that the orders came from me when Walker is the one barking them at the men."

"Nobody instills discipline like a Commando drill sergeant," Walker said from behind them as he walked in the door. "I had good teachers."

"Walker, good to see you again," Macklin said, offering his hand for Walker to shake. "How are you settling in?"

"Like a duck to water," Walker replied. "Some things you just don't forget. It helps to have bosses who know what they're doing. It's easy to enforce a logical order. Not so much when the decisions don't make sense."

"Tell us if that ever happens," Jeremy said immediately. "This isn't a dictatorship."

"I wouldn't be here if it was," Walker replied. "Some of the jackaroos haven't figured that out yet, but they'll come around."

"My brother—"

"Is no longer running the station," Walker interrupted. "I don't speak ill of the dead. So, enough about that, you said you had something to talk to me about?"

Caine laughed. "We just asked and were told no business until after dinner."

"I wouldn't want to spoil anyone's appetite," Sam said. "Our cook may not be up to Kami's standard, but who is?"

"Then let's eat," Walker said. "I'm starving, and Phil might not cook like Kami does, but she's still in a whole different class than what I got in the army."

"Phil?" Caine asked.

"Philippa, but the only thing she hates worse than being called that is being called Pippa." Caine's grin grew wider, and Jeremy could practically see him matchmaking in his head. "What?" Walker said. "It pays to be on the good side of the person making your meals. Just ask Lachlan if you don't believe me."

BY THE time they finished eating, Jeremy had relaxed. Whether that was because of the good company or the beer, he wasn't sure, but he lifted his glass in a toast to the others at the table. "Cheers, mates. Sam and I are lucky to have such good friends."

As if sensing his change of mood, Caine, Macklin, and Walker returned the toast but waited for him to continue.

"Sam and I have been going over the financial records Devlin left," Jeremy continued, "and it doesn't look good. He had a couple of bad seasons, by which I mean four or five, and he took out some pretty hefty loans to cover the losses. Those loans are going to come due, and we don't have the money to pay them off. We might be able to do it if we sold off most of the mob, but then we wouldn't have the resources to get through next year without taking out another loan. And that's no way to run a station."

"The problem," Sam said, picking up the thread of the conversation, "is that the banks won't care about running the station in the long term. Their concern is the repayment of the loan, nothing else. We might be able to renegotiate the terms of the loan on the grounds that Jeremy just took over and needs some time to get his feet under him, but that's not going to change the bottom line. We would need four or five exceptional seasons at least to pay off the loans without doing damage to the long-term viability of the station."

"So what's your p-plan?" Caine asked.

Jeremy winced at the stutter. Caine hated to stutter, but more than that, he only did it when he was upset these days. If Caine was upset at their situation, that was okay. If he was upset at them bringing him into it, they were screwed.

"You have one or you wouldn't have invited us over for d-dinner," Caine said. "You would have told us you were selling and asked if your house was still available."

"We're looking for investors," Sam said. "An influx of capital now in exchange for a percentage of the profit in the future."

"And input into the running of the station," Jeremy added. "We're not asking for anything on blind faith."

"It wouldn't be a small investment," Sam said, "but I know the kinds of expenses Lang Downs incurs, and I've looked at the accounts for Taylor Peak. If we combine operations as much as possible without endangering the organic certification on Lang Downs, we can cut down on a lot of overlap."

"Like what?" Macklin asked.

"Like paying for feed," Sam said. "We pay a delivery fee and so does Taylor Peak. If we ordered one shipment for both stations, we'd only have one delivery fee, and since it would be a larger order, we might even get a better price on the feed itself. We'd have the work of distributing it, but we have to do that anyway. We could look at combining equipment as well. Do we need all the duplicate equipment we would have if we ran the two stations as one? Or could we sell off some things and have ongoing maintenance on fewer pieces of equipment?"

"For that matter, we may not have to hire as many seasonal jackaroos down the line once we get to the point of being able to run a combined mob. That's a couple of years down the road until the organic certification is far enough along that we won't upset your standing, but within three years," Jeremy added.

"Or you add to the mob and keep current staffing," Walker interrupted. "Earn more by expanding rather than by cutting costs."

"That would be the other option," Jeremy agreed. "It comes down to this. We find investors, whether it's the three of you or someone else, or we have to sell or let the bank foreclose. We're out of options and out of time."

"You ran n-numbers, I assume," Caine said.

Sam passed him the sheet. Caine studied it in silence.

"Well, I'm in," Walker said. "I don't know if I have enough to make a difference on my own, but ever since Lachlan came to Lang Downs, I've been thinking about getting a place of my own. I figure this is the best chance at it I'm going to get, and a lot less risky than trying to build something from the ground up."

"I d-don't understand how D-Devlin could have such b-bad years when we didn't have the same problems one station over," Caine said finally.

"He had a lot higher repair costs after the big storm two years ago," Sam said. "The tornadoes mostly missed us or didn't hit anything other than a few fences, but he had some significant property damage and loss of livestock. Another year, he got hit worse by the dry weather and had to buy more feed when prices were higher because of the drought. We rode it out better because you planted drought-resistant grasses and grains when you moved to organic production. I know we had to supplement, but not like Devlin did."

"A run of bad luck like that can do a station in," Macklin said. "We were nearing that point when you arrived, Caine, if you remember. We got it turned around without having to go to the bank for a loan, but money was tight that first year."

"I r-remember," Caine said. He set the paper down and looked across the table at Jeremy. "What do you want to do? You always said brumbies couldn't drag you back here after D-Devlin kicked you out. Are you trying to save the station because you want it or because you think you should?"

Jeremy took a minute before answering the question. He had said those things, but he had also continued to try to fix things with Devlin. It hadn't worked, but it didn't change Jeremy's desire to make things right with his brother. "Lang Downs means something," he said finally. "It's a haven for people who need it. It was a haven for me when I needed it, and I wouldn't have met Sam without it. It's home in a way Taylor Peak hasn't been for me as an adult. But Taylor Peak was home for me once, and it could be again, and maybe with Lang Downs as a model, I can make Taylor Peak somewhere special too."

"In that case, write up a proposal with the amount of initial investment, percentages of profits, terms and conditions and all the rest," Caine said. "We can make the supply run to Boorowa next week, get it all settled at the bank, and combine the accounts at the store in Boorowa and anywhere else we need to."

"Just like that," Jeremy said with a shake of his head.

Caine looked at him, all wide-eyed innocence. "How else would it be? Yes, it's a risk. I've spent enough years on a station to know that. But I came here with a lot less assurance things would work out because it felt like the right thing to do. Taking a chance on you is easy next to that."

"Does Macklin get a say in this?" Jeremy asked with a grin. "He is your partner, after all."

"Caine's the businessman, I'm the stockman," Macklin replied, "but I didn't hear anything to make me think it's a bad idea. I'd have said something if I did."

"And I would've listened," Caine said. "We usually make the supply run on Monday. Does that give you enough time to get something drawn up, Sam?"

"I'm not a lawyer, but I'll write up what I can and we can get someone to look at it in town before we sign it," Sam said.

"Good," Caine said. Then his smile took on a mischievous edge. "So if you're staying here, does that mean you won't need the house on Lang Downs anymore?"

"Why?" Jeremy asked. "You planning on moving out of your house?"

"No," Caine said, "but Seth and Jason need a place of their own, and it seems silly to make them wait for us to build something if your house is going to be empty."

"Seth and Jason?" Sam said. "As in together as a couple?"

"About bloody time," Macklin muttered.

Caine elbowed him, making Jeremy laugh. "Yes, together as a couple," Caine replied.

"When did this happen?" Jeremy asked. "I thought Jason was seeing Cooper."

"Probably the day they met," Macklin replied.

Caine ignored him. "Cooper got tired of playing second fiddle earlier this week and told Jason that where Seth could hear him. That was enough to finally push him to say something. They've been joined at the hip ever since."

"That's not new," Sam said. "I was surprised when Jason started seeing Cooper after the way he always latched onto Seth whenever they were home together." He looked over at Jeremy, who nodded. "The house is theirs if they want it. I hope they'll be as happy there as we were."

"THAT WENT better than I ever expected," Sam said as they got ready for bed that night. "I hoped they'd say yes, but I did think they'd take a lot more convincing." He hung up the clothes he'd worn for dinner—he could wear them again before washing them—and climbed into bed in just his underwear. It was too hot for anything heavier this time of year. He was still getting used to the house, where everything was, and not having all of his and Jeremy's things. Molly had cleared out most of Devlin's personal effects for them, but they needed to make a trip to Lang Downs and decide what they wanted to move and what they could leave for Seth and Jason.

"I can't decide if Caine really thinks it's a good investment or if he just feels sorry for us," Jeremy said as he came out of the bathroom and joined Sam in bed.

"He's got a heart big enough to agree because we're his friends," Sam said, "but I kept his accounts for eight years. He's nobody's fool, and anybody who thinks otherwise has never seen the way he runs Lang Downs. He asked how Devlin had such bad years when Lang Downs didn't, and the answers we gave him were true, but Lang Downs could have had the same problems to the same degree and they would have been in better shape than Taylor Peak. Devlin was a stockman, not a businessman."

"Then I'm doubly glad I have you and Caine in my corner," Jeremy said, "because I've never even pretended to be a businessman. I can take care of the livestock, the equipment, and the buildings, but don't make me deal with money."

"I won't," Sam promised. "You and Walker deal with all of that. I'll keep things running on the other end. I've learnt Caine's tricks, and with the two stations combined, we'll have a lot more pull with distributors."

"I don't know what I'd do without you," Jeremy said as he pulled Sam into his arms.

"Good thing you'll never have to find out, then, isn't it?" Sam replied. He leaned into Jeremy's kiss, and that was the end of their talking for the night.

FOURTEEN

"SAM AND Jeremy are staying at Taylor Peak," Caine told Seth when he found him in the tractor shed the next day.

"I expected as much," Seth said, careful to keep his expression neutral. Caine would expect him to be happy to have a home for himself and Jason, because that was surely where this conversation was going.

"They said you and Jason were welcome to have their house," Caine added. "They're going to come get the rest of their things one day this week, but you can start moving in whenever you're ready."

Nailed it in one.

"Thanks," Seth said. He couldn't tell Caine to leave, but he really needed this conversation to end. He rubbed his hands on his dungarees. "I'd better get this done, then, so I can check out the house and figure out that we'll need. I might need to go into Boorowa on my next day off."

"I don't imagine they'll take many of the household items," Caine said. "They have the house on Taylor Peak and everything in it. Unless it's something special, maybe, like something Ian made for them, they'll probably leave it for you two."

Seth's stomach churned. If he couldn't use needing to go to town as a delaying tactic, he'd have to find some other excuse. He loved Jason, but it was all going so fast. He didn't know how to do this. He didn't know what happy looked like. Chris and Jesse notwithstanding, he didn't have any idea how to make this work. It was too much too fast—everything he'd ever wanted and more—and he didn't know how to handle it. He could ask. Intellectually he knew Caine or Macklin or any of the other couples on the station would give him all the advice he could ever want, about anything from learning to live together to how to have sex with another man—okay, he wouldn't ask Neil about that one unless it was just to watch his face go all red. But to do that, he'd have to admit he didn't know what he was doing. He'd have to admit how much loving Jason scared him. They'd help him, but they'd also feel sorry for him, the poor kid with no parents and a shitty childhood. Fuck that. He was a grown man. He'd do this because he wanted it, and maybe he'd screw it up, but he'd give it everything he had until then because that's what you did and how you loved someone. He'd learned that much despite his mum's and Tony's examples.

"Seth?" Caine said. "Are you okay?"

"Just thinking," Seth replied. "I haven't exactly had the best of luck being happy in my life. I'm having trouble believing it now."

"Believe it," Caine said. "You have a job, a home, a family who cares about you, and a wonderful man who knows you through and through and loves every part of you. Falling in love is always a beautiful thing, but when you can also say he's your best friend, it adds an extra level of amazing."

That was the problem, though. Jason didn't know everything about him. Seth dug his fingers into his thigh. The cut had healed to the point it didn't hurt anymore, but even the reminder of it steadied him. Jason couldn't find out about the cutting. He'd never understand.

"I'll keep that in mind," Seth replied, seeing that Caine was waiting for an answer.

"You're only alone if you want to be," Caine reminded him. "But I'm keeping you from your work, and Macklin would have words with me for interfering with you doing your job."

Seth had a pretty good idea what that would look like. He'd slept in the big house when he and Chris first moved to the station, before Neil had moved into the foreman's house and Chris and Seth had moved into Neil's old house. At sixteen, the sounds filtering down the hall had been somewhere between funny and gross. At twenty-six, he had a slightly different opinion on the matter.

"We wouldn't want to upset the boss. I'll see you at dinner."

"Have a good rest of the afternoon," Caine said, "and as always, let me know if you run out of anything. I don't want equipment breaking down because you couldn't do proper maintenance."

"I'll tell you," Seth promised. "And I'll have plans for the first couple of drover's huts ready by the end of the week, I hope. I have a little more research to do when I'm done in here, but if I can find what I need in the next day or two, we can start thinking about when we want to start installing the first solar panels and generators."

"Wonderful. Come up to the big house anytime. You can even use the office computer if you need to. It's usually more reliable than the wireless Internet." Caine left with a wave.

Seth waved back, trying to corral his wayward thoughts. A house. Caine had just given him a bloody house. That was daunting enough, but Caine hadn't just given it to him. He'd given it to him and Jason. And Jason would want to move into it. They needed privacy. They wouldn't have to worry about Chris and Jesse overhearing, or worse, the seasonal jackaroos. Cooper hadn't said anything to Seth about Jason, and if he'd spoken to Jason since their breakup, Jason hadn't mentioned it, but it still made being in the bunkhouse awkward. A place of their own was the perfect solution.

Except Seth was a fuckup of epic proportions. He'd never managed anything permanent in his life, and this wouldn't be any different. He couldn't count how many places he'd lived before his mum married Tony, and they all knew how that had ended. Chris had done everything he could to provide for them after that, but it had hardly been easy. He'd had three good years at Lang Downs before going off to uni, but that was probably his record. Roommates, girlfriends, advisors—he'd run them all off in record time. It would be hard enough losing Jason when he figured that out as it was. If they were living together, it would be a hundred times worse. Jason would say nothing Seth could do would drive him away, but everybody got tired of him eventually. Chris was the only one who'd never given up on him, but even Chris had other priorities besides Seth now. He wouldn't turn Seth away or kick him out, but Jesse would always be Chris's first concern now.

As it should be, but it still stung.

"Stop it," he muttered. "You're not going for the razor, because life is good. You love Jason, you're home, this is all you've ever wanted. Shut the fuck up and get to work."

He grabbed his toolbox and went back to the tractor he needed to work on. They needed to drag the roads again, and Caine was counting on him to have the tractor working. It wasn't new, although Seth didn't know how old it was. It still worked fine most of the time, certainly enough not to need replacing yet, but it meant the engine was temperamental at times. He'd start with the spark plugs and go from there. He'd fixed it before. He would fix it again.

He lost himself in the familiar rhythm of loosening spark plugs, cleaning them, and replacing them. It worked at first, giving him something to focus on besides his own errant thoughts, but it was too familiar, and his attention wandered after a while, his hands moving by rote as he tried to imagine living with Jason. In one wave of Caine's magic wand, he'd have it all—the house, the dog, the white picket fence, a picture-perfect life. It scared the ever-living fuck out of him. He'd never had the picture-perfect life. He'd never had anything other than what he could hoard away from his stepsiblings and a string of screwed-up relationships. He could argue that the relationships had failed because he was too hung up on Jason to commit fully to anyone else, but that didn't mean he'd do any better now that he had Jason.

He moved on from the spark plugs to the carburetor, but the bolt stuck. He cursed under his breath as his hand slipped off the wrench into a nearby bracket, slicing the back of his hand open. "Well, fuck," he muttered even as the pain pierced through the chaos of his thoughts. He took a deep breath and went in search of a clean cloth to wrap his hand with. He didn't find anything in the tractor shed, so cradling his bloody hand against his chest, he headed toward the kitchen. Sarah and Kami would fix him up.

"Seth! What have you done to yourself?" Sarah exclaimed when he walked into the kitchen.

"Cut myself working on an engine," Seth said. "I didn't have a clean rag and I didn't want to get any more grease in it than is already there from the bracket."

"Come on, then. Let me take a look at it." She ushered him over to the sink and handed him a bar of soap. He scrubbed his hands clean, paying special attention to the cut. He knew how to do this. He could have gone to his own room and taken care of it, but it felt good to have Sarah fussing over him. His mum had never been the fussing type, but Sarah more than made up for it now. "All right, let me see," she said.

He offered her his hand dutifully, hissing at the sting when she poured peroxide over the cut. "It's not that deep," she said. "I think we can wrap it up to keep it clean and it will heal on its own. Just be careful with it for a couple of days."

"I will," Seth promised.

"And stay out of the tractor shed for the rest of the day. Give it that much time to heal before you get it dirty again."

"I have work to finish," he protested.

"And it can wait until tomorrow, or Patrick or Jesse can finish it today if it can't wait. You aren't the only mechanic on this station, Seth Simms, and I won't have you ending up in the hospital because you were too stubborn to ask for help. And if you think I won't tell Jason and your brother, you're sorely mistaken."

"Okay," Seth said, raising his hands in surrender. "I'll stay out of the tractor shed until tomorrow. But if Caine asks, I'm telling him it was on your orders."

"I'll take that blame," Sarah replied. "Jason just came back from checking the mob at Taylor Peak. Go spend the rest of the afternoon with him. You lads deserve some time together. I know you haven't been working together during the day."

They'd been sleeping together at night, curled up in Seth's bed, still mostly dressed because Seth couldn't get past Chris and Jesse down the hall. Jason hadn't pressed, but now Caine was talking about them having their own home and privacy and….

Seth took a deep breath and squeezed his hand into a fist. Pain burned up his arm as the motion pulled the cut open, but it steadied him. He wanted this. He could learn how to do it. Sarah had, even after all the years of abuse at Macklin's father's hands. She'd met Kami and made a new relationship work. Seth could do the same.

"What's on your mind, love?" Sarah asked.

"Trying to figure out how to be happy," Seth replied honestly.

"Oh, love," she said, pulling him into a grandmotherly embrace. "You celebrate it, that's how. One moment at a time. Tomorrow will take care of itself. You just focus on this moment and how good it makes you feel."

Seth had never had that luxury, because tomorrow had never taken care of itself. Tomorrow had always meant the possibility of moving, of not eating, of Tony raising his voice or even his hand, of Chris being bashed. Tomorrow had been something to fear for too long to take it for granted now.

No one here would lift a hand except to help him. He didn't have to worry about his next meal or having a roof over his head, but that only made the rest more fragile. If he didn't have to worry about those things, he'd end up screwing something else up even worse.

"Go find Jason. Everything will feel better when you're with him."

Seth nodded and headed outside. He didn't immediately go in search of Jason, though. He couldn't deal with that yet. Instead he wandered toward Sam and Jeremy's house—his and Jason's house, if he could ever get past freaking out at that thought. It was smaller than some of the other houses on the station, one story with one bedroom and bath, a minimal kitchen with only a counter for coffee or tea instead of an eating area like some of the older houses had, and a utility room with a washer and dryer. The veranda stretched all the way around the house, though, leaving plenty of room for chairs and even a table if they wanted to have people over for a beer or a party. Seth didn't remember them doing it often, but the big table stood in the middle of the back side of the veranda. He ran his hand along the wooden rail that delineated the edge of the veranda. Ian had probably done the woodwork, though Seth didn't actually remember him working on it when they'd built the house.

It was going to be Sarah's house until she'd decided to marry Kami and move in with him instead.

Arms around his waist startled him, but before he could pull away, Jason spoke in his ear. "What do you think? Want to move in with me?"

Seth nodded because any other answer would hurt Jason's feelings, and he never wanted to do that. "It's a little overwhelming," he admitted.

"We don't have to say yes right away," Jason said. "Or you can move in so you're out of Chris and Jesse's hair and I can stay in the bunkhouse until you're ready."

"You've spent almost every night with me for the past week," Seth said. "Talk about closing the barn door once the horse has escaped."

"It's not the same," Jason said. "That house, that's a commitment. It's not trying things out to see if we fit. It's the next closest thing to driving to Boorowa and registering a civil partnership. The minute we both move in there, we're as good as married in the eyes of everyone we care about, because that's what happens here on Lang Downs. The people who make it home, they come here and they make a life for themselves and the ones they love."

"I can't even tell you how much I want that," Seth said.

"I can't even tell you how much it scares me," Jason replied. "It's all I've ever wanted, and now that I have it, I can't quite believe it's real."

"What if I screw up?" Seth asked.

"Forget everything your stepfather ever said," Jason ordered. "You aren't a screwup. You're an intelligent, amazing, handsome man, and you've earned your place here, no matter what you think. My dad even says so, and you know how hard he is on mechanics. What if I screw up? You're not the only one in this relationship, you know."

"If you screw up, you'll fix it," Seth said. "That's what you do."

"That's all anyone can do," Jason replied, "and so that's what you'll do too. Mum told me one time that relationships aren't about being perfect. They're about dealing with the shit that goes wrong together."

"Somehow I don't think those were her exact words," Seth said with a grin.

"No, probably not, but it's what she meant." Jason kissed Seth softly. "We can do this. We just have to believe that whatever goes wrong, we can work it out."

"Then I guess we ought to start packing," Seth said. He didn't know how it could be that simple, but he'd never forgive himself if he didn't try. "Caine said something about seeing if we needed anything and making a supply run to Boorowa on our next day off. I don't even know what we'd need."

"Sheets, towels, maybe a few dishes," Jason said. "I know Ian made Sam and Jeremy a few things they'll want to take with them, but they'll probably leave the rest. We won't have much to buy."

"I have a few things in storage in Sydney," Seth said. "If we need them, that is. They wouldn't fit in the car and there isn't room at Chris's anyway, but if we have our own place, I could go get them and bring them down at some point. I left most everything with Ilene, but I have a dresser Ian made for me. Chris insisted I take it with me so I'd have something of home no matter where I lived. I couldn't leave that with her."

"Of course we'll go get it," Jason said. "We just have to decide when we can be gone overnight."

Seth melted a little at the casual assurance in Jason's voice. Jason might not have said it in the words Seth wanted to hear, but he was committed to their relationship or he wouldn't be talking about going together to get Seth's chest.

"I guess we should go look at our house then, huh?"

Jason grinned and grabbed Seth's uninjured hand "I'm not carrying you over the threshold. You weigh too bloody much."

"I'm not a girl," Seth said as they walked inside. "I don't need that romantic nonsense."

As soon as they walked inside, Jason pinned Seth to the wall. Seth could have gotten away—he was bigger than Jason—but he had no desire to do so. "Romance is not just for girls," Jason said. He kissed Seth tenderly, lovingly even, taking his time with the contact. Seth parted his lips and let Jason take the lead. Silence pressed in on him, driving home to him that they were finally, truly alone with privacy guaranteed. No one would come knocking on the door. No one was listening in the next room. No one even knew they were there, much less what they were doing. They could stand there with Seth's back against the kitchen wall for hours or they could go to the bedroom and fuck like rabbits. They could strip right there and go at it on the living room floor if they wanted. This was *their* space. The intimacy of it left him reeling. He broke the kiss and gasped for breath.

"Let's take a look around," Seth said. He'd been in the house before—he'd even helped build it—but not in years. When he was home for a visit, they either ate in the canteen or at Jason's house. He'd had no reason to come in here.

Jason stepped back and they poked around in the kitchen for a bit. Like Seth remembered, it had a fridge, an electric kettle for tea, and hookups for an oven and stove but had never been installed. "Are you a good cook?" he asked Jason. "Because I suck at it. So unless you want to cook, we can just leave it as it is and eat in the canteen."

"I can put a meal on the table," Jason said, "but I'd rather eat in the canteen. Cooking is too much work if we have other options."

Seth opened the cabinets. A few mugs sat on the shelves, along with a tin of sugar, some biscuits, and a jar of Vegemite. Seth laughed. "That's pathetic, even for two jackaroos on a station. There isn't even a bag of chips to munch on."

"Start a list," Jason said. "We'll go to Boorowa and get anything you can't live without."

The living room was simply decorated, with a couch and a couple of chairs. Nothing fancy, but nothing that would need to be replaced. They didn't lead fancy lives. Sam's desk sat in one corner. "They'll want that," Jason said. "Ian made it for them the year Thorne moved to the station. I remember because I helped them move it in here after Thorne left to go to Wagga Wagga for a couple of months. I'd never seen Ian look so sad."

"I never knew what that was all about," Seth said. "I was only home for a couple of days that year. I actually left the day after Christmas to go back to Sydney because I had a project due."

"He has PTSD," Jason said. "Nasty stuff left over from the Commandos, I guess. He flipped out over something—I don't know what— and punched a wall. He decided he couldn't stay on Lang Downs like that and went to Wagga Wagga to get help. It took a bloody lot of courage, if you ask me."

Seth looked down at his bandaged hand. He hadn't done it to himself this time, not on purpose anyway, but Jason's words weighed on him. Thorne had been man enough to get help, but Seth was too much of a fuckup for that.

"What did you do to your hand?" Jason asked.

"Sliced it open on a bracket," Seth said. "Sarah patched it up. It hurts like a bitch, but it'll heal. I've had worse." He'd done worse to himself. Not often because he didn't want scars he'd have to explain, but once or twice his razor had sliced deeper than he'd intended.

"We'll clean it out and wrap it up again before bed," Jason said. "I may be a vet, but wound care isn't that different. I could probably put a suture in it if you need me to."

Seth cradled his hand against his chest. "I don't think it needs stitches. It was long and messy but not very deep."

"At least let me take a look at it?" Jason said. "It'll make me feel better, even if I can't do anything for you."

"Tonight," Seth said. "So what else do you think we'll need?"

They poked around in the closets a bit, but with Sam and Jeremy's things still there, it felt too invasive. "Maybe we should wait until they've moved out completely before we move in," Seth said. "I know Caine said it was okay, but it feels…."

"Like we're using their space," Jason finished for him. "As much as I want to be alone with you, really alone, you're right. We've waited this long. We can wait a few more days."

A few more days for Seth to try to get over his hang-ups so they had a chance at being happy without his issues ruining everything.

"I THOUGHT you and Jason would already be shacked up in your new house," Chris teased when Seth came back home with him after dinner.

"Not while all Sam and Jeremy's things are still there," Seth said. "We didn't want to invade their privacy that way. We can wait a few more days."

"Uh-huh," Chris said. "I remember what it was like to be young and horny. Do Jesse and I need to volunteer for an overnight shift?"

"You're only four years older than I am," Seth said defensively. He wasn't going to think about being in an empty house with Jason, knowing Chris and Jesse wouldn't be back until after breakfast. He wanted to sleep tonight, thank you very much. "You make it sound like you're old enough to be my father."

"Not quite that old," Chris said, "but old enough to know what you're feeling and young enough to sympathize. Do you know when Sam and Jeremy are coming to get their stuff?"

"Caine said in a couple of days, but nothing specific," Seth said.

"I'll talk to Caine tomorrow," Chris said. "If it isn't going to be tomorrow or the day after, Jesse and I will make ourselves scarce. Give you and Jason some privacy for a night."

"I already said you didn't have to do that."

"I know we don't have to," Chris said, "but you didn't ask. I offered. There's a difference."

Not as far as Seth was concerned.

"Jason probably has everything you'll need since he was seeing Cooper, but there are supplies in the bathroom—"

"I'm not listening to this," Seth said, plugging his ears with his hands. "My brother didn't just offer me condoms and lube so I could have safe sex. This is not my life."

He fled into his bedroom to the sound of Chris's laughter. Let him laugh. Seth wasn't budging, and he wasn't going to ask Chris for advice either. Jason wasn't a novice. He could show Seth what to do. It would still be embarrassing as hell, but at least it wouldn't be his *brother* giving him lessons. That didn't bear thinking about.

He sat down on the bed and unwrapped his hand. Jason had offered to take a look at it, but Carley had waylaid him after dinner. Seth didn't know when or even if Jason would make it back tonight, and he could see blood on the gauze Sarah had used. Better to clean and redress it now.

He went into the bathroom to wash it out again. He could hear Chris and Jesse's voices in the other room, and he just knew Chris was telling Jesse about their conversation. When Jesse's booming laughter resonated through the house, he had all the proof he needed. Chris's teasing was good-natured. He didn't have a mean bone in his body, and he'd never given Seth more of a hard time than Seth gave right back, but this was different. This meant something. It meant everything.

It meant too much.

He was in so far over his head. He had to keep it together. Jason deserved so much more than Seth could give him in his current state. He deserved someone who could love him without flipping out over it. He deserved someone who could be happy instead of searching for flaws every time things looked good. Seth was no good for him, and the only person who couldn't see it was Jason. Oh, everyone had said all the right things, but Seth wasn't fooled. He was a punk from the gutter with no real right to be here with Jason, or with any of these strong, grounded men. He was a broken piece of trash that not even his mother could love. Maybe Jason hadn't figured it out yet, but he would. He'd see Seth for what he was, and when he did, he'd leave, like everyone else had. Seth didn't deserve a happy ending, but Jason did, so he'd let Jason go—back to Cooper or on to someone else, it didn't matter. Jason would have a shot at happiness with someone who could be what he deserved.

With shaking hands, Seth opened the cabinet over the sink to get out a fresh bandage. His razor sat on the bottom shelf where he'd left it after he shaved that morning. He shouldn't pick it up. He already had the cut on his hand. He could pour alcohol on that if he needed pain to get himself back together, and if anyone asked, he'd have an explanation for the cut and the alcohol. If he picked up the razor, he'd have a cut Jason might see and would want an explanation for. An explanation Seth couldn't give him, because how could Jason with his picture-perfect family and happy-ever-after dreams possibly understand what would drive Seth to hurt himself? How could Jason ever understand that controlling the pain helped Seth control everything else too?

If he didn't pick it up, he wouldn't make it out of the bathroom without shaking apart.

He took a deep breath and then another one, trying to steady himself enough that he could ignore the urge to cut, but the longer he stood there, the louder the siren call of pain became. He grabbed the alcohol and dumped it over the cut on his hand. Tears coursed down his face as he bit back the urge to shout from the pain, but it wasn't enough to silence the thoughts in his head. It had never been like this. He'd never spun this far out of control. He had to make it stop. He could make a small cut, just a nick, really, and Jason would never even notice it was there. They kissed and snuggled in bed at night, too aware of Chris and Jesse down the hall to do more than that. Jason wouldn't even see a little scab.

Seth reached for the razor before he could talk himself out of it. He pulled down his jeans and examined his legs. The cut he'd made before had healed to a faded pink line. In another few days it would be gone entirely. He didn't want to reopen it, though. He didn't want a scar because in a few days, they'd move into Sam and Jeremy's old house and when that happened, Jason would want to do more than kiss and cuddle. He'd want to touch and kiss and explore and—

Seth swallowed hard and set the point of the razor to his other leg. Just a little puncture.

"Seth?" The door swung open, startling Seth. The razor dug deep into his leg.

"Get out!" Seth spat, spinning so Jason couldn't see the blood on his leg.

"Seth, what's going on?" Jason said.

"I said get out," Seth repeated.

"No. What is this?" Jason grabbed Seth's wrist and lifted the bloody razor to chest height. "What were you doing?"

"None of your goddamn business," Seth said. He tried to pull his hand away, but Jason didn't let go.

"You're bleeding. Did you cut yourself?"

"No shit," Seth said. He pulled again and this time Jason let him go. He tossed the razor in the sink and reached for the peroxide in the cabinet. It would hurt less than the alcohol, and with Jason standing right there, Seth didn't want any more questions. He didn't expect to get that lucky, but he could hope.

Jason stood there in silence as Seth cleaned and bandaged the cut on his leg. He hadn't meant to cut that deeply. This one would probably leave a scar. It served him right. It would be a good reminder not to hope for things he couldn't have. He pulled his jeans back on and pushed past Jason into the hall. Jason followed him into his bedroom. Seth glared at him, but Jason ignored it.

"What happened?"

"You know what happened," Seth said. "I cut myself with a razor. It bled. I bandaged it up, and now I'm going to bed. And no, you can't stay tonight. I don't want company. I don't want you."

"Stop it," Jason said. "Why are you being like this?"

Seth didn't answer. He just lay down on the bed with his back to Jason. "Turn off the light on your way out."

"Okay, I'll leave tonight," Jason said, "but this isn't over. We're going to talk about this and we're going to find a solution to whatever it is. I meant what I said about not giving up just because things get complicated."

"Good-bye, Jason," Seth said. He could feel tears building in the corners of his eyes, but he fought them back. He wouldn't let Jason see him cry.

"We'll talk in the morning," Jason repeated.

Seth didn't reply. Jason left and turned the light off, and Seth let the tears fall. He should've known better. He didn't belong here with Jason. He didn't belong anywhere. He'd pack his bag in the morning. They were shorthanded on Taylor Peak. Sam and Jeremy would let him stay for a few days while he figured out what to do next.

FIFTEEN

JASON TOSSED and turned in his bunk all night, too worried about Seth to sleep well. He rose early and headed to Chris and Jesse's house, hoping to catch Seth before he went to breakfast. Maybe cornering him before they'd had caffeine was a bad idea, but if he missed Seth that morning, anything could happen before he found Seth again.

The image of the bloody razor haunted him. Why would Seth do that? Why would anyone hurt themselves deliberately? He tried to think back to when he and Seth both lived on the station, and even to the times they'd both been home from uni together, to see if he could find a pattern of odd behavior. Seth's hands were always torn up, but so were Jason's dad's. His mum scolded his dad for it, but he'd always replied that anyone who worked on engines was going to end up with busted knuckles or worse. It was part of the job description. Jason could remember Seth's hands being similarly scraped up, but nothing that would suggest deliberation. That cut on his leg hadn't been an accident, though. He'd intended to do that.

He knocked on the door to Chris and Jesse's house out of habit rather than necessity, but he didn't wait for an answer before walking in. He hadn't needed an invitation in years.

He found Chris and Jesse sitting at the small table in the kitchen.

"Sorry to show up so early," Jason said, "but I need to talk to Seth."

"You'll have to find him first," Chris said. "He's gone. He left a note."

Chris pushed a piece of paper across the table to Jason.

> *Chris,*
> *I can't stay. I'm sorry. I'll call when I get settled, but don't tell Jason where I've gone.*
> *Seth*

"You don't listen very well," Jason said hoarsely as he tried to make sense of the note.

"My brother is a bloody idiot who wouldn't know a good thing if it bit him in the arse," Chris said. "And since you didn't get that chance before he rabbited, I figure he's got it in his head he's doing you a favor by leaving this way."

"How is this supposed to be a favor?" Jason asked. "We were supposed to move into Sam and Jeremy's house. We were supposed to be happy."

"Seth hasn't had a lot of practice with happiness," Chris said. "I don't think he trusts it very much."

Jason tried not to be hurt by that, but he couldn't stop it from stinging. "Does he cut himself a lot?"

"Sure, but every mechanic does," Jesse said. "It goes with the job."

"No, not like that," Jason said. "I walked into the bathroom last night intending to check the cut on his hand from the tractor, and I found him with a razor against his leg and blood dripping down his thigh. Did you know about this?"

Chris shook his head. "You're sure it was intentional? I mean, he didn't just cut himself because you startled him?"

"If he'd cut his cheek or jaw, I'd believe that," Jason said, "but why would he have the razor against his leg? He wouldn't talk to me, so I don't know what he was thinking, but it all seems really odd. I caught him cutting himself, he wouldn't let me stay with him last night, and this morning, he's gone."

"He used to get in fights a lot," Chris said. "Before we came here, but things were tough and we didn't have a lot of stability. I figured that was why. He never started it, and I did my best to keep him out of trouble, but I could only do so much. If he was cutting himself then, I didn't know about it, but I'm not sure I would have noticed. I was working a shit job with ridiculous hours to try to pay for a place to live so he could go to school. Most days I wasn't home before he went to sleep, and he left for school before I woke up. He could have been doing anything and I wouldn't have known."

"This isn't your fault," Jesse said. "Whatever Seth's problems are, you did everything you could to provide for him and protect him."

"He idolizes you," Jason agreed. "He talks trash like nobody's business, but never about you."

"What do we do now?" Jesse asked.

"I don't know about you," Jason said, "but I know what I'm going to do. I'm going to find the stupid dropkick and drag him back here by his short hairs. I'm going to sit him down and explain to him that he doesn't get to do this to the people who love him. He can't tell me he loves me, promise to move in with me when the house is ready, and then run. That's not how relationships work. Now I just have to figure out where he went."

"He said he'd call," Chris said. "He took his phone. I could try calling him. If we have an idea of where he is or where he's going, it would narrow down your search."

"I'd appreciate any help you can give me," Jason said. "I'll fight for him, but I have to find him first."

Chris's phone lit up where it sat on the table. "Hello?"

Someone on the other end spoke.

"Hi, Sam. Seth's there? That's good. Can you keep him there? Jason would like to talk to him, and I think that's best done in person." Chris frowned at whatever Sam was saying. "Okay. If you think that's best. I'll tell Jason. Keep us posted, though, yeah? Thanks, mate. Talk to you soon."

"What did he say?" Jason asked.

"Seth showed up at Taylor Peak this morning asking if he could stay for a few days while he figures out what to do next," Chris said. "Sam and Jeremy could use the help, so they said he was welcome as long as he wanted to stay if he'd help out while he was there. Sam said Seth looked relieved at that. Sam asked us to give him a few days to see if he can get to the bottom of the problem before we go rushing over there. At least if he's there, someone can keep an eye on him. If he runs again, he could end up anywhere."

"I have to take the sutures out of Jeremy's horse day after tomorrow," Jason said. "I can't really delay that. I'll wait that long, but then I'm going to talk to Seth."

"Think long and hard about this," Jesse said. "I don't know what's going on in Seth's head, but I can take a couple of guesses. The longest he's ever lived in any one place is the three years he spent here before you went off to uni. You're the only friend he's kept in all the moving around. I never hear him talk about anyone else. Oh, the girlfriend of the moment, yes, but not his mates. You are every good thing Seth has ever known all wrapped up in one, and if I'm right, that scares the shit out of him. So you have to decide how much he means to you. Do you love him enough to deal with his insecurities and his hang-ups and whatever his issues are? Because if you aren't completely sure you do, you need to let him go. Loving you will be the making or the breaking of him. Obviously we'd prefer it if you didn't break him."

"He's already broken enough," Jason said softly. "I don't care what I have to do to make it better. I just need to know what that is."

"He probably doesn't know," Chris said. "If he did, he'd have told you. I know it doesn't seem like it right now, but he trusts you more than he trusts anyone else. Even more than he trusts me."

"Then why did he run? Why didn't he talk to me?" Jason asked.

"He's the only one who can answer that, but he's probably ashamed of what he did," Jesse said. "I knew a bloke in high school who cut himself. When everyone found out, he tried to commit suicide because he couldn't deal with people knowing. He didn't succeed and an aunt and uncle stepped in to make sure he got help, but it was a touch-and-go thing for a while. It isn't a healthy coping mechanism, but it's better than some alternatives."

"I guess I have some reading to do, then," Jason said. "Maybe I can figure out what he needs, or at least figure out alternatives to give him." He looked at Chris and then at Jesse. "Maybe he can't believe my promises right now, so I'll promise you instead. I love him enough to stay, no matter what."

"Keep telling him that," Chris said. "Eventually he'll have no choice but to believe it."

"I will," Jason promised. "I'd better get to work."

AS SOON as Jason left, Jesse reached for Chris's hand. By the time he'd met Chris, Seth was mostly grown, so he didn't have the same sense of responsibility that Chris did, but even after just the three years Seth had lived with them, learning how much Seth was struggling tore at Jesse's heart. He could only imagine what it was doing to Chris.

Chris grabbed his hand and hung on tight. "I knew things were bad before we got here, but I thought they were better after that. How did I miss this?"

"He didn't want you to know," Jesse replied. It wouldn't give Chris any more comfort than it gave him, but it was the truth. "He wanted you to settle in at Lang Downs and make your own life."

"Taking care of him has been part of my life for as long as I can remember," Chris said. "That didn't stop being important just because I met you."

"Said every parent ever," Jesse agreed, "but part of growing up is learning to take care of yourself, and he wasn't a child anymore when you arrived here, much less now. He's entitled to his secrets."

"You're supposed to be on my side," Chris grumbled.

"I am," Jesse assured him. "I will always be on your side, but in this case, it's not a question of sides. You're beating yourself up for something that isn't your fault, and I'm not going to sit by and watch you do that."

"What do I do now?" Chris asked. "I don't have the slightest idea how to help him."

"I think that depends on him," Jesse replied. "He's an adult now, and as much as your inclination—and mine—is to pull him back here and watch over him, we can't do that unless he asks for help."

"He's hurting himself, Jesse! He's picking up a razor and slicing into his skin. How do we just let him be?" Chris protested. "If he cuts himself the wrong way, he could bleed to death."

Jesse shuddered at the thought of walking into Seth's bedroom one morning and finding him dead in a pool of blood with his razor still in his hand. "Unless I miss my guess, this isn't the first time he's done this. And if he's been doing it awhile, he's figured out how to get what he needs out of it without doing permanent damage."

"That doesn't make me feel better."

"It should," Jesse said. "I told you I knew a kid who used to cut as a way of coping. When he could do it and no one knew, he managed to function pretty normally. The problem came when people found out and started pressuring him to stop. No, it's not healthy, and yes, we want to help him find better ways of coping, but if we hound him into running and make him feel like he can't come to us because of his cutting, things are going to get worse, not better." He tugged on Chris's hand until Chris moved from his chair and settled in Jesse's lap.

"We aren't going to leave him to suffer alone. We're going to offer him what he needs and is ready to accept, whatever that is. And if we can't figure out what that is, maybe Thorne and Ian can help." He nuzzled Chris's shoulder. "And you aren't going to deal with it by yourself, either. I'm not Seth's brother, but I'm still in this all the way."

"You are Seth's brother in every way that counts," Chris insisted. "He looks to you as much as he looks to me when he needs help."

"And I'll give it to him this time too," Jesse promised. "Just like I'm going to give it to you. You can't blame yourself for this, and don't tell me you aren't. You did everything you could and far more than most people would have to take care of him after your mum died. Don't think I don't know it. And don't think he doesn't, either. I said it before, but I'm saying it again. He worships you."

"I still should have known."

Jesse held Chris tighter, offering comfort the only way he knew how. He didn't know what would happen or how they'd make this work, but it didn't matter. He'd stand by Chris—and Seth by extension—no matter what.

"JASON," MACKLIN called as Jason was about to leave the canteen after breakfast. "Ride out with me today? A couple of sheep were acting off yesterday. If they're sick, we need to get them isolated before it can spread to the rest of the mob."

"I was supposed to ride out with Kyle today," Jason said. "Did you let him know he'd be one short?"

"I spoke with him before breakfast. He knows I've borrowed you for the morning. If it's nothing, you can join his crew after we're done. If it's something we need to take care of, he'll make do without you."

"Let me grab a couple of things from my room," Jason said. "I'll meet you at the tack room."

Jason ran back to the bunkhouse and got a stethoscope and a thermometer. He could do that much in the field. If he needed to do a more thorough exam, they'd have to bring the sheep back to the shed. He whistled for Polly when he came back out. She'd be useful if they had to separate sheep from the mob and herd them back to the station. She came loping up with a goofy grin on her face. She was getting grizzled around her muzzle, but her eyes were still bright with intelligence and she showed no signs of slowing down. "You ready, girl? Let's go check some sheep."

She yipped at him excitedly and jogged along beside him as he went to meet Macklin. Macklin had Ned and Brownie saddled already.

"Dani will be jealous," Jason said. "She still thinks Brownie is her horse."

"Just because I let Dani name her doesn't mean she's the only one who can ride her," Macklin replied. Jason grinned. Macklin had perfected the stony foreman act before Jason ever moved to the station, but the station's children had always been his weak spot. Dani and Liam had the entire station wrapped around their little fingers, and Macklin was no exception.

"You said the sheep were acting off," Jason said as they rode north out of the valley. "Can you be more specific?"

"Not grazing, standing off by themselves, acting listless." Macklin ticked the list off on his fingers as he spoke. "Maybe it's nothing. Maybe they ate something they shouldn't have. But since you're here anyway, it's worth having you take a look."

"Absolutely," Jason said. They rode in silence until they'd passed the first gate and were out in the tablelands.

"I see a lot of myself in Seth," Macklin said as they slowed from a canter so they could open the gate.

Jason didn't answer as they opened the gate, rode through, and latched it behind them. "How so?" he asked when they were ready to ride on.

"When you've lost everything, and probably even more when you've never really had anything to begin with, it's hard to believe in permanence," Macklin replied. "I ran away from home rather than getting kicked out like Chris and Seth were, but I still lost everything. Michael took me in, and I will be forever grateful for that, but it took me more years than I care to admit before I stopped wondering when he'd change his mind and I'd have to leave again."

"It's been ten years," Jason said. "Surely he knows by now Lang Downs will always be home if he wants it."

"Maybe, although he hasn't lived here for most of those ten years," Macklin reminded him. "But it isn't just about Lang Downs. It's about people. When you can't even count on your parents, who are supposed to love you no matter what, it's kind of hard to believe anyone will love you enough to stay."

"Is that why you fought so hard against loving Caine?" Jason asked.

"Part of it," Macklin said. "Other than that Yank accent, he blends right in now, a breath of fresh air still but every bit a grazier, but do you remember how little he knew when he got here?"

"He had to ask *me* for advice," Jason said. "I remember."

"And I was supposed to believe he'd stay on the station permanently," Macklin said. "He told me every way he could think of that he was in this for good, but it took nearly losing him for me to get past the worry that he might leave."

"Okay, I can see that. But I've always lived here except when I went away to uni, and I've always talked about coming home," Jason said. "I'm not the same kind of risk Caine was."

"Rationally, no, you're not. But that's the thing about issues—they aren't rational. Seth knows you keep your promises. It's just going to take time for him to believe that applies to him too. Words won't be enough. It'll take a lifetime of standing by him no matter what to convince him. It'll take a lifetime of loving him."

Jason could think of far worse ways to spend his life. "I can do that, but he has to let me."

"And that's the problem," Macklin said. "He doesn't know how to let you. You just have to do it, whether he lets you or not. His fears are this big, immovable boulder. You can't blast it out of the way or even chip at it. You have to flow around it and under it and through the cracks in it and love him despite it, no matter what he thinks. He's scared, so he ran. He thinks you'll give up and forget about him."

"Never."

"Then prove it to him. We can spare you here if you need to work down at Taylor Peak for a few weeks."

"Chris thinks he'll run if I follow him to Taylor Peak," Jason said.

"Maybe he will, but if he does, it's because he doesn't believe you'll follow him again. Prove him wrong," Macklin replied.

"I told Chris and Sam I'd give them until the day after tomorrow since I have to go to Taylor Peak then anyway," Jason said. "I'll take a bag with me in case I need to stay."

"You can go sooner if you want."

"I know," Jason said, "but I think Chris is right. I'll give him a couple of days to settle, and then I'll talk to him. I won't give up, but if he needs a little space to think, I need to respect that too."

"If there's anything Caine or I can do, you only have to ask," Macklin said.

Jason smiled. "That's the one part of this that has never been in question."

MACKLIN WALKED into the office on sock feet.

"Hi," Caine said when he looked up from the computer. "What did Jason think about the sheep?"

"He doesn't think it's anything serious. Their temperature was normal, but we brought them back into the valley for observation, just in case."

"Makes sense," Caine said. "If he's right, it doesn't hurt to have them down here for a few days, and if he's wrong, it'll keep anything from spreading. It'll cost a lot less to treat or butcher two sheep than it would an entire portion of the mob."

"Exactly." He came around to stand beside Caine's chair and wrapped his arms around Caine's shoulders.

"What's wrong?" Caine asked.

"Does something have to be wrong for me to hug you?" Macklin asked. He rested his cheek against Caine's dark head and just breathed him in.

"No, but you don't usually do it during work hours," Caine said. He turned his chair so he could stand into Macklin's arms. "Not that I'm complaining."

"It hasn't been the easiest month," Macklin replied. "With Taylor dying and Sam and Jeremy leaving. And now with Seth and Jason. It feels like there's a hole. Sam's supposed to be here in the office so you can be out in the paddocks with me. Jeremy's supposed to be leading a crew and winding Neil up at dinner. Seth's supposed to be in the tractor shed so Patrick doesn't have to be."

"And you don't like it when all your chicks aren't right where you can watch them," Caine said. "I'm supposed to be the mother hen, not you."

"Do you blame me?" Macklin asked.

"Of course not." Caine kissed Macklin tenderly. "Your soft heart is one of the things I love about you."

"I don't have a soft heart," Macklin grumbled.

"Of course you don't," Caine said. "You just took Jason out to look at the sheep instead of bringing them back to the valley yourself because you've forgotten how to cut two sheep out of the mob by yourself. You didn't want to talk to him about Seth where no one else could hear you."

Macklin didn't sigh. There were downsides to having a lover who knew him so well.

"He doesn't know how lucky he is," Macklin said. "He grew up here with first Michael and then you making sure Lang Downs was a safe, stable place for a child to run wild and find his place in the world. He's the ultimate proof we've done something good because he knows without any doubt who he is and where he belongs. Unfortunately Seth doesn't, and Jason has no frame of reference for that. I tried to give him one."

"I love you," Caine said. "You know that, right?"

Macklin nodded. "It took me long enough, but yes, I know it. That's the part Jason doesn't understand. Seth doesn't know how to believe it. By the time I met you, I'd learnt to trust permanence."

Caine snorted.

"Okay, I didn't trust you would stay, but I trusted that I could have a job and a life and not have it taken away from me on someone else's whim," Macklin said. "Or that if it was, I could find a new job and move on. Seth has to learn that still."

"Do you think Jason can teach him?" Caine asked.

"If he can't, I don't know that anyone can," Macklin replied. "Other than Chris, Jason is the only fixture in Seth's life. Before you say it, we don't count. We're part of the station to him."

"Would it help him to hear that he'll always have a home and a job here if he wants it, regardless of whether he leaves again or how long he's gone?" Caine asked. "I'm trying not to interfere, but I want to help if we can."

"You, not interfere?" Macklin put his hand on Caine's forehead. "Call the doctor, I'm sure you're sick."

Caine retaliated by digging his fingers into Macklin's ribs. Macklin jumped back with a huff of laughter. "I'm so very lucky to have you," Macklin said.

Caine smiled that sweet, gorgeous smile Macklin had fallen in love with the first time he saw it, even if it had taken him almost too long to admit it. "We're lucky to have each other." Caine moved back into Macklin's arms and leaned against him. "Seth and Jason will find their way, and we'll help them when we can. We have to keep believing that."

"And if they don't, we'll help them pick up the pieces."

SIXTEEN

SETH SAT in the corner of the canteen alone. He could have gone to sit with Sam, Jeremy, and Walker. They would have made room for him, but they would have talked to him, and Seth wasn't interested in anything that required him to interact with anyone else. His brain was a field of broken glass, just waiting to shred him if he let his thoughts wander.

Sitting where he was, he could hear snatches of conversation from the other jackaroos, but none of them knew him well enough to draw him in, and Seth didn't make an effort to insert himself. He'd only counted a handful he'd want to know on a good day. Today didn't qualify.

"Did you hear what Taylor ordered today?" one of the jackaroos asked.

"No, but I'm sure I won't like it," another replied. "I swear, we work twice as hard now as we did when his brother was in charge, and we aren't getting paid more. It's bloody unfair."

If they'd worked a little harder, maybe the station wouldn't be in the shape it was in, Seth thought, but he didn't share his opinion. They wouldn't have any interest in hearing it, and Jeremy wouldn't thank him for provoking an argument.

"He had our crew replacing old boards on the shearing shed. Like the way the shed looks matters as long as the sheep can't get out when we're working on them."

"We spent the day moving the mob out of a perfectly good paddock because they'd been there for a week already. When Devlin was in charge, we only moved once a month."

Which explained why some of the paddocks were so overgrazed, Seth realized. Caine and Macklin rotated the mob regularly so they wouldn't denude the fields and let potentially dangerous weeds grow instead. Of course given the chemicals Seth had found in the tractor shed, Devlin had dealt with that problem differently. That would have to change so Jeremy could move toward the organic certification, but the average jackaroo wouldn't know much about that. Caine had to teach everyone at Lang Downs about it, even as invested as they all were in the overall running of the station. These blokes had no thought for anything other than how to do as little work as possible.

The comments continued, scraping along the edges of Seth's hearing and making him want to kick some sense into the drongos, but it was just grumbling. He'd heard plenty of it at the various auto shops he'd worked at, and even occasionally on Lang Downs, enough to know that people would find a reason to complain. As long as they weren't downright insulting to Seth's friends, he'd let it pass.

SETH'S RESOLVE lasted two days. Two days of tossing sleeplessly at night, of working himself as hard as he could during the day and of carefully not thinking about the razor he had left at Lang Downs. He didn't know if Jason had told anyone what he'd seen or if word had made it to Taylor Peak yet, but his reprehensible habit had cost him the only good thing in his life. He wouldn't let it follow him here. If he didn't have his razor, he couldn't cut himself, and if he couldn't cut himself, maybe someday Jason would forgive him and—

That train of thought would get him exactly nowhere. He'd burned his bridges and no amount of changing his ways would unburn them. He would stay on Taylor Peak because Sam and Jeremy obviously needed the help. Walker made sure things got done, but they were shorthanded, and Seth could help fill that need for the summer. When the season was over, he'd see how he felt. He'd never really fit in the city, but that was as much because he still dreamed of Lang Downs and Jason as it was because he didn't like the city. Now that he'd lost all hope of that dream, maybe the city wouldn't be so bad.

Walker had said something last night about one of the utes not sounding right when he was driving it yesterday, so Seth would have to spend the morning under the hood, trying to figure out what was making it act up. He'd hoped to ride out with a crew today because Jason was coming to take out Misfit's stitches, but luck was against him as always.

He'd made it almost to the tractor shed where he'd left his tool belt when he heard a couple of the jackaroos talking.

"… one of those shirt-lifters from Lang Downs. He says he's a vet, but he's just some kid. He probably sucked the boss's dick to get the job."

Seth saw red. He spun on his heel and marched toward the group of jackaroos, fists clenched so tightly his fingernails cut into his palms. "Shut up, you stupid fucker," he said as he plowed into the group. "You all talk shit like it doesn't mean anything and nobody's listening. Well, think again, because I'm listening."

"Yeah, and?" the jackaroo goaded. "What are you going to do about it?"

Seth drew his arm back and slammed his fist into the bastard's gut. Pain radiated up his arm from the impact and the still-healing cut on his hand, but that only drove him on. He didn't have his razor anymore. He couldn't get what he needed that way, but this son of a bitch had given him an excuse even Sam and Jeremy couldn't argue against. He reared back and struck again.

The jackaroo went down hard. "Get up," Seth shouted. "You talk shit like you're a big man. Prove it."

The jackaroo climbed slowly back to his feet, his eyes glittering with anger now. *Bring it on*, Seth thought wildly. He dodged the first punch the other jackaroo threw, but the second landed on his jaw, sending him reeling back. The crowd jeered as he dove back in, fists flying now. Some of his blows landed, some of them missed. He blocked some of the ones aimed at him and bore the ones he couldn't stop. He would take this fucker down because no one talked like that about Jason.

When the jackaroo went down a second time, Seth didn't give him the chance to get back up. He followed him down, pummeling his face as hard as he could.

He heard shouts but ignored them. He wasn't done yet. Not until he made sure the bastard wouldn't say anything like that about Jason ever again.

"Simms!"

The sound of his name drew his attention but did nothing to cool his ire. He'd raised his hand to punch the jackaroo again when someone grabbed his arm. He jumped to his feet, more than ready to have a new target for his emotions. He vaguely registered that Walker had him in his grip, but the recognition didn't slow him down. He'd never beat Walker, but it didn't matter. He never started a fight expecting to win, just to walk away. Walker wouldn't kill him, just pound his arse into the dirt, and maybe that would finally be enough to shut up the voices in his head. He took a deep breath and swung at Walker.

"Dammit, Simms," Walker growled as he dodged the punch. His grip on Seth's wrist tightened, but Seth kept fighting. He didn't know how to stop. Not now. He never saw the blow to his jaw coming.

SETH BLINKED a couple of times as consciousness returned. He turned his head, trying to figure out where he was, but that hurt like a bitch.

He must have groaned because someone pressed an ice pack to his jaw and another to his eye. "Don't move. Nothing's broken, but you're damn lucky."

Phil. That was Phil's voice. He must be in the canteen.

"What happened?" he croaked. It hurt to talk. She'd said his jaw wasn't broken, but it sure felt like it.

"You attacked another jackaroo, and when Walker tried to break it up, you turned on him," Phil said. "If you weren't already a mess of bruises, I'd smack you myself. Do you know how many ways that man could kill you with his bare hands?"

"Forty-five?" Seth said.

"More than that," Walker replied, startling Seth. He jerked his head in the direction of Walker's voice and then gasped when pain lanced through his head.

"Don't move," Phil scolded. "Nick, don't bait him. He isn't in any shape for it."

"He swung first," Walker said defensively. Seth kept his mouth shut. This was far more entertaining than swapping barbs with Walker himself. Maybe he'd stay on Taylor Peak after all, just to see if Phil could henpeck Walker into submission as fully as Molly had cowed Neil. Even Thorne didn't call Walker by his first name. Seth wouldn't have known who Phil was talking about if anyone else had been in the room.

"I'm sure he did. I'm also sure you could have overpowered him without knocking him out."

"Neutralize the threat—that's the first lesson we learnt in the Commandos," Walker replied. "That's not training that goes away. I didn't kill him. That's as good as I can get."

Phil gave him the kind of look that always sent Neil running when Molly directed it at him. Walker didn't flee, but Seth could tell he was squirming. "'S my fault," he slurred. "I wouldn't have stopped otherwise."

"And why is that?" Phil demanded, turning the glare on him. Shit, why had he opened his mouth again? Oh yeah, so he could save Walker's chance of being happy since he couldn't do anything about his own love life.

"Because I'm a stupid, stubborn shit who doesn't know how to back down," Seth said. "That's not Walker's fault."

"That may be true," Walker said, "but you don't strike me as the kind who goes around picking fights. What started it?"

"The bastard opened his mouth one time too many." Seth's stomach soured at the memory of what the jackaroo had said. He wasn't about to repeat it in front of Phil. She'd probably heard worse living on a station full of men, but he wouldn't be the one to say it. "I'd had enough."

"You knew when you walked onto the station that things were tense," Walker reminded him. "You punching the daylights out of someone didn't help. If you can't ignore their talk, report it to me and let me handle that. That's why Sam and Jeremy hired me."

"It wasn't about Sam and Jeremy," Seth muttered. "I don't like it, but I can ignore that. They can fight their own battles or have you fight for them. I get that. But I know how hard Jason worked to earn his degree. I won't let anyone suggest Sam and Jeremy are using him as a vet because he...."

"Because he what?" Phil said.

"You don't really want to know what they said, do you?"

"No," she replied, "but Walker needs to know so he can deal with it."

"They suggested he bribed the bosses with sexual favors," Seth said. "Only they weren't as nice about it."

"He is cute, if you like the type," Walker said. Seth's blood boiled. He struggled to sit up, but Phil stopped him.

"Nick, stop taking the piss. Seth, lie back down. You're still bleeding."

"I realize this is none of my business," Walker said, "but if you love him so much you'd go to this extreme to defend him, what are you doing here instead of on Lang Downs with him? I know Caine and Macklin didn't fire you."

"You're right," Seth said. "It isn't any of your business."

Walker's jaw tightened. Seth braced himself for a dressing-down, but Walker just shook his head. "Fine, but here's the deal, Simms. You get a pass for today because what they said was unacceptable, but next time it happens, you can either head back to Lang Downs or move on somewhere else. You can keep your secrets, but they can't interfere with the job. Get your shit together or get out."

Seth wanted to shout after him that Sam and Jeremy wouldn't let Walker fire him, but that would require more effort than he was capable of at the moment. He closed his eyes and focused on the pain in his nose, jaw, and cheekbone. He had a fine collection of bruises, to be sure, and probably some cuts as well. Phil had said he was bleeding. He checked his nose, but it didn't feel broken. It hurt like a bitch, though, so he prodded at it a little more just to make sure.

"Are you trying to make it hurt worse?" Phil said, pulling his hand away.

He sighed and didn't answer. She wouldn't understand. Turning on Walker hadn't been a conscious decision, but it had been a surefire way to get enough pain to hold him for a while. The jackaroo who'd made the comment about Jason hadn't even come close. Stupid fucker.

"No, just trying to see how much damage there is so I can get back to work," Seth said. "I have a ute to fix."

Phil pursed her lips but didn't stop him when he sat up this time. His head spun momentarily, his vision going swimmy, but he blinked a few times and sat very still until he could focus on her face without feeling like he was going to vomit. The process repeated itself when he stood up, but he finally reached the point that he could walk. "I'll see you at dinner."

If he staggered a little walking out the door, she was kind enough not to say anything.

JASON WAS taking the sutures out of Misfit's leg when he heard the jackaroos talking.

"He just went off like a madman. I thought he was going to kill Perkins. If Walker hadn't pulled him off, I don't know what would have happened."

Not my business, Jason told himself as he kept working.

"I don't know why the bosses let him stay, but Simms is a danger to the station," another one said.

Now it was his business. He couldn't ask them, though. They'd never tell him anything. He'd have to find Seth when he was done with Misfit and make sure he was okay. It sounded like he'd come out on top of the fight, but that didn't mean he was uninjured.

He finished up with Misfit and put him back in his stall. He'd numbed the area so it wouldn't bother Misfit while he was working, so he'd need to wait until the lidocaine wore off before they turned him out. Now he had to find Seth and hope he could get him to talk without running. He didn't know Taylor Peak as well as he knew Lang Downs, but he knew Seth, and that meant finding the tractor shed, or whatever the equivalent of it was here. Seth would go there to lick his wounds even if he didn't have work to do.

He checked the building next to the barn, but that was all storage. As he approached the one after, he heard the distinctive sound of Seth cursing. The sound made him smile. Some things never changed.

He hesitated when he reached the door, and it tore at him. He'd never thought twice about going to Seth before, whether it was to check on him, because he needed something, or simply because he wanted to spend time with him. The need to fix this was almost impossible to ignore, but he wouldn't fix anything if he pressured Seth so much that he ran again.

"Seth?"

Seth looked up. Even in the dim interior, Jason could see cuts on his face and the bruise forming around his eye. If Seth was the winner, Jason didn't want to see the loser.

"Jason."

"You okay?"

"I've been better," Seth said with a shrug. "I was winning the fight until Walker decided to break it up."

"Why were you fighting in the first place?" Jason asked, amused despite himself.

"They were talking shit," Seth replied. "I can put up with a lot, but not that."

"Really, Seth?" Jason said. "You got yourself torn to pieces because some idiot made a comment about you?"

"They weren't talking about me," Seth said. "They were talking about you."

That took the wind out of Jason's sails. "Can I take a look, make sure you aren't hurt too bad?"

"Phil and Walker already checked me out," Seth said. "I've got one hell of a shiner, a bruised jaw, a sore nose, and some cuts. Nothing that's going to kill me."

"I'd still like to see for myself." Jason took a tentative step into the building, hoping Seth wouldn't try to bolt.

"Why are you here, Jase?" Seth said with a sigh, but he didn't try to run, so Jason counted that as a win.

"I came to take out Misfit's sutures," Jason said. "I'd have come earlier, but Chris said I should give you time to calm down before I followed you."

"I told him not to tell you where I was when I called to let him know I was safe," Seth said, but there was no heat in his words.

"I know. He showed me the note you left," Jason replied as he came a little closer. "I don't know why you felt you had to leave, but whatever it was, it's not as bad as you think."

Seth's disbelief was clear on his face.

"You don't have to believe me, but unless you're going to tell me you're a serial killer or something like that, nothing you say is going to change the fact that I love you. So you might as well get used to it. If you run, I'll just keep following until you finally get tired of running."

"You don't want me," Seth said. "I'm a complete fuckup. Nobody wants me."

Jason's heart broke at the self-recrimination in Seth's voice. "I don't know where you got the idea that nobody wants you, but you're wrong. Chris wants his brother. Caine and Macklin need you as a mechanic and an engineer. But most of all, I want you in every way known to man. I want you as my best friend. I want you as my lover. I want you as my partner, if you'll have me. I want the house and the dog and the life together, but only if I can have it with you."

Seth shook his head, but Jason ignored it and went on.

"You don't have to believe me, but it's not going to change how I feel. I know what I want, and I know who I want it with. But here's the thing. If you tell me it can't work the way I need it to work, I'll listen. You just have to tell me how you need it to work. If you need me to drive back to Lang Downs and call you to set up a date, I can do that. If you need me to stay in the bunkhouse while you move into the house on Lang Downs and get used to the idea of having a home, I can do that too. I want it all. I'm not going to lie. But I'm willing to start wherever you're comfortable."

"And if I don't want to start at all?" Seth asked.

The words stung, but Macklin had warned him Seth wouldn't make this easy. "Then I'll wait until you're ready," Jason said, "but I'm not giving up and I'm not going away. I made that mistake two nights ago and you ran from me."

Seth made a helpless sound that tore at Jason's self-control. He crossed the remaining distance between them and wrapped his arms around Seth. "Please," he whispered against Seth's shoulder, "don't run from me again."

Seth didn't reply, but he didn't push Jason away either, so Jason counted that as a win. Slowly, Seth's arms came to rest around Jason's waist, holding him in place. The breath Jason had been holding came out in a rush.

"I don't know how to do this," Seth said so softly Jason could barely hear him. "I don't know how to do anything right."

"That's not true," Jason said. "I've seen you fix more engines than I can count."

"Engines don't count," Seth said. "They're easy. Put the parts together the right way and they work. It's everything else that's hard."

Jason squeezed Seth a little tighter. "We're the right parts. We just have to figure out the best way to fit together. It's a puzzle, and we'll solve it together."

Seth nodded. "Give me a couple of days to get used to the idea?"

"As long as you need," Jason promised. "Just...." He dropped his hand to Seth's thigh, where the razor had dug deep. "Just don't hurt yourself again, okay? I can deal with a lot of things, but seeing blood dripping down your leg like that... I don't know how to deal with that."

"I'll try not to," Seth said.

Jason wanted to press for a promise or answers or an explanation, anything that would help him keep it from happening again, but he'd already pushed more than he'd planned. He could be patient for a little longer. "Then I'm going to head back to Lang Downs. Can I call you tonight to see how the rest of your day went?"

"I'd like that," Seth said.

Jason kissed him gently, trying not to make the pain in Seth's split lip worse, but he couldn't leave without that much. "I love you," he said again. "I'll call you tonight."

"I love you too."

SEVENTEEN

SETH GLARED down at the phone in his hand. Jason had said he'd call, but it was getting late and the phone hadn't rung yet. He could call. He knew Jason's number as well as he knew his own. Hell, probably better, since he never called his own number. He didn't want to call. He wanted Jason to keep his promise and call—

The phone rang, stopping that train of thought. He made himself wait for the second ring to pick it up.

"Hello?"

"Hi, Seth. I'm sorry I'm so late calling. I got back to Lang Downs to another sick sheep. I had to take care of that before I could do anything else, and then Kami insisted I eat something, and Chris wanted to know how you were, and Caine and Macklin wanted an update on Taylor Peak, and—"

"And life was as crazy as always at home," Seth finished. "You don't owe me an explanation. I'm just glad you called. What's this about sick sheep?"

"Macklin noticed a couple of sheep acting oddly. They didn't have a fever or anything, but I brought them back to the valley for observation just to be safe. When I got back today, Ian had brought another sheep down that had the same symptoms, so I had to go back through the check on all three of them to make sure I hadn't missed anything the first time," Jason explained.

"Did you?" Seth asked.

"If I did, I still haven't found it," Jason said. "It's probably nothing, but I have to keep a close eye on them. How was the rest of your day?"

"Fine," Seth said. "I got the ute running right again. I swear, Taylor skimped on everything. All it needed was a tune-up, but it had been let go to the point that much longer would have led to the engine having to be rebuilt, and that's a whole lot more expensive than changing the oil and the spark plugs on time."

"Yeah, Dad always said he was as parsimonious as it came. How are you feeling?" Jason asked. Seth could hear Patrick saying those exact words. Patrick had never had much patience for the Taylors until Jeremy showed up. "Not in too much pain?"

"I took some paracetamol," Seth said, "but nothing's going to make the bruises go away faster. I'll just have to live with not being pretty for a few days."

"I still love you, bruises and all," Jason said so earnestly Seth had to laugh.

"I wasn't fishing for compliments."

"I know," Jason replied, "but that doesn't make it any less true. I didn't fall in love with you because of the way you look, and I'm not going to stop loving you because you have a few bruises."

"Why did you fall in love with me?" The words slipped out before Seth could stop them. They made him sound like an insecure Galah, but it was the one thing he couldn't figure out.

"Because you're funny and amazing and didn't look down on the kid from the outback when you moved to Lang Downs," Jason said. "Because you always had time for me even though I was younger than you. Because you pretended to have trouble with math so I wouldn't feel bad about struggling with it and still managed to explain it to me better than any of our teachers or textbooks ever could. Because you were as lonely as I was, even if you were better at pretending you didn't need anyone. Because your smile lights up a room and I forget other people are around when I look at you. Is that enough or do you need more reasons?"

Seth swallowed hard. He hadn't expected Jason to have an answer for his question, especially not that detailed an answer. "It's enough," he said hoarsely. "It's… fuck, Jase, you can't say things like that to me. I'm not that man."

"Yes, you are," Jason said. "Maybe you don't see yourself that way, but you did all those things. Remember when I got back from Taylor Peak after Misfit got hurt? You're the one I went looking for. Not my parents or Cooper or anyone else. I went looking for you because as soon as I saw you, I felt better. You make me happy just by being there."

"You're a drongo to trust me that much," Seth said. "I'll just fuck it up like I fuck up everything and end up hurting you too."

"You keep saying that," Jason said, "but it's not going to happen. I mean, I'm sure we'll step on each other's toes sometimes. You are a bit of a slob. But that's not enough to make me stop loving you."

"And when I get so freaked out about something I end up doing something stupid to get it to stop?" Seth asked. "Because that's a whole lot harder to control than being a slob."

"What's freaking you out?" Jason asked. "Maybe we can find a better way to cope with it."

"Everything," Seth said. "I don't know how to have a relationship. I don't know how to have sex with a man. I don't know how to be happy."

"I hate to break it to you," Jason said, "but we've had a relationship for ten years, and you're doing fine. So maybe if you know more about that than you think you do, the other stuff won't be that hard either."

"Being friends isn't the same thing," Seth said.

"No?" Jason asked. "Because from where I'm sitting, the only things that'll change are sleeping in the same bed—which we did half the time anyway—and sex. And the only difference there is who you're doing it with. Unless you aren't attracted to me."

"Now who's fishing for compliments?" Seth's voice caught as he spoke. Not attracted to Jason? How could he think that?

"Me," Jason answered easily. "Hearing you say you loved me was a dream come true. Kissing you was something I only let myself think about alone late at night. I'm trying my damnedest to be patient and give you what you need for this to work, but it hit me hard when you ran. I'll stand at your side no matter what comes, but I can't do that if you aren't here."

"I'm sorry," Seth said. "I didn't want you to find out. I didn't want *anyone* to find out how weak I am."

"Do you think you can tell me why you did it?"

Seth tried to figure out how to explain his cutting to Jason. It never made sense later, even to him. "Because sometimes things get so tangled up in my head that I can't think straight," he said finally. "And when that happens, pain is the only thing that breaks the cycle. I can control that. I can choose where to cut and how deeply. Sometimes it feels like the only thing I can control."

"Now it's my turn to apologize. I never meant to make you feel that way."

"You didn't," Seth said. "At least not just you, and not intentionally. I told you. I'm a fuckup, and the way I deal with that isn't any better."

"You aren't a fuckup, and if you don't like the way you deal with it, find a new way."

"It's not that easy," Seth protested.

"I'm sure it's not, but that doesn't mean you can't do it. You've never backed down from a fight, Seth. Hell, you took on Walker today. Next to that, this will be a piece of cake."

"I wouldn't even know where to start," Seth admitted.

"Me either," Jason said, "but I know who might have some ideas."

"Who?"

"Thorne or Ian," Jason said. "They both got help to deal with their PTSD. Some of the things they learnt might help you too. And if they don't, they can tell us who to ask for more help."

"I love you," Seth said because nothing else would do right then. "Anyone else would have run away screaming by now."

"Their loss," Jason replied. "I love you too. You should get some sleep so your body can heal up. I want you well again. I might not love you for your pretty face, but that doesn't mean I like it covered in bruises."

"I miss you," Seth said softly. "The bed is cold without you in it."

"It's summer," Jason said. "Nothing is cold right now. But I miss you too. Say the word and I'll move to Taylor Peak tomorrow. Or you can come home. Whatever you want."

"In a few days," Seth said. He hated making Jason wait, but he couldn't take that final step yet. He needed a few days to just breathe first. "Tell everyone I said cheers."

"Good night, Seth. Dream of me."

"Night, Jase."

Seth disconnected the call and lay in bed, staring at the ceiling. His thoughts chased themselves around in his head, but for once, he let them run without trying to slow them down and channel them toward or away from anything.

Jason loved him. Despite everything, despite the cutting and the running and the fighting and everything, Jason still loved him. It should have scared him, that even when he screwed up this badly, he couldn't shake Jason, but it steadied him instead. Maybe Jason was right. Maybe he could make this relationship work.

He closed his eyes and the thought of a life with Jason followed him into sleep.

SETH DIDN'T wait for Jason to call him when he got back to his room in the bunkhouse the next night. He grabbed his phone and called Jason right away.

"Hello?"

Jason sounded breathless… intriguingly so.

"Hi, it's me."

"Hi, Seth. I was going to call you in a few minutes. I just got out of the shower."

And wasn't that a lovely image? Jason dripping wet from the shower, wrapped in just a towel—a towel Seth could flick out of the way with minimal effort.

"Do you want to call me back?"

"No, just give me a second to put some clothes on."

"Don't go to any trouble on my account," Seth replied. "I kind of like the idea that you're only half dressed while we're talking."

"Oh, so this is going to be one of *those* calls?" Jason teased.

"Do you mind?"

"Not a bit. As long as it won't make you uncomfortable."

"I'm uncomfortable all right," Seth said, adjusting himself to make more room for his awakening cock, "but I'm hoping you'll do something about it."

"When you come home, I'll do anything you want," Jason promised.

"Tell me," Seth whispered. "What would you do if I was there?"

Jason's breath hitched. "We'd come in from dinner in the canteen, probably laughing because of something Molly said to Neil."

Seth could picture it so easily. How many hundreds of times had they left the canteen laughing at how henpecked Neil was? It was a comforting image, safe and familiar and *real*.

"As soon as we got inside, I'd push you against the wall, because laughing with you is a huge turn-on. Almost as much as kissing you."

"Maybe I'd push you against the wall instead," Seth said.

"I'd be fine with that," Jason replied. "As long as you're touching me and letting me touch you in return. I'm a switch through and through."

Seth shivered at that, imagining rolling around on the bed with Jason, changing positions and roles as the mood took them. It felt so right, thinking of being together that way. "What then?"

"Depends on what you want," Jason said, "but I'm thinking we get naked pretty fast. Unless you'd rather go slow and draw things out, of course. Slow can be good too."

Seth could imagine both, but he was already half hard just from listening to Jason talk. He wouldn't have the patience for slow tonight. "Naked is good. We can go slow another night."

"We will." The depth of promise in Jason's voice stole Seth's breath. He couldn't dwell on it, or he'd beg Jason to drive over there right now. He popped open the buttons on his shirt and shrugged it off.

"My shirt's off," he said. "Is that enough?"

"It's a start," Jason said, "although I'm a little farther along than you are. That's okay, though. I'll enjoy stripping you the rest of the way. What do you like? Should I suck on your nipples for a while or keep stripping you?"

Seth didn't even know how to answer. Foreplay with Ilene had been all about getting her ready, her assumption being that touching her would be enough. He couldn't remember the last time someone had taken the time to explore his body.

"Seth?" Jason said softly.

"I'm here. Surprise me."

He could practically hear Jason grinning through the phone. "Oh, baby, you're in for a treat. I have an oral fixation, you know. I've got to have my mouth on something during sex. Your mouth, your neck, your chest, your dick, tonguing open your arse—it doesn't matter as long as my mouth's busy somewhere."

Seth moaned. Oh fuck, Jason was going to kill him before he ever touched him.

"Suck on your fingers," Jason directed. "Get them nice and wet." Seth did as Jason told him. "Ready?"

"Yeah."

"Good. Now run them over your nipple. Doesn't matter which one. That's my tongue learning your body, finding just the right spot and pressure to make you moan for me again."

Seth would've moaned even if he'd felt nothing just because Jason wanted him to, but his nipple tingled and puckered at the touch of his hand, fueled by his imagination and what it might feel like to have Jason licking over his skin. "Feels so good."

"That's what I like to hear," Jason replied. "I want you so bad my hands are shaking. I'm going to drop the phone if I'm not careful."

"Don't do that," Seth begged. "I want to know what happens next."

"We can't do what I have in mind in the living room," Jason said. "Well, maybe we could, but we'd be more comfortable in bed, so I'd dance you through the house to the bedroom because I'm not letting you go, even to get there faster. When we get to the bedroom, I get you the rest of the way undressed. Get undressed for me?"

"As long as you do the same."

"Already there," Jason replied.

Seth stripped as fast as he could. His whole body ached to be touched, but he waited to see what Jason would tell him to do next. "Me too," he said when he picked the phone back up.

"Can you still hear me okay?" Jason asked. "I put the phone on speaker so I'll have both hands free. I have to get myself ready if I'm going to ride you like I've dreamed of doing."

Lust hit Seth low in the belly, his groin tightening with it as he imagined Jason hovering above him. "What should I do?"

"You have to open me up if you want me to ride you," Jason said. "It hurts otherwise."

"I don't want to hurt you," Seth said immediately.

"You won't," Jason assured him. "You'd get your fingers all covered in lube and take your time opening me up so that when we can't stand it anymore, you'll slide right inside me, slick and smooth and easy."

"You'll have to do it for me tonight." Heart pounding, Seth tried to picture what it would feel like to open Jason up the way he'd described, but his imagination failed him. "Tell me what you're doing. Tell me what it feels like."

"You've got big hands, and they feel so good on me." Jason's voice had gone throaty. Seth closed his eyes to better picture what Jason was describing. "Long, thick fingers that will stretch me open so good. You start with just one. You don't need to. We do this often enough—and I want you so bad I'll stretch fast and easy for you—but you like teasing me. You like hearing me beg for your fingers. You like hearing me beg you to fuck me even more, but I'm not quite that desperate yet. It won't be long, but I'm not there yet."

"Jason," Seth moaned. He wanted to see how Jason looked as he fingered himself. What would his face look like contorted with pleasure?

"You keep working your finger deeper, but you're a bastard about it, never touching my prostate because you know I'll go off too fast if you do that. You've done that before, stuck a couple fingers in me and played with it until I can't help myself."

"But not tonight," Seth said, getting into the spirit of the moment. "Tonight I want more than just my fingers inside you."

"Then give me another finger," Jason said. "One won't be enough for you to take me hard."

Seth wrapped his hand around his cock, stroking slowly as he imagined it was Jason's hand keeping him hard while he stretched him. "I've got two fingers in you now," he said. "You're hot and tight, aren't you?"

"Hot and tight and greedy," Jason agreed. "The only problem is you're out of reach. I told you I liked having my mouth on something. Turn around so I can get to your dick. I'll suck you just enough to keep you ready for me."

Seth's hand tightened on his length as he replaced the image of Jason's hand with the image of his mouth closing around the tip. "Shit, fuck, Jase, you're going to kill me."

"No, baby, just love you," Jason replied. "Your fingers feel so good inside me, stretching me open." He gasped out a sharp moan. "You found my prostate that time."

Seth groaned. He wanted more of those needy sounds. If touching Jason's prostate made him sound like that, Seth would milk it for all it was worth. "Not just found it," he forced out around his own grunts and gasps. "I'm going to play with it until you're begging me to fuck you."

"It won't take much," Jason said. "I'm so close already. You know just how to touch me to make me shoot like a rocket."

"What does it feel like?" Seth pressed.

"Like fireworks going off under my skin," Jason gasped. "Like coming home. Making love with you will always feel like coming home. I'm ready, Seth. Fuck me now?"

"Yes," Seth said hoarsely. "Tell me how you want it."

"You're flat on your back," Jason said. "I straddle you and sink down on you like we were made to fit together. You're so thick inside me. If you filled me any fuller, I'd burst. Touch yourself, Seth. Squeeze tight. That's my arse taking you in, making you feel good. Does it feel good?"

Seth didn't have the words for how good he felt right now, not just physically but with the way Jason talked about them, like this was a regular thing, a part of their lives together. But Jason was waiting for a reply, so he forced his thoughts to coherency. "So good. So tight."

"You rock up into me as I push down," Jason said. "You could just lie there and let me do all the work, but you never do. You always take such good care of me. You're getting my sweet spot on every pass now, fucking me just right. It's fast and frantic and I'm not going to last long. Not tonight."

"Me either," Seth gasped. "Come for me, Jase. I want to hear what you sound like."

Jason stopped talking after that, but the moans and gasps that came through the phone were all Seth needed to hear. The sounds sped up. "Talk to me," Jason gasped.

Seth's inexperience caught up with him without cues from Jason to guide him, but he couldn't let Jason down. He might not know what to do, but he could say other things instead. "You're so gorgeous like this. You were made to ride me, weren't you?"

"Made for everything we do together," Jason said. "Seth!"

Harsh panting echoed through the phone. Seth tightened his grip as his climax overtook him. He groaned as his body shook with his release. He tried to say Jason's name, but he couldn't get his mouth to work right.

He lay there for several minutes, just listening to Jason's breathing.

"I love you," Jason said finally.

"I love you too," Seth replied. "I promised Jeremy I'd get the tractor and combine running right again, but as soon as that's done, I'm coming home."

"I'll be here waiting," Jason promised. "Whenever you're ready."

Seth didn't know about ready, but he had to try. Jason had painted a picture of a life together that drew Seth like a moth to a flame. Maybe he'd get burned, but maybe, with Jason there to help him, he'd finally get it right.

EIGHTEEN

IT TOOK another three days before Seth got everything running well enough that he felt comfortable leaving. He excused going through all the utes and other equipment instead of just the tractor and combine with the thought that if it was all done, he wouldn't have to come back in a week or two. He could wait six to eight weeks and then come back for a couple days and do all the maintenance work at the same time. It was a delay—he'd even admitted as much to Jason during their nightly phone calls—but it meant a longer stretch of stability when he finally went home.

He couldn't delay any longer, though. He'd done everything he could around Taylor Peak. It was time to go home.

He packed everything in the boot and headed east toward Lang Downs. Toward Jason.

Toward home.

By the time he crossed the property line between the two stations, his hands were shaking and his breath came in short pants. He'd lost count of how many times he'd reached for his phone to call Jason for reassurance, but Jason would still be working, and Seth didn't want to disturb him. He could handle this. He just had to keep driving until he got to Lang Downs. Jason would be there waiting for him and everything would be okay. Jason wouldn't let him falter.

His phone chirped at him.

Can't wait for you to get here. Come home soon.

Just like that, Seth's breathing eased and the tightness in his chest loosened. He didn't know what he'd done to deserve Jason, but he was going to do his damnedest not to fuck it up because nothing—not even the bite of his razor—settled him like Jason could.

He stopped long enough to text Jason back. *Just crossed onto the station. Home in an hour or so. Love you.*

Love you more.

Seth laughed, as he was sure Jason intended, even if it wasn't possible for Jason to love Seth more than he loved Jason. They didn't need to argue over it, though, so he didn't reply. He didn't stop grinning the rest of the way into the valley.

When he reached the station proper, he debated where to park. The seasonal jackaroos all used the car park behind the tractor shed and drove the utes while they were on the station, but most of the year-rounders left their vehicles near their own houses.

Begin as you mean to go on. How many times had his first-grade teacher said that? He couldn't count, but it had stayed with him all these years. He drove right up to Sam and Jeremy's old house—it would take longer to get used to thinking of it as his and Jason's—and parked there. He'd barely stepped out of the car before Polly came running up to him, tail wagging.

"Hey there, girl," he said as he scratched her ears. "Where's Jason?"

"Right here," Jason said from behind him. "I saw you drive in, but Polly got here first."

"I'm always happy to give her ears a good scratch," Seth said, "but I'd rather say hi to you."

When Jason came close enough to reach, Seth pulled him into a tight embrace. "I missed you."

"I missed you too," Jason said. "It wasn't home without you here. It never has been."

Seth took a deep breath. "Help me take my stuff inside?"

"Here?" Jason asked. "Or at Chris's house?"

Begin as you mean to go on. "Here. I may still fuck this up completely, but I'm going to give it all I have anyway."

"You won't fuck it up," Jason said. "I won't let you."

Seth smiled. "That's what I love about you."

They grabbed Seth's bags from the boot and carried them inside. "I'll unpack later," Seth said as soon as the door closed behind them. He dropped the bag in his hand and reached for Jason. Jason met him halfway, their mouths crashing together as Jason ran his hands up Seth's back. Out of patience, Seth grabbed Jason's hips and pulled their bodies flush. Jason undulated against him, rubbing their growing erections together through their clothes. "Oh, fuck," Seth gasped when he broke the kiss.

"I won't last that long," Jason said with a groan. He pulled Seth toward the couch. Seth crowded behind him, keeping as much contact between their bodies as he could. Jason turned into his arms and fell back onto the cushions, pulling Seth down on top of him. He squeezed Seth's arse and then worked his hand between them so he could attack the button on Seth's jeans.

Seth lifted up onto his knees long enough for Jason to get his jeans open. When he slipped his hand inside and wrapped it around Seth's cock, Seth shuddered. Jason's hand was big and hot and calloused, and it felt so fucking right on his body. He fumbled with Jason's clothes, wanting to return the pleasure Jason was giving him.

Jason groaned the minute Seth found skin beneath the layers of fabric. "God, I love your hands," he said. "So much better than phone sex."

Seth's hand shook as he tried to find the right angle, tension, and rhythm to make Jason feel good, but Jason didn't seem to care beyond getting Seth's hands on him in the first place, and Jason's hand on him was too distracting for him to do more than mimic Jason's motions. His whole body ached, and his pulse pounded in his ears, making it hard to hear Jason's moans.

"Kiss me," Jason demanded, pulling on Seth's neck. Seth braced himself as best he could with one hand and leaned into the kiss. Jason latched on to his mouth, sucking and biting at his lips. Seth moaned into the kiss as his grip on Jason's cock faltered. It was too much all at once and yet not enough, and his head was spinning and sparks jumped along his nerves, and he thought he'd die right there from the sheer fucking joy of it.

He got his hand moving again, determined not to leave Jason hanging when Jason was making him feel so good. Jason moaned and tangled his tongue with Seth's. A second later, Jason's cock twitched in his hand and covered his fingers with stickiness.

He slowed his movements, trying to take in the fact that he'd made Jason come. Holy fuck, he'd made Jason come. He'd done that, inexperience and all. He'd wrapped his hand around Jason's dick and....

His climax broadsided him, and he spilled all over Jason's groin, mixing with the mess already on his hand.

"Oh, God," he gasped as he broke the kiss. He couldn't breathe. He couldn't think. He couldn't....

"Not God, just me," Jason said with a grin.

Seth laughed despite himself. "Better than phone sex?"

"Not even in the same universe as phone sex," Jason said. "But we'd better get cleaned up. It'll be dinnertime soon and we can't go to the canteen like this. Take a shower with me?"

Seth's gut tightened and his throat started closing up again. Before he could find a way to deflect the question, the dinner gong sounded.

"Damn, better not," Jason said. "I'd be too tempted to linger. Give me two minutes to clean up and you can have the bathroom."

"Another time," Seth said. "We don't have to do everything tonight."

Jason laughed. "Good thing. You have to give me time to recover first." He kissed Seth again and sat up. "I hope there are towels in the bathroom."

Seth watched him go with sweaty palms that had nothing to do with mind-blowing sex. He could handle the sex. He might not know what he was doing, but he'd managed to make Jason feel good anyway. Sex wasn't the problem. It turned his brain off. The problem arose when his brain turned back on again. He went to the kitchen sink to wash his hands. Given their positions on the couch, Jason had borne the brunt of their mess. A quick wipe and a thorough hand scrubbing would erase most of the evidence of what they'd done from his body. Nothing could erase it from his mind. He would cherish this memory until the day he died.

He found a washrag under the sink and used it to clean himself up. He'd toss it in the laundry when he was done with it so no one would accidentally use it on any dishes. When he was clean, he zipped up and put himself back together as best he could. His lips felt swollen from the force of their kissing, but their relationship wasn't a secret. Nobody had to know it had gone beyond kissing to a frantic hand job on the couch.

They'd probably all think they'd gone straight to the bedroom to fuck like mad. They'd never hear the end of the teasing tonight at dinner.

He rested his head against the cool metal of the refrigerator. Why had he wanted to come home again?

Jason wrapped his arms around Seth's waist. "You okay?"

Oh yeah, that's why.

"Just thinking we're going to catch hell in the canteen tonight," Seth said. "If my lips are as swollen as they feel, everyone will know what we were up to."

"Do you really care?" Jason asked. "All the year-rounders are living with someone at this point, so it's not like they aren't having sex whenever they feel like it. And the seasonal jackaroos will all be jealous because they aren't getting any on a regular basis. Besides, as often as we've dished it out, we can't be bad sports now that it's our turn. I distinctly remember you giving Chris and Jesse shit about it when they first got together."

Seth grinned. "Yeah, they deserved it."

"Then so do we," Jason said. He pressed a kiss to Seth's shoulder. "I'm glad you're home. Let's go eat and then we can unpack your things and talk a little before bed."

SETH'S CHEEKS still burned from the teasing he and Jason had been subjected to at dinner as they walked back to the house later that night after gathering the rest of his things from Chris and Jesse's house. It had all been in good fun, but Chris hadn't pulled his punches either. And every time Seth had tried to correct an assumption, Neil had made a big deal of covering his ears and going on about not wanting details. Of course Ian had turned on him at that, making Seth wonder what the private conversations between the two best friends were like, but Thorne hadn't seemed bothered so maybe Seth was missing a joke somewhere. He'd been gone long enough for that to be quite likely.

They walked inside and Jason sat back down on the couch, patting the space next to him for Seth to join him.

"Didn't we just do this?" Seth teased as he sat down next to Jason.

"This time we're going to talk," Jason said.

Seth had been afraid that would be his answer. "Yeah, I guess we should."

"We brought your bags in here when you came back, so I take it you're going to move in, but I'm trying really hard not to make assumptions or pressure you. So you have to tell me what you want. Do you want me to stay in the bunkhouse?"

The very thought of Jason moving in made Seth's stomach clench, but he had given in to his panic once. He wouldn't do it again. "No. I can't promise to make it easy, but I want you here with me. I came home for you, not for an empty house."

"It's not either-or," Jason reminded him. "I can keep the room in the bunkhouse as long as I need to, whether I stay with you or go back there to sleep. This isn't an all-or-nothing proposition."

"I know that," Seth said, "but the problem never was sleeping next to you. It's not even the sex. I mean, I still don't know what I'm doing, but I'm not afraid of it. If I do something wrong, you'll tell me what to do instead."

"So what is the problem?" Jason asked gently. Seth felt his defenses rise, but Jason wasn't being nasty. He wanted to know so he could help. If only answering didn't make Seth feel so vulnerable.

"Everybody leaves," he said finally. "And I don't know how to believe it will be different this time."

"I know I'm not going to leave you," Jason said, "but the only way I can prove that to you is by doing it."

"Which is why I said you should move in with me," Seth said. "Maybe I don't know how to believe it now, but I won't know how any better a week or a month or a year from now. Having you here with me is better than having you somewhere else."

"Then I'd better start packing," Jason said. "Because there's nowhere I'd rather be."

"You want a hand?" Seth asked, his heart still pounding. He'd expected the conversation to be harder for some reason, and the unexpected simplicity of it left him unsure about what came next.

"I don't have much in the bunkhouse, but it'll be faster with two sets of hands," Jason replied. "If you don't mind listening to a second set of bullshit."

"What are they going to say that isn't true?" Seth asked. "I don't know most of them anyway. I don't care what they think." And Jason had picked him over the only one Seth really knew anything about, so anything Cooper said would just be sour grapes.

They walked over to the bunkhouse, close enough that their hands brushed at times but without actually holding hands. Jason's room was the first room off the communal living area, but that meant they still had to walk through all the gathered jackaroos to get to it.

"Well, well, look who's back," one of the jackaroos called. "Thought we'd seen the last of you."

"I went down to help out with the machinery on Taylor Peak," Seth said. "It was easier to stay for a few days and get it all done than drive back and forth."

"Yeah?" the jackaroo said. "How'd you get those bruises on your face, then?"

"Stopping an idiot from running his mouth," Seth replied. "I can show you if you'd like."

"Seth," Jason said in quiet warning as he put his hand on Seth's arm. Seth longed to shake it off and have a go at this drongo like he'd done with the last one, but he didn't need a reputation as a brawler.

"Let's get your things and get out of here," he said to Jason. Jason led him through the common area to his room. Seth looked around at the few personal items Jason had on the dresser.

"If you'll pack my books, I'll get my clothes and we can get out of here," Jason said, tossing Seth a duffel.

"I can do that," Seth said as he gathered up the veterinary texts and piled them into the bag. It would be heavy, but he'd manage if it meant they only had to make one trip. He'd be perfectly happy never to set foot in the bunkhouse again. Jason was still packing his clothes when Seth finished, so he grabbed some of the garments from the drawer and started folding them.

"Going to help me with my laundry now?" Jason teased.

"I figure they're all going in the same hamper for the wash," Seth said with a casual shrug that belied how his heartbeat picked up at the thought. "Might as well get used to it now."

"I like the sound of that," Jason said. "I remember being little and Dad coming in complaining because one of Mum's things had ended up tangled in his shorts. Are you going to be upset if I end up wearing your underwear by mistake one day?"

"I've seen your underwear," Seth joked back to hide how much he wanted exactly what Jason described. The image of Jason in Seth's boxers instead of the tight boxer briefs he usually wore sent need curling through his system. "If you wear mine, it won't be by mistake."

"You try spending the day in the saddle with boxers chafing at the insides of your thighs and see how long it takes you to switch to something else," Jason replied easily.

Seth owned three pairs of regular briefs for exactly that reason. He didn't spend much time on horseback, since he spent most of his days working on equipment, but he'd learned his lesson when Jason was teaching him to ride. Deciding he didn't gain anything by sharing that memory with Jason, he went back to folding clothes and handing them to Jason to go in his bag.

They got everything packed and headed back through the common area. Seth diligently ignored the jackaroos who'd gathered while they were in Jason's room, although he noticed Cooper was nowhere in sight. In his more generous moments, he felt sorry for the other jackaroo, but he couldn't regret being the one Jason picked.

He set the duffel he was carrying down as soon as they got in their new house. His throat felt tight and he had to take a few deep breaths to steady himself. He'd asked for this, dammit. He wasn't going to have a panic attack the minute Jason accepted. Jason came up beside him and wrapped his arms around Seth's neck, and just like that, he could breathe again.

"You okay?" Jason asked.

"Probably not," Seth admitted, "but you make it better just by being here."

"Do I need to go back to the bunkhouse?" Jason asked.

"No!" Seth exclaimed. He took a deep breath, trying to calm his racing thoughts. "No, please stay. I want you here. Really. I just have to get used to it."

"Then I'll stay." Jason nuzzled Seth's neck. "We don't have to unpack tonight if you don't want to, but we should get the bags out of the doorway at least. We don't want to trip over them in the morning."

"They'd be a good warning if anyone tried to come in," Seth replied.

"Who's going to try to come into our house in the middle of the night?" Jason asked. "You've lived in the city too long. I bet the door doesn't even have a lock."

And hadn't that taken some getting used to when he first moved to Lang Downs? Caine's office door had a lock, not that Seth had ever seen it closed, much less locked, but that was probably the only lock on the entire station.

"I guess Polly would warn us if anyone came visiting," Seth said. "I didn't see her after dinner."

"She's around," Jason said. "She's probably chasing squirrels or something. She never catches them, but that doesn't stop her from trying. She'll wander home when she's ready."

Seth couldn't have been as sanguine about it if he owned a dog of his own. That was one of the reasons he'd never adopted any of the puppies occasionally on offer at the station. They were working dogs, not pets. He knew that, but the thought of making that kind of attachment and then letting the dog wander at will, to get tangled up with who knows what out in the tablelands, froze him all the way through.

He hefted the bag again and headed back toward the bedroom. Jason might not want all his books in the bedroom now that they had space to spread out, but they could worry about that another night. For now, he could stash the bag in a corner, and they could figure out how to share space in the bedroom.

He set the bag down and started for his own gear, but Jason caught him. "How about we leave all of that for tomorrow? It's been a long day and all I really want to do right now is curl up in bed with you and sleep. We can get clothes out of our bags as easily as out of drawers in the morning."

Relief flooded through Seth. He knew a cop-out when he took one, but he was already on edge. He could handle curling up and sleeping with Jason. It was everything else he didn't know how to handle right now. It might not be any better in the morning, but at least he'd have a night's sleep in Jason's arms to help prepare him for it.

"As long as you don't accuse me of being a slob because of it." He backed Jason toward the bed.

Jason tickled his ribs lightly. Seth winced a little when Jason's fingers hit a bruise, but he kept moving them toward the bed.

"I do want to brush my teeth before bed," Jason said. "Hold that thought and I'll be right with you."

Seth let Jason grab his toiletries and head to the bathroom. While he was gone, Seth gathered his own toiletries. As he pulled everything out, he spied his razor at the bottom of the bag. He couldn't leave it there—he'd need to shave in the morning—but Jason would be back in a minute, and the memory of the last time Jason had seen Seth with the razor in hand still haunted him. He didn't want a repeat when things were finally going his way. He grabbed it and stuck it in the middle of the rest of stuff. That way if Jason saw it, it would be clear Seth was just carrying it to the bathroom, not contemplating using it.

"Bathroom's all yours," Jason said as he came back into the room. Seth nearly jumped out of his skin. "Seth?"

"I'm just putting it away," Seth blurted. "I'm not going to cut myself."

"I know you aren't," Jason said. "You promised me you wouldn't, but you do have to shave, so you should put it in the bathroom where it belongs."

Seth nodded and walked down the hall to the bathroom. His skin felt thin, like he was going to shake apart any second, just shatter into pieces like a dropped glass. He set his toothbrush and toothpaste on the sink and tossed his shampoo in the tub. He set the razor next to his toothbrush, but it stared at him accusingly until he grabbed it and stuffed it in a drawer. He couldn't look at it. It represented everything he had to leave behind him if he wanted this relationship with Jason to work. Next time someone went to Boorowa, he'd have them buy some disposable razors for him. Then he could toss this one in the trash and never have to be tempted again.

If only that would solve his problem.

He brushed his teeth quickly so Jason wouldn't worry about what was taking him so long and then hurried back to the bedroom. Everything would be better once he had Jason's arms around him again. Jason was already lying on the bed in just his boxer briefs, such a welcoming smile on his face that Seth's fears melted like snow in the January sun.

Seth stripped off his shirt and joined Jason on the bed.

"You aren't really going to sleep in dungarees, are you?" Jason teased.

Seth shook his head, but the scab on his thigh taunted him. Things were going so well. He didn't want Jason to see it and remember what a fuckup Seth was. If he turned the light off first....

He reached for the lamp, but Jason stopped him. "Not yet. We can turn it off when we're ready to sleep, but I want to lie here and kiss you for a while first, and it's even better when I can see your face."

Seth rolled back to face Jason, keenly aware of being alone with him in the house. Chris and Jesse weren't asleep down the hall. They weren't in the bunkhouse with jackaroos on the other side of the wall. It was just the two of them.

Before his thoughts could derail further, Jason leaned in and kissed him tenderly. Seth relaxed into the kiss. He could do this. He could lie here and kiss Jason. They'd done that already, even if they weren't alone in the house when they'd done it.

"Stop thinking," Jason whispered against his lips. "I'm going to wonder if you aren't as caught up in this as I am."

That was the problem. He was too caught up in their relationship, to the point that he couldn't think about anything else. He pushed his worries out of the way and concentrated on Jason—on the scratch of his stubble, on the warmth of his bare chest against Seth's own, on the overpowering feeling of rightness.

Jason twined his fingers into Seth's hair and scooted closer. Not sure what else to do with his hands, Seth wriggled one beneath Jason's shoulder and draped the other around his waist. Jason hummed into the kiss and adjusted so Seth's arm lay in a more comfortable position.

The deep, lazy kisses lulled Seth into a sense of security. They weren't rushing toward anything like they had the couple of nights on the phone. They were just enjoying each other. He ran his hands over Jason's back, feeling the broad muscles of his shoulders and lats flex beneath his touch. Jason reciprocated the caress with one hand, never stopping the drugging kisses that stole Seth's wits along with his breath. He would be happy never to leave their bed if Jason kept kissing him like this. Jason angled his other hand between them and smoothed it over Seth's chest. Memories of everything Jason had promised to do to him when they were alone and in bed together swamped him. He shifted a little to give Jason better access. Seth wouldn't push, but he certainly wouldn't say no if Jason wanted more.

Jason pulled away from Seth's mouth despite his moan of protest, to press openmouthed kisses along his jaw and down his neck. Seth rocked his hips, seeking friction, but Jason stilled them with a gentle touch.

"We did that already," he said. "We're not rushing tonight. We're just exploring. You could take your jeans off, though. We'd both be more comfortable without them."

Seth shimmied out of his dungarees but left his boxers on. Jason was still that dressed too. He kicked his feet free and sent the garment flying. When he rolled back into Jason's embrace, he groaned as their bare legs brushed. Why had he not wanted to get undressed before?

Jason snuggled in close again. Seth's skin tingled everywhere they touched. He got his arms back around Jason and held on tight—not that Jason was trying to get away. If anything, he was trying to get closer. That was fine with Seth. Jason could crawl right inside Seth's skin and stay there.

"Love you," Jason murmured against Seth's shoulder.

Seth spread his hands wide across Jason's lower back, trying to touch as much skin as he could to ground himself in the moment, this wonderful, powerful, intimate moment that had everything to do with them and nothing at all to do with sex for all that they were mostly naked together.

His fingers brushed the waistband of Jason's briefs.

"Hold on," Jason said. He rolled to his back and stripped off his underwear before rolling back into Seth's arms. "There. Unrestricted access."

Seth's hand had moved to Jason's arse before he could formulate the desire to touch. He squeezed the hard muscle and then spread his palm over as much of the silky skin as he could reach. He didn't need more than that. He just needed to touch.

Jason tipped his head back up so he could reach Seth's mouth again. Seth fell into the kiss like a parched man at an oasis. He sucked on Jason's lower lip, eliciting a groan and a roll of his hips against Seth's. He squeezed Jason's arse again, encouraging him to keep moving, but Jason didn't take the hint. Instead he licked his way into Seth's mouth, taking his time but taking thorough possession of it nonetheless. Seth shivered. Fuck, he could get used to this. Jason wasn't kissing him like he wanted to get off. He was kissing him like he could go on kissing him forever. This wasn't sex. Seth didn't know what it was, but it wasn't that. He'd had sex—never with a man, but he didn't think that was the difference. No, the difference was Jason. Jason loved him. By whatever miracle, Jason wanted to be here with him, lying in bed mostly naked, kissing him like they had all the time in the world.

"Love you too," Seth said when they paused for a breath.

"Ready to go to sleep?" Jason asked.

Seth could have said no. He could have insisted they take the arousal shimmering between them to its logical conclusion, but saying yes came so naturally.

"Then turn off the light," Jason said.

Seth rolled away to reach for the lamp, but he stopped for a moment before he clicked it off to look at Jason in all his naked glory and to marvel that he was here with Seth.

"Turn off the light," Jason repeated. "You can ogle me in the morning."

Seth laughed and switched off the light. Jason pulled the covers over them and snuggled back against Seth, his arse pressed firmly against Seth's groin. He reached back and popped the waistband on Seth's boxers. "You could take those off too."

Seth almost said no out of habit, but he didn't want to say no. He finished undressing and spooned back up behind Jason. His cock fit perfectly against the crease of Jason's arse. Jason let out a breathy sigh and pulled Seth's arm around him.

"Sleep well."

Seth squeezed Jason's hand. "You too."

NINETEEN

"THANKS AGAIN, Chris," Seth called as he escaped his brother's clutches with two bottles of Tooheys. He and Jason really needed to make a trip to Boorowa. They couldn't keep drinking Chris's beer forever. He had a day off coming up, if his trip to Taylor Peak hadn't forfeited it, so maybe he could go then. He'd have to talk to Caine. For now, though, he needed to get these in the fridge at home before the February sun sucked all the cold out of them. Jason would be home soon, and Seth hoped he'd enjoy the cold beer.

He heard the water running as soon as he crossed the threshold. An image of Jason naked and dripping wet flashed through his mind. He stashed the beer and headed toward the bedroom. He didn't have to just imagine anymore. He had every right to walk into the bathroom and join Jason in the shower if he wanted. They were lovers. They'd moved in together and everything. He didn't have to torture himself with the thought of Jason with someone else now. Jason was with *him*.

The sound of the water stopped. Seth grinned. That meant Jason was done and would be coming out of the bathroom soon. If he got lucky, maybe Jason wouldn't have taken clothes into the bathroom with him. Seconds later, the bathroom door opened and Jason stepped out in only a towel, short dark hair still dripping water onto his shoulders—his completely bare, broad shoulders. Seth stopped and just drank in the sight of him, all toned muscle hewn by years of work on the station. He couldn't count the number of times he'd dreamed of seeing Jason this way. He'd seen Jason shirtless before, as many times as they'd slept over at each other's houses as kids, but it had never been like this. Even curling up naked to sleep last night hadn't been like this. This was…. Seth didn't have the words for it, but words didn't matter. Jason was here, warm and clean and wet, and Seth could act on all the fantasies he'd never allowed to come to full fruition. He could pick any one of them or any of the scenarios Jason had woven on the phone while Seth was at Taylor Peak or he could invent something new all on his own.

"Like what you see?" Jason teased.

"Fuck yeah," Seth replied roughly.

"Then what are you waiting for?" Jason's voice rubbed along Seth's skin like velvet, making every hair on his body stand up on end. He took a step forward without realizing he'd moved, but once he was in motion, nothing could stop him. He crowded into Jason's space and grabbed his hips, pulling their bodies together. Jason grinned at him, that same shit-eating grin that had tortured Seth in his dreams for ten years. Nothing would do now but to kiss that grin away until Jason was too breathless to look at him like that.

Jason kissed him back desperately, all teeth and tongue and burning passion. Seth tugged on the towel until it fell away, leaving Jason completely naked in his arms. Jason took a step toward the bedroom, causing Seth to stumble. They fell against the wall with Jason pinned between it and Seth's body. Seth ran his hands over Jason's flanks. "Didn't you tell me a story that started out like this?"

"Do you remember how it ended?" Jason said in reply.

Fuck, did he ever. He'd never come so hard from his own hand as he had that night, imagining Jason riding his cock. He reached around to cup Jason's arse in his hand. "You'll have to show me what to do."

Jason wriggled out from between Seth and the wall and grabbed Seth's hand. "Gladly." He tugged Seth toward the bedroom. Seth followed eagerly, although not without taking the time to ogle Jason as they went. He didn't know what he'd done to get this lucky, but he sure as hell wasn't going to complain.

When they reached the bedroom, Jason turned back to Seth and tugged his shirt over his head. Seth lifted his arms to help, then popped the button on his jeans and shrugged them off. He was still acutely aware of the healing cut on his leg, but it hadn't interfered the night before. He wouldn't let it interfere now. He couldn't very well make love to Jason the way he wanted to with his trousers still on.

Seth had seen Jason toss condoms and some lube on the table by their bed that morning when he unpacked some of his belongings, looking for clean socks, but as tempted as he was to reach for them, Jason's body was a feast of epic proportions that Seth could finally explore without restriction. Rushing straight to the main course would be a waste of the perfect opportunity.

Jason grinned at him like he knew what Seth was thinking and stretched out on the bed. He patted the space beside him encouragingly. "Join me?"

Seth threw himself on the bed next to Jason. Jason turned to meet him with a torrid kiss. Seth ran his hands frantically over as much of Jason's body as he could reach. He needed to touch, to prove to himself that this was real, not just another dream that would disappear with the first hint of morning. It couldn't be a dream. His dreams had never taken place in any recognizable location. Jason was just as eager, if the way he touched Seth in return was any indication. Seth arched and turned into Jason's hands. It felt so fucking good to be touched. Jason kept his mouth as busy as his hands, licking and kissing along Seth's neck and shoulder as Seth writhed beneath the touch. He had a flash of Jason listing all the places he'd like to put his mouth. His whole body throbbed in anticipation. Which ones would Jason act on tonight? How soon could Seth talk him into the ones he didn't act on tonight?

It would be so easy to lie back and let Jason take charge. He had the experience to blow Seth's mind, but Seth wasn't a selfish lover. He knew what it felt like to be the one doing all the work with little to no reciprocation before the final act. He wouldn't do that to Jason.

He focused on Jason's reactions through the haze of need disrupting his concentration and ran his hands over Jason's torso, seeking his sensitive spots and how he liked to be touched. The brush of his fingers over Jason's nipple elicited a soft hiss, the rush of air tickling Seth's neck. A firmer touch made Jason groan and squirm against Seth. Firmer touch it was.

He pinched and tweaked and rubbed over Jason's nipple until he was gasping more than he was kissing Seth's neck. Seth propped himself up on one elbow so he could see Jason's face. He didn't doubt the sincerity of his reaction, but he wanted to *see*. He was the one who was making Jason feel this way. He was the one Jason wanted.

"See?" Jason said between groans. "I told you you'd figure it out. It's not all that different than sex with a woman."

Seth huffed out a laugh and moved his hand down Jason's body to encircle his cock. "This is."

Jason's eyes rolled back in his head as Seth stroked him, much to Seth's delight. "That's—" Jason swallowed hard and focused back on Seth. "That's no different than taking care of yourself."

That's where Jason was wrong, though. Touching Jason was nothing like touching himself. When he jerked off, he had one goal in mind: getting off as fast as possible. With Jason, he didn't want to rush the pleasure. He wanted to watch the expressions cross Jason's face as things built between them to more than just physical release. They'd climax at the end of it, sure, but it wasn't just about the rush to get there. This was so much more than sex. Last night had taught him that. It was about all the little gestures that went into getting to that point.

Jason retaliated by twisting on the bed so he could suck Seth's nipple into his mouth. Seth groaned at the sensation, sparks dancing along his nerves. Fuck, it felt good to be touched. It felt even better knowing it was Jason touching him.

"You don't have to stop," Jason murmured against his skin. "Or you can get the lube and get me ready."

Seth's hands trembled as he reached for the little bottle on the table. He knew what to do in theory and from Jason's descriptions on the phone, but that didn't settle his nerves. He wanted this. He only hoped he didn't fuck things up like he always did.

"Hey," Jason said, drawing Seth's attention back to his face. "We don't have to do this tonight. We don't ever have to do this if you don't want to. Not all gay men like anal sex."

"But you do," Seth said.

"Well, yeah, but that's not the point. There are plenty of other ways to make each other feel good. I give a mean blow job."

Seth fell a little more in love at the thought that Jason wouldn't pressure him. "I'll take you up on that another night. I want to try. If I don't like it, we can do other things instead."

"Want me to talk you through it?"

Tempting as that was, Seth had his pride. "I'll let you know if I have any questions." He slicked his fingers and slipped his hand between Jason's legs, spread wide to give him access. Jason went back to sucking at Seth's skin, freeing Seth from the weight of his gaze. Seth worked his finger into the crease of Jason's arse and found his target. He fumbled a little, not sure how much pressure to apply, but the muscles ceded easily to his touch, surrounding his finger in smooth heat. He pumped in and out a few times, trying to see what would feel best to Jason. Jason hummed his pleasure against Seth's skin and arched into the caress. "A little deeper."

Seth did as instructed and probed a little deeper until he felt a spongy bump. He started to ask Jason if that was the right spot, but Jason's moan answered the question before the words could leave Seth's mouth. He rubbed back and forth across it for the sheer joy of watching Jason react to his touch. Every pass elicited another moan and a jerk of Jason's hips. His cock rested against his belly, hard as nails and shiny at the tip. Seth wondered what Jason would taste like. He'd find out another night. One thing at a time and all that.

Remembering Jason's descriptions, he added a second finger.

"Fuck, you feel good," Jason gasped. "You sure you haven't done this before?"

"It's like you said. Not so different, at least not from this end. My dick isn't going in your arse without some foreplay."

"Smartarse," Jason teased, but he pulled Seth down for a kiss. Seth kissed him hungrily, not stopping the movement of his fingers, even if the angle made it awkward now. Jason didn't expect him to be a suave, experienced lover. He loved Seth despite his inexperience.

"You could turn around a bit so I could suck you while you finish stretching me," Jason said, so hopefully Seth almost said yes despite his better judgment.

"I'll go off the second you put your mouth on me. It'd be amazing, but it wouldn't end with me fucking you tonight. I really want to fuck you tonight."

Jason reached for a condom. "Then get this on and get busy. I've been waiting ten years for this."

"No way you were thinking about me like this ten years ago," Seth said as he did as Jason directed.

"I started having wet dreams about you a week after you arrived," Jason replied. "I never said anything because you never gave the slightest hint of being gay or bi. How many times did I hear you tell Chris and Jesse that not everyone in the house was gay? I knew you wouldn't care that I was gay— and you didn't when I finally told you—but I didn't figure you'd want to know I was dreaming about you."

They'd wasted so much time. Seth didn't want to wait anymore. He rolled between Jason's legs and lined up with his target. "This okay?"

Jason laughed and lifted his hips to rub his arse against Seth's cock. "It will be as soon as you move. I want you inside me. Now."

Seth pressed forward, fighting the lingering resistance, and then his cock popped through and he was inside Jason. He couldn't breathe. It was so much more than he'd imagined. He thought he might shake apart from the import, the overpowering intimacy of the moment. Ten years he'd waited for this, and now he had it. He had the whole fucking shebang—house, dog, lover, love of his life. He was *home*.

"I'm not going to last long," he warned Jason.

Jason grunted and clenched around him. "Then you'd better make the most of it."

Seth tried to summon a glare, but he was sure he only managed to look like a besotted fool. He didn't care. Jason knew Seth was totally gone over him. He thrust experimentally, trying to find a rhythm and range of motion that would make Jason feel as good as Seth already felt. Jason grabbed his shoulders and tilted his head up for a kiss. Seth didn't know if he could do both at once, but he wouldn't deny Jason a kiss. He lost himself in Jason's mouth, lingering over the caress until Jason smacked his arse.

"Move."

Seth buried his face in the crook of Jason's neck as he began to thrust again. Jason clenched around him again, his chest heaving beneath Seth's. A couple more thrusts were enough to push him over the edge. His whole body spasmed as he climaxed.

Jason's cock pressed against his abdomen. Feeling guilty, Seth rolled to the side and wrapped his hand around Jason's erection. "I'll do better next time," he promised as he stroked the thick shaft.

"You're fine," Jason said hoarsely. "Just keep doing that and loving me." Seth obliged. It only took a few strokes for Jason to come as well, spattering Seth's hand with hot fluid. Seth dealt with the condom and grabbed his discarded boxers to clean them up a little. Jason watched him with thinly disguised impatience. As soon as Seth dropped the soiled cloth on the ground again, Jason pulled him down and cuddled against him. "Better than any fantasy," he murmured sleepily.

Seth held on tight and stared at the ceiling as Jason fell asleep next to him. He only hoped Jason didn't change his mind about that down the road.

TWENTY

"EVERYTHING LOOKS in order," Caine said as he picked up a pen to sign the paperwork Sam had drawn up to codify the investment partnership they had proposed the week before. He set the pen to paper and then glanced up at Macklin. "Do you want to read over it first?"

Macklin shook his head, much to Jeremy's amusement. "You're the businessman, not me," Macklin said. "Sign it so I can."

Caine chuckled and signed at the end of the document. He handed it to Macklin to do the same.

"Walker already signed his copy," Sam said. "His terms were a little different since the investment wasn't the same amount."

Caine looked across the room at Walker. "The amount of money isn't important. You still have equal say in any decisions we have to make."

"Sam and Jeremy already made that quite clear," Walker replied. "I haven't seen anything on Lang Downs or in any of the decisions Sam and Jeremy have made on Taylor Peak that I would question, so I don't see it being a problem. We seem to share the same opinions on running a station and dealing with the men."

"Good. That's the formalities taken care of. Shall we celebrate?" Caine asked.

"I asked Neil to gather up the year-rounders," Macklin said. "They should be on their way over. We'll tell them first and then tell the seasonal jackaroos at dinner. It won't have nearly as much effect on them as it will on the year-rounders."

Jeremy preferred it that way anyway. They'd get to tell their friends the way they would share any good news with friends, instead of a more businesslike announcement in the canteen.

"We won't all fit in here," Caine said. "Let's go into the living room."

Macklin led them into the living room. Jeremy turned to look for Caine, but he had disappeared deeper into the house. Jeremy had been in the office and living room countless times, but he had always considered the rest of the house private. Caine and Macklin didn't come into his house uninvited. He wouldn't take an invitation into the living room as permission to go elsewhere in the house.

Moments after they settled, the front door opened and Thorne and Ian came in.

"Hi, Nick," Ian said immediately. "Neil didn't say you were here."

"Hi, Ian, Lachlan. I'll let Caine and Sam explain," Walker replied. Jeremy didn't know how Ian had graduated into the very elite—two as far as he knew—group who called Walker by his first name, but it reminded him again that Walker was already part of this funny little family even before he invested in Taylor Peak.

"Settling in at Taylor Peak?" Thorne asked Walker.

"Yeah," Walker said. "Getting to know the place and the people who work there."

"Getting to know Phil, you mean," Sam teased.

To Jeremy's surprise, Walker flushed.

"Phil?" Thorne repeated.

"Philippa, the station cook," Walker said, "but your life's in your own hands if you call her by her full name."

"Walker has taken to spending his time off haunting the kitchen," Jeremy added.

"I'll be damned," Thorne said. "All these years and finally snared by a station cook."

"I'm not snared," Walker grumbled. "I enjoy her company and her cooking. I can't very well socialize in the bunkhouse, and the year-rounders aren't ready to count me as one of them either. Phil doesn't care if I sit with her as long as I stay out of her way."

Thorne and Ian exchanged amused glances. "Snared," Thorne repeated.

"Who's snared?" Neil asked as he walked in the door with the rest of the year-rounders.

"Nobody," Walker said as Thorne pointed straight at him.

"Who did the snaring?" Neil asked as if Walker hadn't spoken.

"I'm not snared," Walker said again.

"The cook at Taylor Peak," Sam said. "He'll tell you it's just because she doesn't care if he sits in there, but the rest of us know the truth."

"That gives us another reason to celebrate," Caine said. "I don't have enough champagne flutes for everyone, but I don't suppose anyone will complain about having it in regular glasses, will they?"

"What are we celebrating?" Seth asked.

Jeremy smiled to see him looking relatively relaxed and standing at Jason's side like he belonged there. Whatever bump in their road had sent Seth running to Taylor Peak, they seemed to have resolved it.

"Let me pour the champagne and I'll tell you," Caine said. Macklin took the glasses and passed them out while Caine poured the sparkling wine for everyone. Once everyone had some, Caine stepped back toward the stone fireplace that dominated one wall of the room. "This is probably Sam and Jeremy's news to tell instead of mine, but I'm going to tell you anyway. We just signed a partnership with Taylor Peak with the goal of ultimately running the two stations as one large spread, with Sam and Jeremy, Walker, and Macklin and myself as the governing board. In the short term, while we go through the steps to get Taylor Peak certified as organic, very little will change. Eventually, though, we'll be looking at merging the mobs and staff to increase efficiency. You all will be the backbone of that, and knowing we have all of you to rely on made this decision one of the easiest I've ever made. Here's to Sam and Jeremy and a new era in the neighborhood."

Everyone cheered and drank, but when they were done, Jeremy clinked his glass to get their attention.

"Caine talks like we're doing him a favor," Jeremy said when he had their attention, "but the reality is that he and Macklin and Walker are the ones doing Sam and me a favor. Things aren't good on Taylor Peak. Devlin was cutting corners left and right, trying to make up for several bad years in a row. With the investment from Walker and Lang Downs, we can put things right and move forward toward making Taylor Peak profitable again for everyone. Caine may say it was the easiest decision he's ever made, but it's a show of incredible faith from where I'm sitting. I'm not surprised, since he's gambled on all of us at one time or another, but it doesn't make it any less humbling that he's gambling on us now." He lifted his glass. "To Caine."

The cheers this time were deafening. Good, Jeremy thought. Caine deserved it. He'd say he was only doing what anyone would do, but Jeremy had plenty of experience with "anyone," and Caine didn't fit any definition of that word.

"You realize you're probably going to lose a second round of jackaroos when you tell the blokes at Taylor Peak," Neil said. "Some of them objected to having the station owned by two poofters. Don't hit me, Molly, that's what they said." Jeremy snickered at the way Neil instinctively dodged Molly's hand the moment the derogative term left his mouth. "But even more common was the objection that Lang Downs was taking over. I'd have stayed longer otherwise, but I was obviously making things worse instead of better."

"The thought has occurred," Sam said, "but the choice was losing jackaroos or losing the station. If we lose enough men that we're dangerously shorthanded, we'll look into options to share the crew between both stations now instead of later."

"Who are you more in danger of losing?" Thorne asked. "Crew bosses and year-rounders or seasonal jackaroos?"

"My impression is most of the seasonal jackaroos are new to Taylor Peak," Jeremy said. "They don't care about the rivalry with Lang Downs because they haven't been around to really know it existed. Some of them had issues with Sam and me being together, but they either left or they've accepted it enough to finish the season. I don't see them having a problem with anything that guarantees they get paid. It's the year-rounders we risk losing now because they're the ones who absorbed Devlin's animosity."

"There are enough of us to send an extra crew boss a day on our days off without impacting Lang Downs at all," Thorne said as he looked around the gathering.

"Or to send each of you not on your day off without unduly impacting Lang Downs," Macklin interjected. "Not that many of you take your days off regularly anyway, but that's a different discussion. If you want to use your day off as a second day at Taylor Peak, that's up to you."

Macklin didn't qualify as "anyone" either. Jeremy didn't know what he'd done to deserve such amazing friends, but he would always be grateful for them.

"Do you need bodies?" Caine asked. "Do we need to assign some of the seasonal jackaroos to Taylor Peak to balance out your crews? Or is it the leadership you need most?"

"Right now we're holding it together," Walker said. "We may lose a few year-rounders, but I think most of them will give us a chance to prove nothing has changed. They may not have the same sense of family that you have here, but they've still built lives for themselves on Taylor Peak. They have houses and the like. The seasonal jackaroos almost all have winter accommodations they can return to, but the year-rounders may not have anywhere else to go without some planning first. And if they stay long enough to make those plans, we might convince them nothing has changed. As much as I appreciate everyone's offers of help, I think it would be less disruptive if we changed as little as possible beyond what we've already done until it becomes necessary. We'll be better off in the long run if the crew bosses at Taylor Peak step up and do the job, and that's more likely to happen if they don't feel like we've already started replacing them."

"That makes sense," Caine said. "My inclination is always to help—and I hope you'll take us up on our offer of help if you need it. I just forget help isn't always necessary or appreciated."

"It's appreciated," Jeremy said. "Don't ever think it's not. But Walker is right. If we can ease the year-rounders into the merger, it might go over more easily. It might also go over more easily for things like Jason coming to take care of the vet needs and Seth coming to work on the equipment. They aren't taking jobs from anyone on Taylor Peak since Devlin called in a vet when he needed one and didn't seem to bother with routine maintenance, only with calling a mechanic in if something broke too badly for him to fix it. It also helps that they're younger and less established here. *I* know they're as much a part of Lang Downs as any of us, but the men will look at them and assume they're new to the station."

"I'm happy to help," Seth said, "but I don't want to stay for several days like I did last time, if I can avoid it. I finally have a place of my own. I want to come home to it every night."

"We'll be thankful for any hours you can give us," Sam said. "We'll also come by the house before we head back to Taylor Peak and pick up anything that's left. I hope you'll be as happy there as we were."

"Cheers," Jason said as he put an arm around Seth's waist. "We'll certainly try."

"We're about to have hungry men waiting for dinner," Kami interrupted. "We'll see you over there."

Everyone else finished their drinks and headed toward the canteen as well. "You should stay for dinner," Caine said to Sam and Jeremy. "You can be here for the announcement for the jackaroos, many of whom you worked with, and you can get your things from your house after that. No reason to drive home hungry."

"Not to mention Kami's a better cook than Phil. Don't get me wrong. She puts a good meal on the table, but it's not the same," Jeremy said.

Caine grinned. "All the more reason to stay, then."

They trooped over to the canteen and joined the serving line. Jeremy didn't worry about being last. Kami always made more than enough, something Jeremy had taken pains to pass on to Phil. Devlin might have skimped on orders for provisions, but Jeremy wouldn't do the same. The men needed to eat and eat well if they were going to work as hard as Jeremy expected them to. It had been one of the few changes he'd made that had won instant approval.

After everyone had been through the line, Caine stood and moved to the front of the room.

"If I can have everyone's attention for a moment," he called. The noise quieted down as jackaroos turned from their plates to look at Caine. "We're happy to announce tonight that Taylor Peak and Lang Downs have entered a cooperative partnership with the long-term goal of running the two stations as a single entity. For most of you, that will have little impact on your daily routine. We may ask a few of you to take some shifts at Taylor Peak over the course of the summer, but that would be in place of your regular shifts here, not in addition to them. If you have any questions, I'm happy to answer them individually."

Caine returned to his seat with Sam, Jeremy, Macklin, and Walker.

"That was easy," Sam said when Caine was settled.

"No reason for it to be anything else," Caine said. "It doesn't really affect them."

"Excuse me."

They looked up to see Cooper standing near their table. "Did you have a question about the partnership, Cooper?"

"Not a question, really," Cooper said, shifting from one foot to the other. "Just… well, if you're looking for people to cover at Taylor Peak, I'd like to volunteer. It's…." He glanced toward where Seth and Jason were sitting. "It's not exactly comfortable here for me these days. I'm glad they're happy, but I don't need to have it rubbed in my face all the time."

"You're welcome to come to Taylor Peak if Caine and Macklin can spare you," Jeremy said.

"Of course," Caine replied. "We wish you all the best."

"If you can pack up tonight, you can ride back with us," Walker offered. "Or you can come tomorrow or whenever you're ready."

"I'll be ready," Cooper said.

"JASON, COULD I have a word?"

Jason looked up at the sound of Cooper's voice. Beside him, Seth tensed. Jason squeezed Seth's thigh in reassurance. "What can I do for you, Cooper?" It was the first time Cooper had approached him since their rather public breakup. Jason wasn't sure what Cooper wanted now, but he would hear him out.

"I talked to Sam and Jeremy. I'm going to transfer to Taylor Peak for the rest of the season," Cooper said. "I just wanted to say good-bye."

"You don't have to leave on our account," Jason said. "We never meant to make you uncomfortable."

"I know you didn't, but this will be better for everyone. I wish you all the best."

"Cheers," Seth said. He stood and offered Cooper his hand. "Good luck on Taylor Peak."

Jason held his breath for the moment it took Cooper to shake Seth's hand. He wouldn't have been surprised if Cooper refused. Without intending to, they had embarrassed Cooper pretty publicly. He'd worried that would cause problems at inconvenient times.

Cooper left after that and Seth sat back down. "I'm proud of you for not gloating," Jason murmured.

Seth grinned at him, the light in his eyes sending desire curling along Jason's skin. "You can show me how proud you are later," he murmured just loud enough for Jason to hear. "You keep promising to ride me."

"You keep taking over," Jason retorted. Seth might claim to know nothing about sex between two men, but he'd taken to it with gratifying ease. Jason hadn't sat a horse comfortably since Seth moved back from Taylor Peak. Not that he was complaining.

Seth's grin turned into a self-satisfied smirk that Jason wanted to wipe right off his face. He hoped Sam and Jeremy got the rest of their belongings quickly because Jason had plans for tonight, plans that involved him and Seth and an otherwise empty house.

TWENTY-ONE

LIGHTNING FLASHED ominously across the sky as Seth closed up the tractor shed for the evening. He'd spent the day doing routine maintenance on the utes no one was using—oil changes, spark plugs, and the like. It wasn't difficult work, but it had kept his hands busy. Jason had left right after breakfast to go to Davidson Springs, the station north of Taylor Peak, on a vet call. He'd been so excited to be called by a grazier who wasn't family—he'd expected it to take longer than the four months since he came home—and he'd told Seth he'd be gone most of the day and not to worry, but it hadn't made it any easier for Seth to watch Jason drive away that morning.

"He's working, not leaving," Seth had repeated frequently throughout the day when no one was around to hear him. Another roll of thunder rumbled over the hills.

"Seth!"

Seth turned at the sound of his name. "Yes, Macklin?"

"There's a storm blowing in. The weather radio says it's a bad one. I've radioed everyone out in the paddocks to go to ground wherever's closest, but that means we've got to shut things up down here. Get everyone you see and tell them to close windows and shutters on all utes and buildings. Anything that might get blown around needs to be moved inside, either in a house or in the tractor shed. I'm going to move the horses into the shearing shed."

Adrenaline burst through Seth's system, making his fingers tingle and his skin feel tight. Macklin never ordered the horses brought inside. They were working animals, perfectly capable of dealing with a little rain or even snow. He eyed the horizon where the storm hovered, full of harnessed fury waiting to be unleashed. *Drive safely, Jason.*

"Has anyone tried to reach Jason to tell him not to try to get home?" Seth asked. "If it's going to be as bad as you say, he should stay at Davidson Springs and come home tomorrow."

"Go call him," Macklin said. "Then you can help get everything ready."

Seth sprinted for the house. He'd left his cell there that morning so he couldn't compulsively check for messages all day. Now he wished he hadn't. Having it on him would have saved him the time it took him to get to the house. He ran into the bedroom and grabbed the phone from the dresser. He had a text from Jason saying he'd reached Davidson Springs that morning, but nothing else. Hoping that meant Jason was still there, he called Jason's number, but it flipped straight to voice mail.

"Fuck," he muttered. He sent Jason a text telling him to stay put and ran for the main house.

"Caine!"

"I'm here," Caine said from the back veranda. "I'm closing up windows. What's wrong?"

"Do you have the number for Davidson Springs? Jason is there and I need to tell him to stay there until the storm passes or even until morning."

"You don't think he has enough sense to make that decision on his own?" Caine asked.

"Probably, but I'd feel better if I knew he'd got the message."

"The number is in the office. There's an old Rolodex that belonged to Uncle Michael. I keep it as a backup in case something happens to my cell. Out here, you never know."

"Thanks," Seth said. He ran into the office and flipped through the cards until he found the one he was looking for. He punched in the number with trembling fingers and waited for someone to pick up.

"Hello?"

"Hello, this is Seth Simms from Lang Downs. Is Dr. Thompson still there?"

"No, he left about an hour ago. He was hoping to beat the storm."

"Thanks," Seth said around the agonizing tightness in his chest and throat. It would take Jason at least two hours to get back even if the storm didn't slow him down, which meant he would almost certainly be caught out in it. He sent another quick text to Jason.

Find shelter wherever you are. Text me that you're safe.

He tucked his phone into his pocket where he'd feel the vibration even if he couldn't hear the chime when a new message came in. Worrying about Jason wouldn't do any good, and they had a station to prepare for the storm.

The wind had picked up when Seth stepped back outside. A quick glance around the station showed men working on closing up various buildings, so Seth headed back to his and Jason's house. He'd shutter the windows and pull the chairs Ian had made inside. The table wouldn't fit, but he'd flip it over and hopefully it would be heavy enough not to blow away. Lightning crackled across the sky, visibly closer than before. Seth picked up the pace until he reached the shelter of the veranda. Even there, the wind buffeted him from all directions: not quite hard enough to knock him off his feet, but definitely enough to make him feel it.

When the house was secure, he dashed toward Chris and Jesse's house. He hadn't paid much attention that morning to who had been assigned to ride out and who was staying closer to home. If they were out in the paddocks, he needed to make sure their house was secure too. He found Chris on the veranda fighting with one of the shutters. He added his weight to Chris's and it finally swung shut. "Get Jesse to fix that hinge when the storm passes," Seth shouted over the sound of the wind.

"I will," Chris said. "Have you checked Thorne and Ian's house?"

"No, Caine was working at the big house, and I've done my house, but that's it."

"Check Thorne and Ian's house and then the others. I'm going to check on Molly and the kids," Chris yelled.

Seth nodded and headed toward Thorne and Ian's house. Raindrops splattered his shoulders as he ran. He should have grabbed his drizabone when he was at the house, but he hadn't expected the rain to start this soon. Thorne and Ian's house was already closed up, whether by them or someone else, so he ran on to the next. He was on his way to the tractor shed to make sure it was secured when Macklin intercepted him.

"Everything is as ready as we can make it. Get inside."

Seth waved to show he'd heard and headed back to the house. Before he could get to the shelter of the veranda, the heavens opened, soaking him to the skin in seconds. The wind whipping around him turned cold as he ducked onto the veranda out of the rain. He left his boots in the mudroom and stripped off his wet clothes. Rain pounded on the roof over his head and gooseflesh puckered his skin as he walked through to the bedroom to dry off and get dressed again.

He toweled off, the friction warming his skin. He was tempted to take a hot shower, but he didn't want to be away from his phone that long if Jason called or texted. He pulled on dry clothes and went back to rescue his cell phone from the sopping mess he'd left on the mudroom floor. Days like this made him glad he'd invested in a waterproof case for it. He checked the phone, but Jason hadn't called or texted. When he looked more closely, he realized the phone didn't have service. "Bloody hell," he cursed. "Jason, you better be somewhere safe."

He moved to the door in the lee of the house and cracked it open so he could peer outside. Normally he could see most of the buildings on the station from that vantage point, but the torrential rain and the unnatural early darkness from the clouds made it impossible to see anything beyond the edge of the veranda. Shit, Jason had better have found a drover's hut to hole up in because no one could drive in this weather. He'd run off the road and get stuck or run off the edge of a cliff and get killed.

He couldn't think that way. Jason was a responsible, rational adult. He wouldn't take stupid chances just to get home a little sooner. As soon as the storm started, he would've found a place to take shelter and wait it out. Worst-case scenario, he'd simply stop where he was and ride out the storm in his car. It wasn't ideal, but the chances of someone else coming upon the stopped vehicle and causing an accident on the station roads in this kind of weather were negligible. Jason was fine. The drover's huts were all stocked with firewood and provisions. He could start a fire, wrap up in a blanket, and eat tinned soup for dinner.

Thunder clapped overhead, making Seth jump. The power flickered for a moment, then came back on. Seth frowned. The house had to have candles in it somewhere. They all stocked them because power outages were a fact of life out here. He just didn't know where they were. He shut the door, making sure it latched tightly, and went into the kitchen to search for candles or a torch. He should have made a point of finding them when they first moved in, but the weather had been so clear that he hadn't thought about it. He'd pay for it now if the power went off and he was stuck in the dark.

He found a long taper and several squat nubs in the back of a drawer, along with a lighter. The power flickered again, taking longer to come back on this time. Seth went ahead and lit the candles. It wouldn't be long before the power went out for good. He got two of them lit before the room went black again.

The flare of the candles tossed odd shadows on the wall, making Seth wish he were anywhere other than alone in his house. Even if he'd had to sit around in wet or borrowed clothes, having company would have been better than being alone in the eerie light of the candles, listening to the rain pound on his roof, and worrying about Jason. It wasn't worth getting soaked again, though. The storm would pass, and he could go find Chris or someone else when it did. He wasn't a baby. He could deal with an hour or two alone in his own house, even with the power out.

He shivered in the cool air. It was the middle of the summer. He shouldn't be cold, but that was beside the point. He walked into the living room and laid a fire in the fireplace. He lit it using the candle and held his hands up to the flames, refusing to acknowledge how badly they were shaking.

A particularly loud crash of thunder made him jump so much he dropped the candle. He cursed as he grabbed it and stamped on the wooden floor to make sure it hadn't caught on fire. He didn't see any sign that it had, not even a scorch mark, but it was hard to see anything in the inky darkness.

Jason was out in this weather somewhere, either in a drover's hut—shelter, but not as sturdy as the house—or stuck in his car.

The thought chilled him to the bone despite the warmth from the fire. He set the candle on the mantel and paced restlessly around the room. Jason was an adult. More than that, he'd grown up in the tablelands. He didn't need anyone to tell him how bad a storm was going to get. Seth would bet Jason's weather sense was as good as Macklin's. He would have realized the storm was getting bad and headed for the nearest drover's hut. He would even have known where it was. He had a lifetime of familiarity with Lang Downs. He was fine.

He checked his cell phone again, not that he expected there to be any change since the last time he had looked, but he had to see for himself that he hadn't missed a text or a call.

No Service.

He resisted the urge to throw the phone across the room. Damaging it wouldn't change the situation and would make it that much harder for Jason to reach him when he could. *Jason's fine*, he told himself. *He hasn't called because he doesn't have service either. Or he's called and there's a message waiting for you as soon as your phone is working again.*

Yes, that was it. Jason had found shelter and left a message and was waiting out the storm. All Seth had to do was hold it together until his cell service came back on and everything would be fine. Jason might not come home until tomorrow since the roads would be a bloody mess with this much rain, but he would call or text and Seth would be able to relax.

Lightning struck somewhere nearby, bright enough to be visible around the cracks in the shutters. He shuddered as the thunder made the whole house rattle. God, he hated storms like this. He could deal with it if Jason was here beside him, keeping him calm. He could even deal with it if he knew Jason was somewhere safe, still on Davidson Springs or even in a drover's hut between here and there. It was the uncertainty that was killing him.

Something crashed toward the back of the house. He nearly jumped out of his skin. Adrenaline made his fingertips tingle as he reached for the candle to go investigate. If something had broken one of the shutters, he had to fix the hole before the downpour flooded the house.

He checked the bedroom first but couldn't find the cause of the noise, so he went into the bathroom to check the window there. As small as it was, he doubted that was the source, but better to check. The shutters were closed over the window still, but the candlelight caught his razor where he hadn't put it away after he'd used it that morning. His fingers tingled again as another shot of adrenaline swamped him.

He didn't need to cut himself. It was just a storm. It would pass and Jason would call and everything would be fine. He could leave it sitting right there on the counter and walk back into the living room to wait. Or he could go into the bedroom and lie down, surrounded by Jason's scent and the lingering muskiness of sex. He could close his eyes and imagine their reunion and forget about everything else until Jason got home.

He picked up the razor to put it away, but he couldn't make himself reach for the drawer. Now that the razor was in his hand, the temptation to soothe his troubled thoughts with the one thing he could control grew almost irresistible.

He couldn't do it in the dark. It was hard enough to control when he had adequate light and nothing to startle him. As jumpy as he was with all the thunder, he'd probably hit an artery if he tried to cut himself now.

"No," he said as he wrenched the drawer open and tossed the razor inside. "I told Jason I wouldn't cut anymore. I'm not going to break that promise now."

He jerked back out of the bathroom and went to the living room to put more wood on the fire. He wasn't cold anymore—his skin burned now with nerves and fear—but it gave him something productive to do. He couldn't cut—he'd *promised*—so he'd control the fire instead.

He built the fire up to a blaze, but the heat rolling out of the grate pushed him back to the other side of the room. He cursed under his breath. That wasn't what he'd hoped to achieve. He gripped his thighs hard, digging his fingers into the muscle. He didn't need to panic. The fire would burn down, the storm would pass, Jason would call or text, and in the morning he'd come home. Everything was under control, even if it didn't feel like it.

The lure of the razor beckoned, but he ignored its siren call. He'd promised Jason. Once, maybe he could have hidden the marks left behind, but they knew each other's bodies too well now. If he cut himself, Jason would see it, and he'd ask about it. Cuts on his hands from working on the engines got fussed over but accepted. Jason had grown up with a mechanic. He knew how that worked. A nick on his cheek or his jaw where his hand slipped and he caught himself shaving would earn him a look for being distracted and hurting himself, but again, it happened. A slice anywhere on his body because he'd lost control of himself and gone for his razor would earn him a look of such disappointment it would break his heart. Jason would forgive him because that was the kind of man he was, but how many times would he be able to let it go before it became too much and he decided Seth wasn't worth it?

No, Seth couldn't cut himself. Losing Jason would destroy him. He couldn't do something he already knew would hasten that process.

He didn't realize he was moving until he stood in the bathroom doorway again. The candlelight reflected off the mirror, casting his face in shadows. He stared at his reflection because it was safer than looking at the sink with its drawers and his razor inside. His hair stuck up in tufts where he'd dried it with the towel and not bothered combing it. His skin looked sallow in the strange light, so unnaturally pale that his eyes stood out like bruises against his skin, dark and wild in his panic. He held his own gaze in the mirror and made himself breathe slowly, in and out, in and out.

Jason had made him breathe that way the first time they'd had sex, when he'd been sure he'd come the second he got inside Jason's hot, tight body.

The irreverent thought startled a laugh out of him, but it only increased the ache in his chest. Jason wasn't there. He hadn't called or texted. He could be anywhere now, lying in a ditch hurt or dead, trapped in his car if he'd lost control.

Seth swallowed hard and reached for the drawer with trembling hands. He couldn't do this. He couldn't stay here with his worries and temptation incarnate. He made sure the razor was closed, stuffed it in his pocket, and went back to the mudroom. His boots were still wet, but he forced his feet into them anyway. He pulled on his drizabone and turned up the collar so it would protect his neck. He jammed his hat on his head and hunkered down against the rain. Chris and Jesse's house was only two minutes down the road.

The wind and rain stung his cheeks and soaked his dungarees below the hem of his coat, but he ducked his head into the wind and pushed toward his goal. He couldn't break his promise to Jason. He had to get help because he couldn't do it on his own.

He stumbled onto their veranda and fell against the door. He managed to get the handle to turn so he could get inside out of the weather. He stripped off his drizabone, boots, and hat.

Chris heard him and came into the mudroom. "Seth? What's wrong?"

Seth pulled the razor out of his pocket and pressed it into Chris's hands. "Take it. I promised Jason I wouldn't cut anymore, but I can't do it. Take it. I don't want to break my promise."

"Okay," Chris said. He tucked the razor in his pocket and pulled Seth into his arms. "You don't have to do it by yourself. I've got you now. It's going to be okay."

"How?" Seth asked brokenly. "Jason hasn't called or texted. He's out there somewhere in this storm. He could be dead for all I know. I just found him. How can it possibly be okay if I lose him now?"

"You aren't going to lose him," Chris said. Chris had always been the one to soothe his hurts and fears. Even when their mum was still alive, Seth had always taken his scraped knees to Chris. Then Tony came along and had solidified their brotherly bond forever. Seth supposed he ought to be grateful to his bastard of a stepfather for helping him create an unbreakable bond with his brother. "He's safe in a drover's hut, and he'll call as soon as the storm passes. You just have to hold on until then."

"I don't know how," Seth said through the tears that dampened his cheeks along with the rain. He gestured toward Chris's pocket. "That's all I've ever had."

Chris hugged him tighter. "Come on. Standing here won't fix anything. Come in the kitchen. I can't make you tea, but we can keep you company."

Seth followed obediently and took his seat at the kitchen table. Jesse came in a second later. "Hi, Seth. I didn't expect to see you until the storm passed."

Seth didn't even look up.

"He's half soaked. Could you get us a blanket?" Chris asked.

Jesse came back a minute later with a thick blanket that Chris wrapped around Seth's shoulders.

"Is he okay?" Jesse asked. Seth wanted to shout no, but he couldn't get his body to cooperate. He just sat there shivering and crying.

"I don't think so. I hate to ask with the storm still so bad, but...." Chris said.

"I'll go get Thorne and Ian," Jesse said. "Don't let him go anywhere until I get back."

"He's not going anywhere," Chris replied. "He's going to stay right here where he belongs until Jason gets back."

TWENTY-TWO

THORNE SHOOK out his drizabone and took off his boots when they got inside out of the rain. Jesse hadn't said much, just that Chris and Seth needed them, but Thorne had survived hell—he wouldn't let a little thing like a summer storm keep him from helping his friends. He'd told Ian he could stay behind if he wanted. Ian had laughed in his face. Thorne glanced over to where Ian was removing his rain gear as well. God, he loved that man.

Jesse led them into the kitchen, where Chris and Seth sat at the table. Seth had his head buried in his arms and a blanket wrapped around his back, but Thorne could see the minute shivers that racked his whole body. Chris had his arm around Seth's shoulders. He gave Thorne a look of such desperation that Thorne's heart broke for them. "What happened?"

"I don't really know," Chris said. "He came tearing in here in this weather with wild eyes and shaking hands and all but threw his razor at me. He's been like this pretty much ever since."

"He cuts?" Ian asked.

Chris nodded. "I didn't know until a few weeks ago. I swear I didn't or I'd have found a way to help him a long time ago. He promised Jason he wouldn't do it anymore, but Jason left Davidson Springs before the storm started and hasn't checked in since, and, well…."

Thorne could imagine the rest. He had lived with the kind of panic that came from not knowing the status of a loved one, and he had lived with the loss of his entire family and the survivor's guilt that came with it. He gestured for Ian to take the seat next to Seth while he sat down across from him. "Seth?"

Seth didn't look up, but the tremors eased a bit.

"I can guess what you're thinking right now," Thorne went on. "You're sitting there imagining the worst because Jason hasn't checked in. You're thinking he's hurt or dead out there in this weather with no one to watch him. You're thinking he's scared as well as hurt because he doesn't know if anyone is coming for him. And you're thinking that if the worst happens, you'll never forgive yourself for not going looking for him or not stopping him from going to Davidson Springs in the first place."

Seth's shoulders tightened as he tried to muffle his sobs. Thorne hated adding to Seth's turmoil, but he had to get it out in the open.

"You're thinking you've failed him somehow, that because you aren't omniscient and omnipotent, you're worthless, and he shouldn't love you because you'll never do anything but make him miserable." Ian reached for Thorne's hand and squeezed it softly. Chris and Jesse looked horrified, but Thorne couldn't stop. He had to get Seth to admit to the poison inside him or they'd never get it out.

"Or else you're thinking he changed his mind about you and instead of heading home when he left Davidson Springs, he went to Cowra or somewhere beyond to get away from you."

"No!" Seth sat up at that and glared viciously at Thorne. "No, he wouldn't do that. Even if he decided to end things, he wouldn't do it that way. He'd come home and tell me. He wouldn't be that cruel."

"Good," Thorne said. "You still have some sense of reality in there. You're doing better than I was. Now you just have to get rid of the rest of the shit in your head."

"I've tried," Seth said, "but the only thing that works is the one thing I promised Jason I wouldn't do anymore."

"It pretty much sucks when life takes away your only coping mechanism," Ian agreed. "I wish I could tell you learning new ones is easy. I can tell you that you don't have to do it alone."

"Ian's right," Thorne said at Seth's skeptical look. "Yes, ultimately the choice to cut or to do something else instead is yours and no one can make it for you, but you have people who care about you and want to help you. And you know that or you wouldn't have come to Chris when you reached the point of not being able to cope anymore. If you'd truly believed you were alone, you would have used that razor instead of tossing it away, promise or no promise."

"Believing you're alone is the hardest part to get past," Ian said. "Fifteen years on this station—*this* station, Seth, with everything that entails and all the amazing people who would do anything for each other—and it took Thorne to make me see I hadn't been alone since the day I arrived here."

"And you know all the year-rounders on Lang Downs stayed because they landed here when they had nowhere else to go," Thorne added. "Caine's uncle took some people in. Caine has taken in others. But the fact remains that no one who came and stayed had it easy before they got here. It might have been Michael's or Caine's decision to offer them a job and a home, but it's the decision of everyone who stays to help the people who come after us. That includes you."

"What do I do?" Seth asked. "I don't even know where to start."

"There's no magic cure," Thorne warned. "This isn't something that's just going to go away. It's been four years and I still have bad moments. Not as many, but it's something you learn to cope with rather than getting rid of. Beyond that, you have to figure out what works for you. Ian and I can suggest things. You can do online searches for techniques for coping with panic attacks. You can find online support groups if you want to go that route, to talk to people with your specific problems instead of just people who know what it is to have a shit hand in life. Ian or I can give you the name of a therapist if you want to talk to someone that way."

"The real thing, though," Ian said, "is that you have to do it for yourself. Jason will support you just like we will, but if you're only changing for him, that puts a huge burden on him. You need to do it for yourself."

Seth nodded. "I don't think I can handle it tonight."

"No, not tonight," Ian agreed. "You need to sleep if you can. Tomorrow when you're rested and Jason has come home and you can put the panic behind you, we can talk specifics. Tonight just remember you aren't alone."

"I can't go back over there without him," Seth said.

"You don't have to," Chris replied. "You still have a room and a bed here. The sheets are clean. You can sleep here. Or we can pull a couple of mattresses onto the floor in the living room and all sleep there together. Whatever makes you most comfortable."

"Pretty fucked up reason to have a slumber party," Seth said.

"If it's what you need to make it through the night or the next day, and it doesn't hurt you or anyone else, it's not fucked up at all," Thorne said. "After you realize you're not alone, that's the next lesson you have to learn. Taking care of yourself isn't selfish or fucked up or anything else. It's what you have to do so you can deal with everything else. I've seen men drink themselves into oblivion. I've seen men overdose on drugs. I've seen men eat their own guns when it all got to be too much. A slumber party is a hell of a lot better than any of those options, so if that's what you need tonight, accept Chris's offer. If it isn't, figure out what you need and ask for it."

Seth still didn't look convinced, but Thorne knew from experience that acceptance had to come from within, not from someone else. They would keep supporting and encouraging him until he could make those choices on his own.

"The rain is tapering off, it sounds like," he said. "Ian and I are going to head home before it gets worse again, but we'll talk more tomorrow, and we're never far away if you need us."

"Thanks," Chris said.

"Thank you," Seth echoed. "I don't want to feel this way anymore."

"And you've just done the hardest part," Thorne said. "Now that you've decided to do something about it, it will get easier. We'll talk again tomorrow."

SETH LAY in his old bed and stared toward the ceiling, not that he could actually see it since the power was still out and the shutters all still closed. The rain had slowed to a gentle patter on the roof, but Jason still hadn't called. Even a light rain could disrupt cell service—it was why they carried radios in the outer paddocks—but knowing that wasn't enough to settle his fears. He needed to hear Jason's voice, or at least see his name next to a new text before he could stop worrying completely. He clung to the promise Thorne and Ian had made. No matter what happened, whether Jason showed up in the morning or never came back, he wouldn't face it alone. How many times had he watched the inhabitants of Lang Downs rally around someone in need? They had rallied around him and Chris when they'd first arrived and were still strangers. They would be there for him if he needed them now. He just had to hold on to that thought. He wasn't alone unless he wanted to be, and he had far more than just Chris in his corner now. He'd grown so used to the idea of only having Chris, of never knowing what a real family felt like, that he'd failed to recognize it when he finally had one. Maybe they weren't a family anyone outside of Lang Downs would recognize, but it was far more real than anything else in his life had ever been. He'd always had Chris. Now he had a station full of brothers and sisters, uncles and aunts, friends who wouldn't let him fall no matter what. Hell, the look on Carley's face when he'd called her "Mum" should have clued him in. He wasn't quite ready to call Patrick "Dad," but he could accept him as an uncle. Or a father-in-law.

How the fuck had he got this lucky without seeing it? He didn't deserve it, but he'd long since learned Lang Downs wasn't something a person earned, but something they fell into and held on to for all they were worth. He'd just always applied it to Chris, not to himself. He'd been a tagalong to Chris's rescue and subsequent adoption by Lang Downs, the annoying little brother they had to keep if they wanted Chris to stay.

He'd been blind. Not willfully so but rather spectacularly, regardless. He hadn't registered how Caine had welcomed him back immediately and with far more responsibilities and fewer checks than he'd give the typical new employee. Caine had treated him as a year-rounder from the moment he'd brought up staying. Seth had shouldered the responsibility without hesitation, never pausing to consider everything else that came with that title. He'd stepped up to help Sam and Jeremy because that's what the year-rounders did for each other, but he hadn't had faith that they would do the same for him in his time of need.

He owed them one hell of an apology when this was over and Jason was back safe and he could breathe again. He still didn't understand why they had adopted him the way they had, but he couldn't argue against the fact that they had. He had a family. A real, honest-to-God family who believed in him and accepted him, warts and all, and who would move heaven and earth for him if that's what he needed them to do. If Jason hadn't texted in the morning, they'd head out toward Davidson Springs, some of them stopping to check each drover's hut, others going straight along the road to look for him. They'd do it for Jason, whom some of them had watched grow up, but they'd also be doing it for Seth, because Seth needed Jason, and Seth was family too.

He had a family. He didn't know what to do with a family. His father had abandoned him before he was born. His mother had never been reliable. Tony and his stepsiblings had been a nightmare. He'd only ever had Chris. Now he had Jason—he would never stop being grateful for that miracle—and a station full of people who would do everything they could to build him up instead of tear him down. He wouldn't be subjected to anything like Ilene's domineering ways or his stepsiblings' malicious taunts. He might never understand why they believed in him the way they did, but he couldn't argue with the fact that they accepted him for who he was and would support him in whatever came.

A rather hysterical laugh escaped him despite his attempts to muffle it. He had a *family.*

"Seth, are you okay?" Chris called.

Seth nearly laughed again. It was a good thing he and Jason hadn't had sex in here. Jason wasn't quiet when he came—Seth loved wringing as many noises out of him as he could—and Seth would miss them if he had to muffle them because of Chris and Jesse.

"Yeah," he called to Chris. "Maybe for the first time in a long time."

Chris stuck his head in the door, the light from the candle in his hand illuminating his worried expression. "You sound better than you did earlier. Can I come in?"

Chris always asked. No one else had ever bothered, but Chris and Jesse always asked. Seth patted the bed next to him. "Sure. I could use the company."

Chris set the candle on the nightstand and stretched out on the bed next to Seth.

"Do you remember our father at all?" Seth asked.

"Not really," Chris said. "I was only four when you were born and he wasn't around much even then."

"Long enough to get Mum pregnant and then scarper," Seth said with a nod. "How do you do it? We came from hell. What do we know about loving anyone? About staying with anyone?"

"We aren't them," Chris said. "They gave us life, and then they gave us the example of what not to do. We aren't limited by that. We aren't doomed to repeat their failures. We have other examples to follow now. Good ones. You want to know how you stay? Look at Caine. Hell, look at Macklin. He's got Sarah now, but his father wasn't just absent—he was abusive. Macklin got away, and he got here, and now he has Caine. Thorne lost his family in a fire when he was eighteen and then he moved from place to place in the Commandos."

"And now he has Ian."

"That's right. We're surrounded by people who have done exactly what you're worried about not being able to do. Maybe Mum didn't give us much of a foundation to stand on, but we've got one now. We have the kind of family now that doesn't let you down."

"Yeah, I'm starting to realize that," Seth said.

"Starting to?" Chris asked.

"I'm a little slow on the uptake."

"A little?"

Seth shrugged. What he could he say? Chris was right.

"Ten years," Chris said with a shake of his head. "It's been ten years since Caine saved the life of a complete stranger and took him in—along with his kid brother—and let him cut vegetables in the kitchen until he could earn his living another way." Chris bopped Seth on the shoulder. "Ten years!"

"Yeah, but I wasn't here for a lot of those years," Seth said. "Somebody insisted I go off to uni and get a degree."

"A degree that has made you irreplaceable on the station, I might add," Chris said.

"Not the point," Seth retorted. "The point is I haven't been here. You've had ten years to soak up everything that goes with living here. I haven't."

"You're here now," Chis said, "with everything that means."

"I'm figuring that out, like I said. I just have to make it register in my brain."

"It takes some adjustment," Chris admitted, "but you'll figure it out eventually. The thing about family is, you can take them for granted. You get caught up in the everyday stuff and you don't think about it. You get comfortable. You don't worry about them constantly. You may even forget a little how tight that bond is. Then something happens and they're right there and you remember. I don't know if I ever told you this, but the day I was bashed, when I told you to run and you did, I never doubted—not even for a second—that you'd look for help and you'd bring whoever you found back to try and help me. I wondered if you'd get there fast enough, but I never doubted you'd come back. I just hoped I'd still be alive when you did. Never in a million years did I dream you'd stumble on the one man in all of Yass guaranteed to rain fury on them like an avenging angel."

"How could you have that much faith in me?" Seth asked. "I don't have that much faith in myself."

"You're my brother, that's how."

The simplicity of the statement left Seth trembling. He and Chris had grown apart somewhat in recent years, with Seth away at uni and Chris wrapped up in his new life with Jesse. Seth had accepted it as inevitable—miserable, but inevitable. Now he realized it wasn't inevitable at all, and indeed hadn't really happened. He hadn't needed Chris, so Chris had let him stretch his wings, but he'd always been there, ready to catch Seth if he faltered.

"Thanks, Chris."

"For what?"

"For being my brother."

Chris rapped him on the forehead. "I didn't have anything to do with that."

"Maybe not, but you chose how you've acted all the years since. You had faith in me when no one else cared what happened to me, and because you did, I'm here now, about to have my dreams come true. Mum's boyfriends and Tony didn't teach me how to be a man. I learnt that all from you."

"Go to sleep," Chris said. "We'll have to clean up from this bitch of a storm tomorrow. You'll be miserable if you don't sleep."

"Yes, Dad," Seth teased, but his eyelids finally felt heavy, like he might fall asleep. He pulled the covers tighter around his shoulders and closed his eyes. He felt the mattress shift as Chris got up and left, taking the candle with him, but Seth didn't need the light anymore.

TWENTY-THREE

CLEANUP BEGAN after breakfast the next morning. Every building in the valley was missing at least a few shingles. They had fences down and broken branches everywhere. Seth volunteered for the roof crew mostly so he could have a better view of the road into the valley as he worked. Jason still hadn't called or texted, and worry was gnawing at him again. He'd made himself eat breakfast because it was a long time until lunch, but the food sat heavy on his stomach, making him wish he hadn't. He'd tried calling Jason again that morning, but it had gone straight to voice mail so he either had his phone off or his battery had died. He'd have words with Jason about that when he got home, but that could wait until after he'd reassured himself Jason was unharmed.

They started on the canteen because it had the most damage.

"Is it worth patching or would we be better off tearing the whole roof off and starting over?" Seth asked Ian as they surveyed the damage. "I'm not sure we can get some of the new shingles on without damaging the ones around them."

"We'd have to be careful," Ian agreed, "although I think we could do it. But we can get Macklin up here to check it out before we start if you think we should."

Seth tried to push aside the sense of wonder that Ian, with all his experience, would value Seth's opinion so highly that he would set aside his own opinion on the matter in favor of Seth's engineering training. He knelt down and picked at the edge of an intact shingle. "We'd have to pull the nails out so we could get the new shingle underneath the old one without breaking the old shingle, and then nail them both down again. If it was only a few shingles or even a few dozen, it could be worth it, but this is easily a quarter of the roof. I just think we'd be doing a lot of unnecessary work on a roof that looks like it's as old as the station anyway. It would take a couple of days, but if we get a whole crew working, we could get it done pretty quickly."

"Let's talk to Macklin," Ian said. "If he agrees, we'll get a crew started tearing the old shingles off today."

While Ian started back down the ladder, Seth looked up the valley road. He didn't expect to see a car yet, but he couldn't stop himself from checking. The empty road mocked his concerns. He swallowed them down and followed Ian down the ladder.

"How bad is the damage?" Macklin asked when they found him repairing the fence around the horses' enclosure.

"Seth thinks we should scrap the whole thing and start over."

"There's a lot of damage. I'm afraid we'd either do more damage trying to put on new shingles or else wind up with a roof that isn't waterproof," Seth explained. "We'll do it however you want, of course, but I didn't want to do repairs only to have a leak in a month or two and have to redo the whole roof then."

"What do you think, Ian?" Macklin asked. "You were up there with him."

"He's got a good eye," Ian said. "And he's right about how much of the roof is damaged. I think we could do repairs, but I'm not sure it wouldn't be faster to start over."

"That's good enough for me," Macklin said. "Get a crew up there to tear off the shingles and check the other roofs. I'd rather not redo all of them if we don't have to, but I want it fixed up right."

"Sure thing, boss," Ian said. "Come on, Seth. Let's check the bunkhouse and then we can move to the individual houses and the barns and sheds."

"Seth," Macklin said as they started to walk away. Seth turned back. "Any news from Jason?"

"No. My calls go straight to voice mail. His battery probably died. He forgot to take his car charger. I found it in the kitchen this morning."

"You'll have to break him of that habit," Macklin said. "It's dangerous not being able to get in touch when you're out."

"I'll work on it," Seth promised. "Just as soon as he comes home."

"If he's not back in another hour, we'll go find him," Macklin said, "but let's give him time to get home on his own first."

Seth nodded. He'd decided to wait until lunch before asking so he wouldn't be overreacting, but an hour sounded better. "Thanks. I'll be on a roof somewhere. I'd like to go with you to look for him if it comes to that."

"Of course," Macklin said. "Hopefully he'll be home before that."

The bunkhouse roof hadn't suffered nearly as badly as the canteen had, Seth discovered when he joined Ian on the roof. "We can have this done in a couple of hours."

"That's what I thought," Ian said. "Grab two hammers and some nails. I'll get the shingles and we'll knock this out in no time."

Seth got his hammer and an extra for Ian and a box of nails from the tractor shed and climbed back up to the roof. He started pulling off the damaged shingles and prying loose the nails. Ian joined him eventually, but Seth didn't resume their conversation. They both knew what needed to be done. They didn't need to talk about it. Eventually he'd need to talk to Ian about his offer from the night before, but this wasn't the time. They had work to do and Jason still wasn't home. Seth was holding it together by sheer force of will, and talking about it would shatter what little control he had left. Fortunately Ian accepted his silence, only asking him from time to time to pass the box of nails. Seth looked up the road for the umpteenth time and saw a small white dot moving toward the valley. Jason's car was white.

"Go on," Ian said. "I'll get someone else to help me finish up here. You won't be any good to anyone until you know he isn't hurt."

"Thanks," Seth said. He scrambled down the ladder and ran toward the end of the station buildings so he could follow the progress of the car down the valley. He bounced on the balls of his feet as he waited. Going out to meet Jason would be ridiculous since they would just have to come back to where he was now, but he had a hard time staying where he was.

Finally the car reached where he was waiting, and Jason rolled down the window. "My phone got soaked," Jason said by way of greeting.

"You need a better case," Seth replied hoarsely. "You scared me. I... I had a bad night."

"Are you okay?" Jason asked.

"I should be asking you that," Seth said. "You're the one who spent the night out in the storm somewhere."

"I found a drover's hut when it started getting bad," Jason said, "but I dropped my phone and it wouldn't work when I got inside. But you're okay?"

"I spent the night with Chris and Jesse. I kept my promise. I didn't cut myself."

"I'm proud of you," Jason said.

The words made Seth feel so good, but at the same time, he hadn't told Jason the whole story. "It wasn't a good night. I nearly broke down, but I'd promised you, so I went to Chris instead. They have my razor. I think I'll use disposables for a while until I'm sure I can trust myself again. Thorne and Ian came over. They're going to help me come up with better ways to cope."

"Good. Get in. I need to change clothes, and I imagine there's work to be done."

Seth climbed in the passenger seat. There was work to be done, but not until after he'd assured himself Jason was as unharmed as he appeared. No one would blame him. He'd heard stories about Caine and Macklin and how they finally got together.

Jason parked in front of the house. "I should tell my parents I'm back."

Seth grabbed Jason's hand before he could walk away and pulled him onto the veranda. "Ian will tell them. He saw your car. You need a hot shower and dry clothes."

"Is that what I need?" Jason teased.

The heat that had been pooling in Seth's groin flared now that they were alone and Jason was safe. "Well, maybe the clothes can wait."

Jason grinned and pulled his shirt over his head. "Maybe the shower can wait too. You're just going to make a mess of me. I might as well wait to clean up after."

Seth grinned back. "What are we waiting for, then?" He herded Jason into the bedroom and stripped them both quickly. Jason's jeans were still damp and his skin was cool to the touch beneath them. Seth hesitated. "Maybe you should warm up first."

Jason pulled Seth down on top of him. "What do you think we're doing? I'm never cold when you're in bed with me."

Seth rolled to the side so he could reach Jason better and started at Jason's feet, rubbing his hands over the clammy skin and kissing his way up Jason's legs. Heat bloomed beneath Jason's skin and color returned quickly, reassuring Seth. Jason was wet, not sick. By the time he reached Jason's groin, his cock was fully hard.

"Is this for me?"

"There isn't anyone else in here," Jason replied. Seth sent him a reproving look, but Jason just blew him a kiss.

That was fine. He could be as cheeky as he wanted. Seth had learned his weak spots now. He'd have Jason reduced to begging in no time. Holding Jason's gaze, he licked his way up Jason's cock from root to tip.

"Fuck," Jason gasped.

"We will," Seth promised, "but not yet. I have a whole lot of fear to work out first."

Jason pulled Seth up so he could kiss him. Seth melted into the kiss, taking comfort from the contact between their bodies. Jason was with him, alive and safe. Seth might never let Jason out of his sight again, but for this moment, he could forget the fear that had driven him out into the rain the night before. Jason pushed up onto his elbow, rolling Seth onto his back. Another time, Seth might have protested the position or tried to take back control, but being surrounded by Jason now felt so right. He tugged on Jason's arm, urging him to move more fully onto him. He opened his legs so Jason could settle between them, the movement bringing their cocks into contact. Seth hissed into the kiss and slid his hands down to grab Jason's arse.

Jason rocked his hips, increasing the friction between them. Seth hissed again and bent one knee to create more space for Jason to move.

"Careful, there," Jason murmured against Seth's neck. "If you keep moving like that, I'm going to think you're offering things."

Seth moaned as need swamped him. Jason had told Seth early on that he was perfectly happy as a switch and had no problem letting Seth fuck him. He'd been the epitome of patience, never pressing Seth to try things the other way. Some men, he'd said, never bottomed, and Seth had left it at that, but Jason wasn't a true bottom. He was a switch, and the thought of letting Jason top him now appealed in a way it never had before. If Jason could fuck him senseless, Seth would have incontrovertible proof that he was home and safe and that he was Seth's as fully as Seth was his. "What if I am offering?"

Jason froze above him, tension investing every line of his body. "Are you sure?"

Seth wasn't at all sure he was ready for this, but he wanted it, so he nodded. Jason all but fell on Seth, kissing him so fervently that Seth's head spun. He kissed Jason back with all the passion he could put into it, but just in case he hadn't made his point clear enough, he bent his other knee and opened himself to Jason as completely as he could. "Just remember I've never done this before."

"Believe me, baby, I haven't forgotten," Jason replied. "I was just hoping you'd want to try it someday."

"You like it so much," Seth said. "It has to be worth a try."

"Trust me," Jason said as he rocked back on his heels. "I'll take care of you."

Trusting Jason was easy. In the worst of his panic last night, he hadn't once worried that Jason had left him on purpose. He'd worried Jason was hurt or dead, but not that he had decided to break things off and leave. After that, trusting Jason with his body was a lark. Seth tensed when Jason ran his fingers over Seth's balls and down into his crack.

"Just relax," Jason said. "Let your body get used to me touching you." He left his hand where it was and shifted down on the bed until he could bend down and take Seth in his mouth. Seth groaned in delight and completely forgot about the foreign feeling of Jason's fingers between his cheeks. Jason swallowed around him, making Seth cry out again. Fuck, he loved the things Jason did to his body. He'd never come as hard as he had at Jason's hands... and mouth... and in Jason's arse. This would be just as good because he'd be doing it with Jason.

He was panting hard and fighting not to come by the time Jason lifted his head, eyes glittering in the light of the lamp by the bed. "You'd be more relaxed if you came now."

Seth shook his head. "Then you'd have to wait until I was ready again. I recover fast, but not fast enough for this time." He grabbed the lube from the bedside table and handed it to Jason. "Get me ready and fuck me until I can't walk straight."

Jason's gaze darkened at Seth's provocative words. He pressed a little harder against Seth's entrance. Not enough to push the tip inside, but definitely enough to draw Seth's attention back to his fingers. Anticipation sparked along Seth's skin and eased his nerves.

"Do it," Seth said.

"Not dry," Jason said, squirting lube onto his fingers. The gel was cool despite the heat of Jason's skin when he touched Seth again, but Seth pulled his knees up in encouragement anyway. The gel would warm up quickly, and Seth didn't want Jason to have any doubts about how much he wanted this.

"Bloody hell," Jason cursed. "Look at you, spreading yourself out for me. You really do want this."

"I told you I did. Did you not believe me?"

"I believe you," Jason said. "I'm just having a hard time convincing myself I'm awake." He rubbed the gel over Seth's entrance, the same patch his fingers had explored before he added the lube. Instead of feeling strange now, Seth craved the touch. Jason applied more pressure, and with the lube to ease the way, the tip of his finger slipped into Seth with only a little resistance. "Damn, you're so tight. You're going to squeeze the come out of me before I even get a chance to fuck you."

"So loosen me up," Seth challenged. "I'm not letting you out of bed until you've fucked me properly."

"That's not much incentive to do it right the first time," Jason retorted. "I could keep you here in bed all day making love."

"The bosses might have something to say about that." Their next day off, Seth would take Jason to bed and keep him there all day. Now that he'd put the idea in Seth's head, nothing else would do.

Jason twitched his finger, wringing a cry from Seth's throat. "I've got my finger up your arse and you're talking about the bosses? I'm obviously doing something wrong."

"Then do it right," Seth said hoarsely. Jason pushed his finger deeper and twisted it, running the pad over the walls of Seth's passage. Fireworks exploded behind Seth's eyes. "Oh, fuck!"

"What was that about not doing it right?" Jason prodded that spot again before Seth could form a reply. He couldn't think with Jason doing that. He could only pull his knees back and lift his hips into Jason's touch. Jason gave it to him, pushing his finger in to the hilt before withdrawing it slowly and putting pressure on Seth's prostate as long as he could. Seth's eyes rolled back in his head and wordless sounds fell from his lips. He wanted to beg for more, but his brain couldn't find the words. All the blood in his body had rushed to his cock and that one little spot inside him that Jason was playing with mercilessly.

Then Jason pulled his hand away. Seth opened his eyes and made a sound of protest.

"I need more lube," Jason said. "I won't hurt you."

Seth didn't even care. He could live with a little pain to have those incredible feelings again. Jason returned his attention to Seth's arse, pushing in with two fingers this time. The stretch burned, but Seth was too far gone to care, especially when Jason found his prostate again. He didn't immediately start fucking Seth with his fingers, choosing instead to tease Seth's prostate until he was reduced to breathless pleas.

"One more finger," Jason said, pulling his hand away again. "When you can take that, I'll give you what you want."

The third finger hurt enough to bring Seth back from the edge of completion, even with Jason pressing the pad of his fingers to Seth's prostate. He breathed through the pain as he had learned to do when he cut himself, but that didn't stop his erection from flagging. He still wanted Jason with a need bordering on desperation. He just wasn't sure he could come from Jason fucking him.

"Relax," Jason murmured as he moved his fingers in and out of Seth in a steady rhythm. He never let them come all the way out so Seth's entrance stayed stretched, but each withdrawal eased the pressure a little, giving him a brief respite. He caught the rhythm of Jason's hands and moved to meet each inward push.

"That's it," Jason said. "Fuck yourself on my fingers. Let your body open up and take them."

Finally the burn faded. Seth reached for a condom, but Jason snatched it out of his hand. "I won't hold out if you put it on me," Jason admitted. "I need you too much."

"I'm all yours," Seth replied huskily. "Only ever yours."

Jason rolled the condom on and moved between Seth's thighs. He slotted his cock between Seth's cheeks and then stopped.

"You're not getting out of this, Thompson," Seth said. "Fuck me already."

Jason shook his head. "I'll make love to you as often as you want, but my fucking days are over."

Seth wanted to roll his eyes at the sentimentality and accuse Jason of playing with semantics, but the intensity of his voice stilled the words before they could form. He pulled Jason down for a kiss. The change in position pushed Jason's cock against his entrance more firmly. Seth took a deep breath and lifted his hips. Jason met him halfway and breached Seth's body.

Seth's breath caught in his throat. It stung a bit despite Jason's careful preparation, but not as much as his fingers had done at first. More importantly, Jason was inside him. He wrapped his legs around Jason's hips and urged him to push the rest of the way inside.

"You're so tight," Jason said against his ear.

"Because no one else has ever been inside me like you are," Seth replied.

"Sap," Jason teased, but he kissed Seth tenderly. When he lifted his head, he added, "I love you."

"I love you too," Seth said, "but if you don't move, I won't be responsible for my actions."

"Going to flip me over and ride me?" Jason asked.

"The thought had occurred."

"Tomorrow," Jason said. "If you're not too sore. Let me have the reins right now."

Seth nodded. Jason began moving slowly, just rocking his cock in its berth until Seth was delirious with need. At some point his strokes lengthened, but Seth knew only the incredible feeling of Jason inside him, his cock hitting Seth's prostate with every pass. He writhed beneath Jason, wanton with desire, but it wasn't enough. He grabbed Jason's arse, round and sculpted from hours spent on horseback, and squeezed in time with Jason's thrusts. Jason groaned and drove his cock harder into Seth. Seth cried out and urged Jason on.

Every pass over his prostate pushed Seth closer to release. Jason reached between them to stroke Seth's cock, but he pushed Jason's hand away. He knew what Jason's hand on his dick felt like. He wanted to focus on the new sensation of Jason inside him.

"Can you come just from that?" Jason asked.

"Fuck it out of me," Seth replied.

Jason slammed into Seth, thrilling Seth with his loss of control. He wanted Jason as wild as he was. He'd feel it later—and he'd probably hear about it from the other year-rounders—but he wanted that. He wanted Jason's claim written as deeply on his body as it was already inscribed on his soul. He clung to Jason's shoulders and gave himself over to the thorough ravishing. As the emotion built, every touch to his gland became its own mini-orgasm until he was flying so high he thought he'd never come down. His climax blindsided him, bubbling up from his balls without warning and spouting over his stomach and Jason's chest. He cried out as he came, his whole body spasming with his release.

Jason's rhythm faltered. He pushed deep and stayed there, rocked by his own climax. Seth hated the condom between them at that moment. He wanted Jason's spunk filling him up and running down his thighs. Forget spending the day in bed the next time they had a day off. They were going to Boorowa to get tested so they could ditch the condoms for good.

Jason collapsed on top of him, his breath hot and wet against Seth's shoulder. Seth held him tight as he waited for the high to fade. It passed slowly, but Jason still moved before Seth was ready. Seth let him dispose of the condom, but he pulled Jason back down beside him before he could start toward the shower and the rest of the day.

"I'm a mess of problems and probably about the worst risk you could take," Seth said. Jason started to protest, but Seth put his finger on Jason's lips. "Let me finish, okay? I'm every definition of a bad risk, but I love you, and that's never going to change. And by some miracle, we've both ended up on Lang Downs, surrounded by people who have proven that even bad risks can have happy endings. Last night when I was scared you were hurt or dead, I realized something: you're it for me. I don't want to envision a life without you. I know it's not really legal yet, but will you take a chance on me, Jason? Will you marry me?"

Seth moved his fingers away from Jason's lips and braced himself for the answer.

"First of all, you're not a bad risk. You have some issues, but that's nothing we can't overcome, so stop putting yourself down that way. And to answer your question, yes! God, yes! We can go to Boorowa today and register our partnership if you want."

"Your mum will kill us if we don't let her plan a party at least," Seth said.

"After today, she's your mum too, so don't put that all on me."

Seth grinned. "I guess she is. She has been for a long time, but it'll be nice to make it official."

Jason kissed him hard and fast.

"One more thing," Seth said.

"Yes?"

"Get a better case for your phone," Seth said.

"Bosses' orders?"

"Husband's orders."

Jason smiled, all radiant joy and sappiness. "The best kind."

EPILOGUE

MACKLIN JOINED Caine on the veranda of their house and wrapped his arm around Caine's waist. "Did you imagine, when you moved here eleven years ago, that things would turn out like this?"

Caine smiled up at Macklin before turning back to continue watching for Seth and Jason's return from Boorowa. The party couldn't start without the guests of honor. "Define 'this.'"

"The success of the station, the family we've built, seeing kids we watched grow up getting married and carrying on our legacy," Macklin said.

"You make it sound like we've got one foot in the grave already," Caine teased. "I'll have you know I'm still a man in my prime."

"Oh, so I'm the old one?" Macklin countered.

"If the shoe fits…," Caine replied as he leaned into Macklin's embrace. "But to answer your question, no, not in my wildest dreams did I believe things could turn out this well. My best-case scenario was to not end up losing the station through mismanagement. I hope Uncle Michael is looking down on us right now. I'd like to think he'd be proud of us."

Macklin's arm tightened around Caine's waist. "There's no 'think' about it. He'd be proud of you. You've taken his legacy and built on it. Lang Downs still stands as a place for the people who need it most."

Caine smiled. "And it always will. I see Seth and Jason's car. We should gather the others. We want to be there when they arrive. The 'ceremony' in Boorowa might just be signing a few papers, but Carley's planned a wedding reception they'll never forget."

"Did the Taylor Peak crowd make it?"

"Yes, Sam and Jeremy arrived half an hour ago with Nick and Phil. Ian and Thorne came back last night as scheduled, and I told Kyle to wait until tonight to go back, even though he was scheduled to go help out today. Jeremy's crew bosses can run things without our help for a few hours."

"Good. Let's go celebrate."

Chase the Stars

Lang Downs: Book Two

By Ariel Tachna

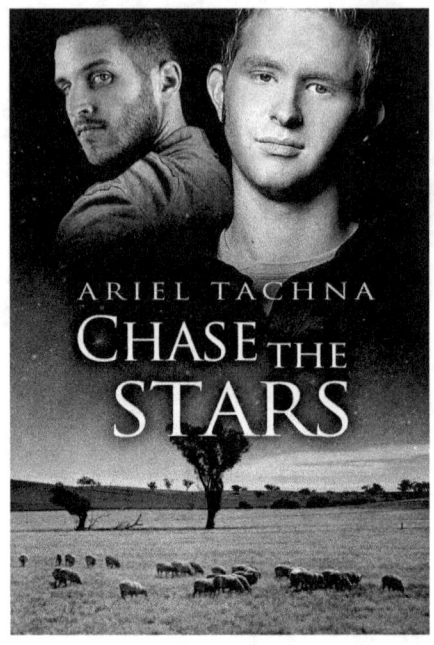

Twenty-year-old Chris Simms is barely keeping his head above water. After losing his mother and his home, he struggles to provide for himself and his brother. When homophobes attack him, he thinks his life is over, but then he's rescued by jackaroos from a nearby sheep station. He's as stunned to be offered a job there as he is to discover both the station owner and foreman are gay.

For Chris, Lang Downs is a dream—one that only gets better when Chris realizes the jackaroo he's crushing on, Jesse Harris, is gay and amenable to a fling. Everything goes well until Chris realizes he's falling for Jesse a lot harder than allowed by their deal.

Jesse is a drifter who moves from station to station, never looking for anything permanent. Convinced Chris is too young and fragile for a real relationship, he sets rules to keep things casual. Watching the station owner and his foreman together makes Jesse wonder if there are benefits to settling down, but when he realizes how Chris feels about him, he panics. He and Chris will have to decide if a try for happiness is worth the risk before the end of the season tears them apart.

http://www.dreamspinnerpress.com

Outlast the Night

Lang Downs: Book Three

By Ariel Tachna

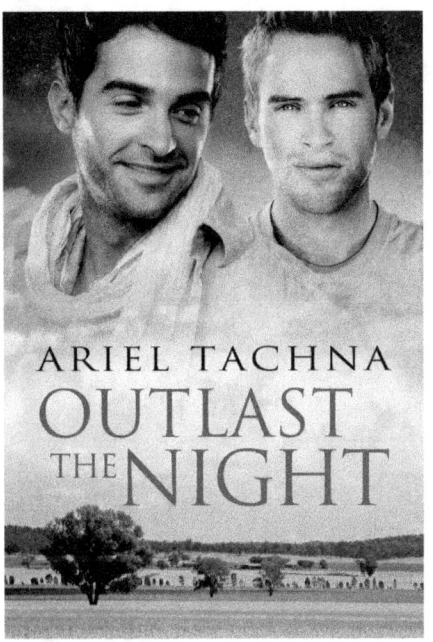

Office manager Sam Emery is unemployed and out of luck. When his emotionally abusive wife demands a divorce, he contacts the one person he has left, his brother, Neil. He doesn't expect Neil to reject him, but he also doesn't expect the news of his divorce—and of his sexuality—to be met with such acceptance.

Neil takes Sam to Lang Downs, the sheep station Neil calls home. There, Sam learns that life as a gay man isn't impossible. Caine and Macklin, the station owners, certainly seem to be making it work. When Caine offers Sam a job, it's a dream come true.

Jeremy Taylor leaves the only home he's ever known when his brother's homophobia becomes more than he can bear. He goes to the one place he knows he will be accepted: Lang Downs. He clicks with Sam instantly—but the animosity between Lang Downs and Jeremy's home station runs deep, and the jackaroos won't accept Jeremy without a fight. Between Sam's insecurity and Jeremy's precarious position, their road will be a hard one—and that's without having to wait for Sam's divorce to be final before starting a new life together.

http://www.dreamspinnerpress.com

Conquer the Flames

Lang Downs: Book Four

By Ariel Tachna

Thorne Lachlan knows a thing or two about getting himself safely out of a blaze. For years he fought in the world's hot spots, a Commando with the Australian Army. Now, retired, he fights flames for the Royal Fire Service. When a grassfire brings him to Lang Downs, the next sheep station in danger, Thorne meets Ian Duncan and sparks fly that neither man can put out. But both men have ghosts from the past that stand in the way of moving beyond mutual attraction.

While Thorne longs for the home he could share with Ian at Lang Downs, he fears his own instability might make him a danger to others. And Ian's always believed that the foster care nightmare he escaped before coming to Lang Downs would make any relationship impossible. Trust doesn't come easily to Thorne or Ian until the fire's aftermath forces them to see past the scars keeping them both from healing.

http://www.dreamspinnerpress.com

ARIEL TACHNA lives outside of Houston with her husband, her daughter and son, and their two dogs. Before moving there, she traveled all over the world, having fallen in love with both France, where she found her husband, and India, where she dreams of retiring someday. She's bilingual with snippets of four other languages to her credit, and is as in love with languages as she is with writing.

Visit Ariel:
Website: http://www.arieltachna.com
Facebook: https://www.facebook.com/ArielTachna
E-mail: arieltachna@gmail.com

DANCE OFF

ARIEL TACHNA & NESSA L. WARIN

http://www.dreamspinnerpress.com

THE PATH

ARIEL TACHNA

http://www.dreamspinnerpress.com

ARIEL TACHNA

Home for Chirappu

http://www.dreamspinnerpress.com

HER TWO DADS

DADS

ARIEL
TACHNA

http://www.dreamspinnerpress.com

http://www.dreamspinnerpress.com

http://www.dreamspinnerpress.com

ARIEL TACHNA

A Summer Place

http://www.dreamspinnerpress.com

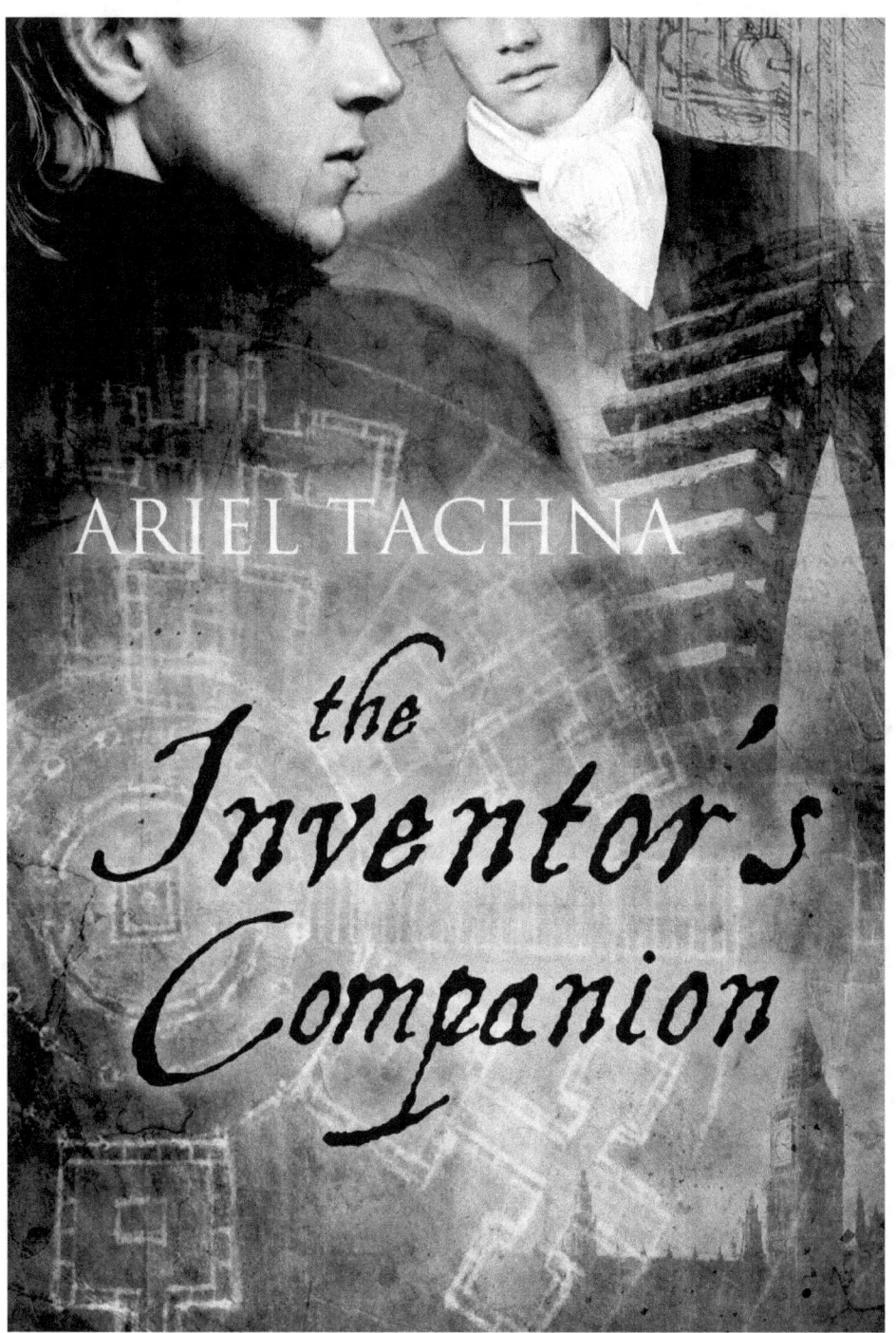

ARIEL TACHNA

the
Inventor's
Companion

http://www.dreamspinnerpress.com

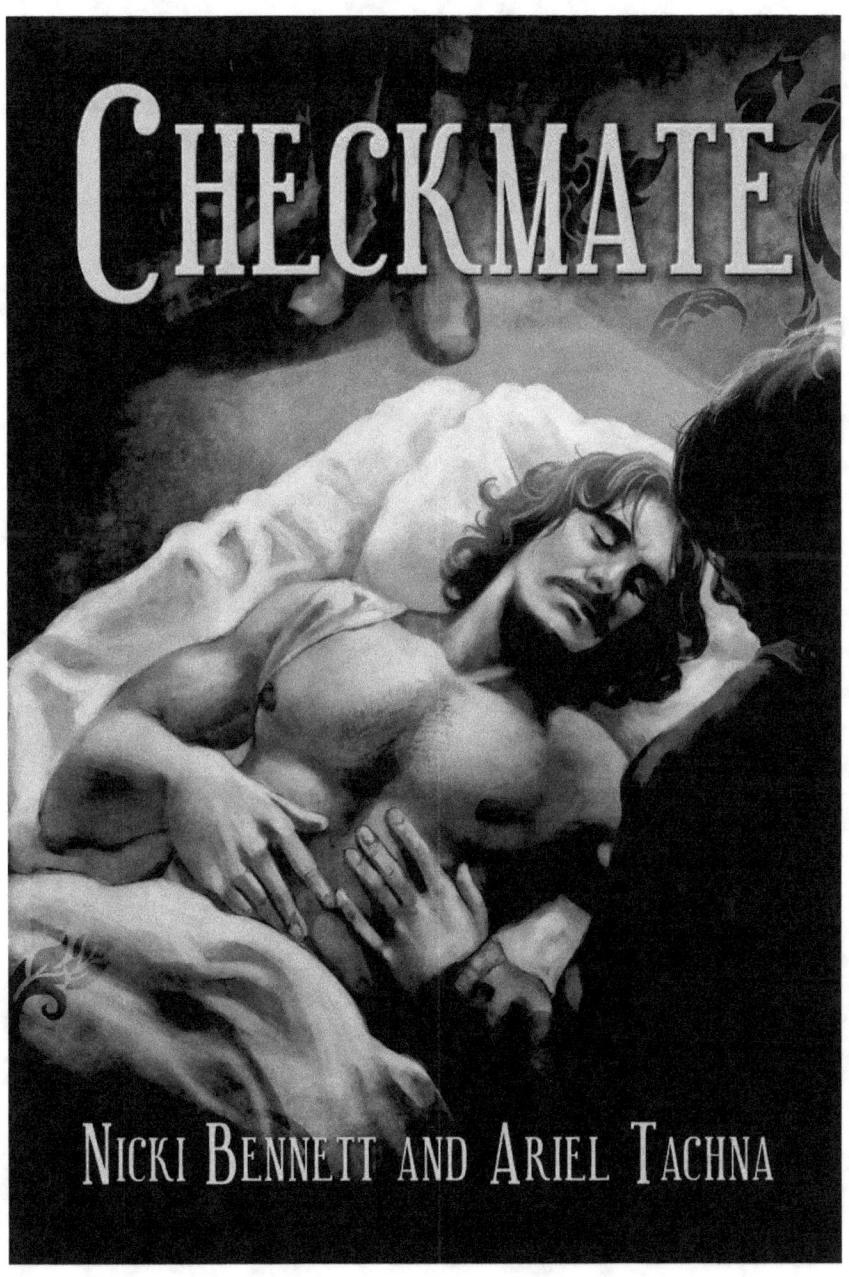

TESTAMENT TO *Love*

ARIEL TACHNA

http://www.dreamspinnerpress.com

the Matelot

Ariel Tachna

http://www.dreamspinnerpress.com

Once in a
LIFETIME

ARIEL TACHNA

http://www.dreamspinnerpress.com

ARIEL TACHNA

CHÂTEAU
D'ETERNITÉ

http://www.dreamspinnerpress.com

Partnership in Blood

Partnership in Blood

www.ingramcontent.com/pod-product-compliance
Lightning Source LLC
Chambersburg PA
CBHW070114260626
47160CB00004B/1458